The Spoilt Child

The Spoilt Child

A Tale of Domestic Life

Peary Chand Mitra

MINT EDITIONS

The Spoilt Child: A Tale of Domestic Life was first published in 1983.

This edition published by Mint Editions 2021.

ISBN 9781513215488 | E-ISBN 9781513213484

Published by Mint Editions®

 MINT
EDITIONS

minteditionbooks.com

Publishing Director: Jennifer Newens
Design & Production: Rachel Lopez Metzger
Project Manager: Micaela Clark
Translated by: G.D. Oswell
Typesetting: Westchester Publishing Services

Contents

PREFACE

The author of this novel, Babu Peary Chand Mitter, was born in the year 1814.

He represented the well-educated, thoroughly earnest, and courteous Bengali gentleman of the old school.

His life was devoted to the good of his fellow-countrymen, and he was especially eager in the cause of female education. In the preface to one of his works, written with that object in view, he writes:—"I was born in the year 1814. While a pupil of the Páthshálá at home, I found my grandmother, mother, and aunts reading Bengali books. They could write in Bengali and keep accounts. There were no female schools then, nor were there suitable books for the females. My wife was very fond of reading, and I could scarcely supply her with instructive books. I was thus forced to think how female education could be promoted in a substantial way. The conclusion I came to was that, unless womanhood were placed on a spiritual basis, education would never be productive of real good. For the furtherance of this end I have been humbly working."

Amongst the books he published with this end in view are the "Ramaranjika," the "Abhedi," and the "Adhyátwiká." The "Ramaranjika" deals with female education under different aspects, and gives examples drawn from the lives of eminent Englishwomen, as well as biographical sketches of distinguished Hindu women, drawn from history and tradition. Of the "Abhedi" the author says:—"It is a spiritual novel in Bengali, in which the hero and heroine have been described as earnest seekers after the knowledge of the soul, and as obtaining spiritual light by the education of pain." Of the "Adhyátwiká," the author tells us:—"It brings before its readers the conversation and manners of different classes of people, in different circumstances, which have been pourtrayed in different styles, and which may perhaps be useful to foreigners wishing to acquire a colloquial knowledge of the Bengali language."

Babu Peary Chand Mitter was a man who keenly felt the evils in society around him, and he used his pen in the cause of temperance and the purity of the domestic circle as against drunkenness and debauchery; amongst his writings having this object in view is the "Mada Kháoya bara dáya," or "The great evils of dram-drinking." It is a novel marked by great humour, and shows the author to have been a satirist of no mean power.

Besides these novels he wrote "The Life of David Hare" both in Bengali and in English. He also contributed essays to *The Calcutta Review*, and an American publication called *The Banner of Light*, besides writing articles for the Agri-Horticultural Society of India.

Babu Peary Chand Mitter died in 1883.

The novel "Alaler Gharer Dulál," or "The Spoilt Darling of an Ill-regulated House," was written more than forty years ago, and was very well received, as the criticisms of the day show. *The Calcutta Review* of the day says:—"We hail this book as the first novel in the Bengali language. Tek Chand Thakur has written a tale the like of which is not to be found within the entire range of Bengali literature. Our author's quiet humour reminds us of Goldsmith, while his livelier passages bring to our recollection the treasures of Fielding's wit. He seems to be familiar with Defoe, Fielding, Scott, Dickens, Bulwer, Thackeray, and other masters of fiction."

Other critics of the day compared him to a Moliére or a Dickens.

Mr. John Beames, in his "Modern Aryan Languages of India," writes:—"Babu Peary Chand Mitter, who writes under the *nom de plume* of Tek Chand Thakur, has produced the best novel in the language 'Alaler Gharer Dulál.' He has had many imitators, and certainly stands high as a novelist. His story might fairly claim to be ranked with some of the best comic novels in our own language for wit, spirit, and clever touches of nature. He puts into the mouth of each of his characters the appropriate method of talking, and thus exhibits to the full the extensive range of vulgar idioms which his language possesses."

In an introductory essay on Bengali novels, in his translation of Babu Bunkim Chandra Chatterjee's novel "Kopal Kundala," Mr. Phillips writes:—"The position and character of Bengali literature is peculiar. A backward people have, so to speak, rushed into civilization at one bound: old customs and prejudices have been displaced, *uno ictu*, by a state of enlightenment and advanced ideas. The educated classes have suddenly found themselves face to face with the richest gems of Western learning and literature. The clash of widely divergent stages of civilization, the juxtaposition of the most advanced thought with comparative barbarism, has produced results which, though perhaps to be expected, are somewhat curious. If one tries to close a box with more than it can hold the lid may be unhinged,—new wine may burst old bottles. The colliding forces of divergent stages of civilization have produced a literature that for want of a better expression may be called a hybrid compromise between Eastern and Western ideas. So we find that the Bengali novel is to a great extent an exotic. It is a hot-house plant which has been brought from a foreign soil; but even crude imitations are better than the farragos of original nonsense, lists of which appear from time to time in the pages of the *Calcutta Gazette*.

The above remarks are merely general, and there exist, of course, bright and notable exceptions, among whom may be mentioned the names of Peary Chand Mitter (the father of Bengali novelists), Bunkim Chandra Chatterjea, Romesh Chandra Dutt, and Tarak Nath Ganguli.

The 'Alaler Gharer Dulál' of Peary Chand Mitter may be called a truly indigenous novel, in which some of the reigning vices and follies of the time are held up to scorn and derision. A deep vein of moral earnestness runs through all the writings of Peary Chand Mitter, and he takes the opportunity to interweave with the incidents of his story disquisitions on virtue and vice, truthfulness and deceit, charity and niggardliness, hypocrisy and straightforwardness. Not only general vices, such as drinking and debauchery, but particular customs, such as a Kulin's marrying a dozen wives, and living at their expense, are condemned in no measured terms. The book is written in a plain colloquial style, which, combined with a quiet humour, procured for it a considerable degree of popularity."

As further evidence, if such were wanting, of the popularity of this novel, it may be mentioned that it has been dramatized, having been published in the form of a *natak* or play, by Babu Hira Lall Mitter.

The leading characteristics of the novel, as they have appeared to the translator, are the humour, pathos, and satire that pervade almost every page of it.

The humour, though it may occasionally be broad, can never be called coarse, and much of it is the cultured humour that might be expected from a writer well acquainted with his own ancient classics. If Thackeray is the type of the cultured humorist of the West, Peary Chand Mitter is the type of the cultured humorist of the East.

The pathos is especially noticeable in some of the scenes which the author has pourtrayed for us with such vivid reality where the poor are brought before us. We see the utter dependence of the poor upon the generosity of the rich, a generosity that is rarely appealed to in vain:

there is pathos too in the scene that brings before us the ryot and his landlord; and in the scenes in the zenana and the bathing-*ghât* where we have an insight into the lives and the thoughts of both the upper and lower classes of the women of the country. There is a deep pathos in the scene that brings before us the old man at Benares, spending the evening of his days in reading and meditation, in "The Holy City": it is a scene that gives us an insight into the deeper religious side of the Hindu character.

The satire is only merciless where it is directed against the vices of drinking and debauchery, or against the custom of the much marrying of Kulins, or the marrying of old men to young girls, or solely for money. In other cases it is not unkindly, especially where it is directed against that not uncommon failing both in the West and the East, which Shakespeare has immortalized as "too much respect upon the world," and which is largely exhibited in the East in the form of lavish expenditure, regardless of debt, upon social and religious ceremonies.

Amongst other characteristics of this novel may be noted that deep vein of moral earnestness, already referred to, which runs through the whole book, and which is chiefly exhibited in the form of moral reflections, such as are so common in many of the Sanscrit tales.

Dramatic vividness is another noticeable feature of the book: a few strokes of the pen suffice to bring before us, as living realities, characters that are drawn from every class of life, and scenes that deal with almost every incident of life in Bengal. In fact a far more vivid picture of social life in Bengal, both in its inner and outer aspects, is presented to us in the pages of this book, than is presented in the pages of many books purporting to give us an account of that life.

And, with this dramatic vividness, there is a general faithfulness to reality that will be appreciated by those who have lived for anytime amidst the scenes described; for, though the book describes life in Bengal as it appeared to the eyes of an acute observer writing more than forty years back, the picture, in its general outlines, is as true of the life of the people now as it was then.

Another noticeable feature of the book is the rhythmic flow which marks its language. This is a feature which appears to characterize all books written for the people in the language best understood of the people, no matter what that language is.

As regards the language in which Peary Chand Mitter wrote this novel, the *Calcutta Review* of the day writes "Endowed, as he was, with strong common sense, as well as high culture, he saw no reason why this idol of unmixed diction should receive worship at his hands, and he set about writing 'Alaler Gharer Dulál' in a spirit at which the Sanscritists stood aghast, and shook their heads. Going to the opposite extreme in point of style, he vigorously excluded from his works, except on very rare occasions, every word and phrase that had a learned appearance. His own works suffered from the exclusion, but the movement was well-timed. He scattered to the winds the time-honoured commonplaces, and drew upon nature and life for his materials. His success was eminent and well-deserved."

One feature that has especially struck the translator in transferring this novel from its original Bengali into English, is that he has found it necessary to omit nothing, on the score of indelicacy, or bad taste,—a remark which could not be made of every Bengali novel. The author has written with the maxim of the old Roman satirist ever before his eyes,—*maxima debetur puero reverentia.*

The translator has had three classes of readers before his eyes, in making this translation.

It seemed to him that so excellent a picture of social life in Bengal could not but be interesting to those Englishmen and Englishwomen who are interested in the lives of their fellow-subjects in India.

It also occurred to him that as the rising generation of Bengalis no longer read Bengali literature as of old, it might interest them to see, in an English dress, a novel that has been so popular amongst their older compatriots.

English students of the Bengali language and its literature may also find the translation of use, as it has been made literal as far as was possible.

The task of translation, though it has been a pleasant one, has not been easy, owing to the many difficulties in the way of adequately rendering into English, without the qualities of the original suffering in the transfer, a book so essentially colloquial and idiomatic in style and character. The fact that Professor Cowell at one time contemplated a translation of this novel, but abandoned the idea owing to this very difficulty, has made the translator still more diffident of success, and he can only leave it to the indulgence of his Bengali readers to decide how far he has succeeded in his translation, in doing justice to the spirit of the original.

The translator's thanks are due to Babu Mohiny Mohun Chatterjea, Solicitor, Calcutta, for his kindness in revising the translation for him, and to Babu Amrita Lall Mitter, the Honorary Secretary to the Society for the Prevention of Cruelty to Animals in Calcutta, and son of the author, for allowing him to publish it.

The Principal Characters

Baburam Babu	A Zemindar
Matilall	His Eldest Son
Ramlall	His Youngest Son
Baburam's First Wife	Mother of his Children
His Second Wife	A Young Girl
Pramada	His Married Daughter
Mokshada	His Widowed Daughter
Beni Babu	A Friend
Becharam	A Friend
Barada Babu	The Kayasth Reformer
Bancharam	A Lawyer's Clerk
Thakchacha	A Mahomedan Friend
Bahulya	A Mahomedan
Haladhar	
Gadahar	
Dolgovinda	Friends of Matilal
Mangovinda	
Matilall's Wife	
Mr. John	A Calcutta Merchant
Mr. Butler	A Solicitor
Mr. Sherborn	A School-master
Premnarayan Mozoomdar	A House Clerk

I

MATILALL AT HOME

Baburam Babu, a resident of Vaidyabati, was a man of large experience in business affairs: he was famous for his long service in the Revenue and Criminal Courts. Now to walk uprightly without taking bribes when engaged in the public service, is not a very long-established custom. Baburam Babu's procedure was in accordance with the old style, and being skilful at his work, he had succeeded, by servility and cringing, in imposing on his superior officers; as a consequence of which he had acquired considerable wealth within a very short time. In this country a man's reputation keeps pace with the increase of his riches or with his advancement: learning and character have not anything like the same respect paid to them. There had been a time when Baburam Babu's position had been a very inferior one, and when only a few individuals in his village had paid him any attention; but later, as he came into the possession of fine buildings, gardens, estates, and a good deal of influence in many ways, he found himself with a host of friends as his followers and advisers. Whenever during his intervals of leisure he went to his house, his reception-room would be crowded with people. It is always the case that when a man has a sudden accession of wealth there is a rush of people to him, just as the shop of a sweatmeat seller will become full of flies as long as there are sweetmeats to be had. At whatever time you might visit Baburam Babu's house you would always find people with him: rich and poor, they would all sit round and flatter him, the more intelligent among them in indirect fashion only, the lesser folk outright and unblushingly, agreeing with everything he said. After sometime spent in the way we have described, Baburam Babu took his pension, and remained at home occupied in the management of his estates and in trade.

Now in this world, entire happiness is the lot of hardly anyone, and it is rare to find intelligence displayed in all the concerns of life. Baburam Babu had turned his attention solely to amassing wealth: the questions which had alone exercised his mind had been how to increase his resources, how to make the whole village aware of his importance, so that all might salute him properly, and how to celebrate his religious festivals on a larger scale than those of his neighbours. He had a son and two daughters: being himself a descendant of the great Kulin, Balaram Thakur, he had, with a view to the preservation of his caste, married the two girls at great expense almost immediately after their birth; but their husbands, being Kulins, had taken to themselves wives in a number of places, and would not so much as peep into the house of their father-in-law of Vaidyabati, except on condition of receiving a handsome remuneration for their trouble.

His son, Matilall, having been indulged in every possible way from his boyhood, was exceedingly self-willed; at times, he would say to his father: "Father, I want to catch hold of the moon!" "Father, I want to eat a cannon-ball!" Now and then he would roar and cry, so that all the neighbours would say: "We cannot get any sleep owing to that dreadful boy." Having been so spoilt by his parents, the boy would not tolerate the bare idea of going to school, and thus it was that the duty of teaching him devolved upon the house clerk. On his very first visit to his teacher, Matilall howled aloud, and scratched and bit him. His tutor therefore went to the master of the house and said to him: "Sir, it is quite beyond my power to instruct your son." The master of the house replied: "Ah, he is my only darling, my Krishna! use flattery and caresses if you will, only do teach him."

Matilall was afterwards induced by means of many stratagems to attend school; and when his teacher was leaning up against the wall, nodding drowsily, with his legs crossed and a cane in his hand, reiterating—"Write boys, write," Matilall would rise from his seat, make contemptuous gestures, and dance about the room. The teacher would go on snoring away, ignorant of what his pupil was doing, and when he opened his eyes again, Matilall would be seated near his writing materials of dry palm-leaves, drawing figures of crows and cranes. When later in the afternoon he had commenced the repetition lesson, Matilall, amid the confused babel of tongues, would utter cries of Hori Bol, and cleverly outwit his teacher by uttering the last letters only of the words that were being recited. Occasionally when his teacher was napping, he would tickle his nose or throw a live piece of charcoal into his lap, and then dart away like an arrow. When the hour for refreshment came, he would occasionally get some boy to give the master lime and water to drink, pretending that it was buttermilk. The teacher saw that the boy was a thorough good-for-nothing, who had made up his mind to have nothing more to do with education; so he concluded that as the boy had profited naught from all the canings he had had, but only learnt the art of playing tricks upon his teacher, it was high time to be released from the hands of such a pupil. The master of the house however would not hear of it, so he had to have recourse to stratagem. The occupation of clerk seemed to him to be better than that of teacher: in the latter occupation his wages were two rupees a month besides food and clothing, while his gains over and above that would be merely a present of rice and a pair of cloths or so at the time of the boy's being first initiated into school-life: on the other hand, in the occupation of a clerk who superintended all purchases in the market, there were constant pickings. Revolving such thoughts in his mind, he went to the master of the house and told him that Matilall's education was complete so far as his writing was concerned, and that he had also been thoroughly taught to keep accounts, so far as estate-management was concerned. Baburam Babu was overwhelmed with joy on receiving this intelligence, and all his neighbours in conclave with him said: "Why should it not be so? Can a lion's whelp ever become a jackal?"

Baburam Babu now thought that he ought to have his son taught the rudiments of Sanskrit grammar and a smattering of Persian. Having come to this determination, he called the priest who was in charge of the family worship, and said: "You sir! have you any knowledge of grammar?" This Brahman was the densest of blockheads, but he thought to himself: "I am now getting only rice and plantains, quite insufficient for me: here I see at length a means of making a living." So he replied: "Yes, sir, I studied grammar for five years continuously in the Sanskrit Tol of Ishvar Chandra Vedanta Vagishwar of Kunnimora. But I have been very unlucky: I have gained nothing from all my learning: I am no more than your humble servant in spite of it all, and my food is but coarse grain and water." Baburam Babu thereupon appointed him to teach his son the rudiments of Sanskrit grammar from that day. The Brahman, inebriated with hope, speedily got by heart a page or two of the Mugdha Bodh Grammar, and set about teaching the boy.

Thought Matilall to himself:—"I have escaped from the hands of my old teacher; how am I to get rid of this rice-and-plantain-eating old Brahman? I am my father and mother's darling, and whether I can write or not, they will say nothing to me. The only object of learning after all is to gain money, and my father has boundless wealth: what then is the good of my learning? It is quite enough for me to be able to sign my name; besides what will my intimate friends have left to do if

I take to learning? their occupation in ministering to my pleasures will be gone! The present is the time for enjoyment: has the pain of learning any attractions for me just now? surely none!" Having come to this determination, Matilall thus addressed his preceptor:—"Old Brahman, if you come here anymore to plague me with this grammatical rubbish, I will throw away the family idol, and with it your last hope of a livelihood; and if you go to my father and tell him what I have said to you, I will just drop a brick onto you from the roof: then your wife will soon become a widow, and have to remove her bracelet from her wrist." The Brahman, distressed by such remarks about his teaching, thought to himself: "For six months past I have been labouring at the peril of my life, and I have not yet been paid anything: the whole occupation is one that is most repugnant to my feelings, and I am in constant danger of my life. Let me now only get clear of him and I care not what happens to me afterwards." As the Brahman was revolving all this in his mind, Matilall looked in his face and said: "Well, what are you in such a brown study about? Are you in want of money? Here, take this! But you must go to my father, and tell him that I have learned everything." The Brahman accordingly went to the boy's father and said to him: "Sir, your Matilall is no common boy! he has a most extraordinary memory; he will remember forever what he may have heard only once." There was an astrologer at the time with Baburam, who observed to the Babu: "There is no necessity for you to give me an introduction to Matilall: he is a boy whose birth was at an auspicious moment; if only he lives he is bound to become a very great man."

Baburam Babu next set about searching for a Munshi to teach his son Persian. After a long search, the grandfather of Aladi the tailor, Habibala Hoshan by name, was appointed to the post on a salary of one rupee eight annas a month, together with oil and firewood. The Munshi Saheb was a man with toothless gums, a grey beard, and a moustache like tow: his eyes would get inflamed whenever he was teaching, and when he bade his pupils repeat the letters after him, his face became hideously distorted in pronouncing the guttural Persian letters kaph, gaph, ain, ghain. The benefit that Matilall derived from learning Persian was pretty much what might have been expected from his possessing no taste whatever for the pursuit of knowledge, and having such a preceptor. As the Munshi Saheb was one day stooping over his book, repeating the maxims of Masnavi in a sing-song manner and keeping time with his hand, Matilall seized the opportunity to drop a lighted match from behind onto his beard. The poor Munshi's beard at once flared up, crackling as it blazed, upon which Matilall remarked: "How now, O Mussulman? you will not teach me anymore after this, I expect." The Munshi Saheb left speedily, shaking his head and exclaiming "Tauba! Tauba!" Then as the pain of the burn intensified, he shrieked: "Never, never have I seen so mad and wicked a boy as this: of a surety field labour in my own country were better than such slavery: it is cruel work coming to a place like this! Tauba! Tauba!"

II

MATILALL'S ENGLISH EDUCATION

When Baburam heard of the evil plight of the Munshi Saheb, the only remark he made was: "My boy, Matilall, is not a boy like that. What can you expect from such a low fellow as that Mussulman?" He then considered that as Persian was going out of fashion, it might be a good thing for the boy to learn English. Just as a madman has occasional glimmerings of sense, so even a man lacking in intelligence has occasional happy inspirations. When he had come to this decision, it occurred to Baburam Babu that he was a very indifferent English scholar himself: he only knew one or two English words: his neighbours too, he reflected, knew about as much of it as he himself did: he must consult with some man of learning and experience. As he went over in his mind the list of his kinsmen and relatives, it struck him that Beni Babu, of Bally, was a very competent person. Business habits generate promptness of action, and he proceeded without delay to the Vaidyabati Ghât, taking with him a servant and a messenger.

In the first two months of the rainy season, the months Ashar and Shravan, most of the boatmen occupy themselves in catching hilsa fish with circular nets, and at midday are generally busy taking their meals. Thus it came about that there was not a boat of any description at the Vaidyabati Ghât. Baburam Babu, full-whiskered, the sacred mark on his nose, dressed in fine lawn with coloured borders, with smart shoes from Phulapukur, a front like the front of Ganesh, a delicate muslin shawl neatly folded over his shoulders, and his cheeks swollen with pán, was walking impatiently up and down, calling out to his servant: "Ho, there, Hari! I must get to Bally quick; you must hire a passing boat for me for four pice." Rich men's servants are often very disrespectful, and Hari made answer: "Sir, that is just like you! I had only just sat down to take my food and I have now had to throw it away and leave it in order to attend to your repeated calls. If there had been any boat going down-stream, it might have been hired for a small sum, but it is flood-tide just now, and the boatmen will have to work hard rowing and steering. You might get across for three or four pice if you would arrange to go with others. I cannot possibly hire a passing boat for you for four pice;

you might as well ask me to make barley-meal cakes without water." Baburam Babu scowled and said: "You are a very insolent fellow; if you speak like that to me again, you get a sound smacking." Now the lower orders of Bengalees tremble even if they make a slip, so Hari endured the rebuke, and quaking all over said to his master: "Sir, how can I possibly find a boat? I had no intention of being insolent to you."

While he was still speaking, a green boat that was being towed up the river on its return journey, approached the ghât where they were. After a long argument with the steersman of the boat a bargain was struck, and he agreed to take them across for eight annas. Baburam then got into the boat with his servant and his messenger. When they had got some way on their journey, he began looking about him in every direction, and said to his servant: "Hari, this is a fine boat we have got! Hi, steersman! whose house is that over there? Ho! surely that is a sugar factory. Ha! Now prepare me a pipe of tobacco, and strike me a light." Then he pulled away at the gurgling hooka, now and again raising himself to look at the porpoises tumbling in the water, and hummed a song of the loves of Krishna:—

> *"When late to Brindabun, O Krishna! I came,*
> *"Your home there, alas! I found only a name."*

As it was the ebb, the boat dropped quickly down-stream and the boatmen had no occasion to exert themselves: one sat on the edge of the boat; another, bearded like an old billy-goat, keeping his look-out on the top of the cabin, sang in the Chittagong dialect the popular song which goes:—

> *"E'en the earring of gold shall loosen its hold,*
> *"By the lute-string's languishing strain cajoled."*

The sun had not yet set when the boat reached its moorings at the Deonagaji Ghât. Four boatmen, panting and puffing with their efforts, lifted Baburam Babu, a mass of solid flesh, out of the boat, and set him safe on land.

Beni Babu received his relative very courteously and begged him to be seated, while his house servant, Ram, at once brought some tobacco he had prepared for him. Baburam Babu was very fond of his pipe: after a few pulls he remarked: "How is it that this hooka is hissing?"

A servant who is in constant attendance upon a man of intelligence soon becomes intelligent himself: Ram, divining what was wrong, put a clearing-rod in the hooka, changed the water, supplied it with some fresh tobacco, sweet and compact, and brought it back with a larger mouthpiece. Finding the hooka placed by him, Baburam Babu took entire possession, as though he had taken a permanent lease of it, and as he puffed away, emitting clouds of smoke, chattered with Beni Babu.

Beni.—Would you not like to get up now, sir, and take some light refreshment?

Baburam.—It is already rather late: I don't think I will just now. I am quite at home, thank you; I would have called for it if I had wanted it. But please just listen to what I have to say. My son Matilall has shown that he possesses remarkable genius! You would be quite delighted to see the boy. I am anxious to have him taught English; do you think you can get me a master to teach him for some mere trifle?

Beni.—There are plenty of masters to be had, and a man of moderate ability might be got for from twenty to twenty-five rupees a month.

Baburam.—What, so much as that? Twenty-five rupees! Oh my dear friend, these religious ceremonies you know are a constant source of expense in my establishment: I have about a hundred people to feed everyday; and besides all this, I shall very soon have my son's marriage to arrange for. Why did I go to the expense of hiring a boat to come here and see you, only to be asked for as much as that after all?

With this, he put his hands on Beni Babu's shoulders, and laughed immoderately.

Beni.—Then put him at some school in Calcutta: the boy might live with some relative, and his education need not in that case cost more than three or four rupees a month.

Baburam.—What, as much as that? Couldn't one manage to get the prices down with a little haggling? And is a school education any better than a home one?

Beni.—Home education is a very excellent thing if you can secure a really first-rate teacher, but such a teacher is not to be had on a small salary. School education has its good points and also its bad points. A healthy spirit of emulation of course springs up amongst a number of boys who are being educated together; but at the same time some of the boys will always be in danger of being corrupted by bad company. Besides when twenty-five or thirty boys are reading in one class, there is a good deal of confusion, and equal attention cannot be paid everyday to all the boys alike: consequently all do not make similar progress.

Baburam.—Anyhow I will send Matilall to you; and when you have looked about you, do try and make some cheap arrangement for me. None of the English gentlemen for whom I once did business are here now: if they had been, I might have got some of them to secure him schooling which would have cost me nothing: it would only have needed a little importunity. However it will be quite enough if my son obtains just a smattering of learning: if he becomes a scholar, he may not remain in the religion of his fathers. So kindly make it your business to see that he becomes a man: I lay the whole responsibility upon you, my friend.

Beni.—If a boy is to grow into a man, every attention is necessary both when he is at home and when he is away from home: the father must see everything with his own eyes and enter thoroughly into all the boy's occupations. There is a good deal of business that may be done through commission agencies, but the education of a boy is not one of them.

Baburam.—That is all very true: regard Matilall then as your son. I shall now get some leisure for my ablutions in the Ganges, for reading the Puranas, and for looking after my concerns; for at present I have no time even for these: besides, all the English training that I possess is training of the old school. Matilall is yours, my dear friend, he is yours! I will rid myself of all anxiety by sending him to you. Adopt any course you think fit, but my dear friend, do take care that the expense is not heavy: you know my position as a man with a number of young children to look after: you can understand that thoroughly, can you not?

After this conversation with Beni Babu, Baburam Babu returned to his home at Vaidyabati.

III

MATILALL AT SCHOOL

M en engaged in business all the week spend very lazy Sundays. They avail themselves of any excuse to postpone their bath and their meals: after they have bathed and eaten, some of them play chess and some cards: some occupy themselves in fishing, some play on the tomtom and some on the sitar: some lie down and sleep, some go for a walk, and others read; but very little attention is paid to the improvement of the mind by study or conversation of an improving character. A good deal of idle talk is indulged in: perhaps somebody's real or fancied disregard of caste-rules may be discussed, and how Shambhu ate three jack-fruit at a sitting. Such is the style of conversation with which the time will be wiled away. Beni Babu's intelligence was of a different order. Most people in this country have a general notion that when school-days are over, education itself is complete; but this is a great error. However much may be the attention paid to the acquisition of knowledge from birth to death, the further shore of learning is never reached. Knowledge can only increase in proportion to the attention that is paid to learning: Beni Babu understood this well and acted accordingly.

He had risen as usual one morning, and having first looked into his household affairs, had taken up a book in order to prosecute his studies, when suddenly a boy of fourteen, with a charm round his neck, a ring in his ear, a bracelet on his wrist and an armlet on his arm, appeared before him and saluted him. Beni Babu was engrossed in his book, but was roused by the sound of approaching footsteps, and guessing who the boy was, said to him: "Come here, Matilall, come here! is all well at home?" "All is well," replied the boy. Beni Babu bade Matilall stay with him for the night, and promised the next morning to take him to Calcutta and put him to school. Some little time after this, Matilall, having finished his meal, perceived that time was likely to hang heavy on his hands, as it would not be dark for a long time yet. Being naturally of a very restless disposition, it was always a hard thing for him to sit long in one place; so he rose very quietly from his seat, and proceeded to explore the house. First he tried to work the mill for husking rice with his feet; then he tramped about on the terraced roof of the house; then commenced throwing bricks and tiles at the passers by, running away when he had done so as hard as he could. Thus he made the circuit of Bally, tramping noisily about, stealing fruit out of people's gardens and plucking the flowers, or else jumping about on the top of the village huts and breaking the water-jars. The people, annoyed by such conduct as this, asked each other: "Who is this boy? Surely our village will be ruined as Lanka was by Hanuman the house-burner." Some of them, when they heard the name of the boy's father, remarked: "Ah, he is the son of Baburam Babu! what then can you expect? Is it not written: 'Men's virtues are reflected in a son, in renown, and in water?'"

As the evening drew on the village resounded with the cries of jackals and the humming of innumerable insects. As many men of position reside in Bally, and the shalgram is to be found in the houses of most of them, there was no lack of the sound of handbells and conch shells. Beni Babu had just risen from his reading and was stretching his limbs preparatory to a smoke, when a great commotion suddenly arose. "Sir, the son of the zemindar of Vaidyabati has been throwing bricks at us!" "Sir, he has thrown away my basket!" "He has been pushing me about!" "He has grossly insulted me!" "He has broken my pot of ghee!" Beni Babu, being very tender-hearted, gave each of the men a present, and dismissed them; then he fell to musing on the kind of training this boy must have been given to behave in such a fashion. "A fine bringing up the lad must have had," he said to himself, "in the short space of three hours he has thrown the whole village into a state of panic: it will be a great relief when he goes." Presently some of the oldest and most respected of the inhabitants of the place came to him and said: "Beni Babu, who is this boy? We were taking our usual nap after our midday meal, when we were aroused by this clamour: it is most unpleasant to have our rest broken in upon in this way." Beni Babu replied: "Please say no more; I have had a very heavy burden imposed upon me: one of my relatives, a zemindar, a man rather lacking in common sense if possessed of great wealth, has sent his son to me to put to school for him; and meanwhile I am being worn to a mere shadow with the annoyance. If I had to keep a boy like this with me for three days, my house would become a ruin for doves to come and roost in."

As this conversation was proceeding, several boys approached, Matilall in their rear, all singing at the top of their voices the refrain—

"To Shambhu's son all honour pay,
"Shambu, the lord of night and day."

"Ah!" said Beni Babu, "here he comes: keep quiet, perhaps he may take it into his head to beat us: I shall not breathe freely till I have got rid of the monkey." Seeing Beni Babu, Matilall seemed somewhat ashamed of himself, and looked a little disconcerted: to his question however as to where he had been, he replied that he had merely been trying to form some idea of the size of the place. When they had entered the house, Matilall ordered Ram the servant to bring him some tobacco, but it was no good giving him the ordinary make; he smoked pipe after pipe of the very strongest, and Ram could not supply him fast enough. It was "Ram bring this!" "Ram, I do not want that!" in fact, Ram could not attend to any other work, but had to be constantly in attendance upon Matilall, keeping him supplied with tobacco. Beni Babu was astounded at such behaviour, and kept turning his head and glancing curiously in his direction. When the time for the evening meal came, Beni Babu took Matilall with him into the zenana side of the house and regaled him with all sorts of luxuries; then having taken the usual betel by way of a digestive, retired to rest. Matilall also retired to his sleeping chamber and got into bed, when he had chewed pán and smoked enough. For sometime he tossed restlessly about, now on this side, now on that; and every now and then he would get up and walk about, singing snatches of the love songs of Nil Thakur, or the old story of the separation of Radha and Krishna as told by Ram Basu. At the noise he made, sleep fled from all in the house.

Ram and Pelaram, the gardener, an inhabitant of Kashijora, had been asleep in the common thatched hall used for the family worship. After the work of the day, sleep is a great relief, and to have it rudely disturbed is naturally a source of much irritation. Both Ram and Pelaram were roused from their rest by the noise of the singing. Pelaram exclaimed: "Ah, Ram, my father! I can get no sleep while this bull is bellowing in this way: I might just as well get up and sow some seeds in the garden." Ram, turning himself round, replied: "Ah, it is midnight! why get up now? The master has done a fine thing in bringing this brat here: it means ruin to us all. The boy is a terrible nuisance: we shall not breathe again till he goes."

Early next morning, Beni Babu took Matilall away with him to the house of Becharam Banerjea of Bow Bazar. This gentleman was the son of Kenaram Babu, and a man of very old family: he was a childlike, simple-minded man, hair-lipped from his birth, and highly excitable on the smallest provocation. Seeing Beni Babu, he called to him in his peculiar nasal tone: "Come, tell me what is in your mind now?"

Beni.—Well, seeing that Baburam Babu has no relative like yourself in Calcutta, I have come to request of you that his boy Matilall may live in your house while he is attending school, going to Vaidyabati for his Saturday holiday.

Becharam.—Well, there can be no possible objection to that. He is perfectly welcome to come and stay in my house: this is as much his home as his father's house is. I have no children of my own, and only two nephews; let Matilall then stay with me as long as he pleases.

On hearing Becharam Babu's nasal twang, Matilall burst out laughing. Beni Babu gave a sigh of disgust, thinking to himself that there would be little peace here so long as such a boy as this was about. Becharam noted the jeering laugh, and observed to Beni Babu, "Ah! friend Beni, the youngster appears somewhat ill-mannered and boorish. I imagine that he must have been constantly indulged from infancy."

Beni Babu was a very shrewd man. His former history was known to all. He too had led a wild life, but had remedied everything by his own good qualities. He now told himself that if he were to express his real opinion of Matilall, the boy might be ruined: there would be an end to his remaining in Calcutta and to his school education, and it was his own earnest wish that the boy should grow to man's estate with some sort of training at least. So after exchanging ideas on many other topics, he took his leave of Becharam Babu and went with Matilall to the school of one Mr. Sherborn. Owing to the establishment of the Hindu College, this gentleman's school had somewhat diminished in numbers: it required all his attention, and constant toil day and night, to keep it going. He himself was a stout man with heavy and bushy eyebrows; was never seen without pán in his mouth and a cane in his hand; and would vary his walks up and down his classes by occasionally sitting down and pulling at a hooka. Beni Babu having placed Matilall at his school, returned to Bally.

IV

MATILALL IN THE POLICE COURT

When the British merchants first came to Calcutta, the Setts and Baisakhs were the great traders, but none of the people of the city knew English: all business communications with the foreigners had to be carried on by means of signs. Man will always find a way out of a difficulty if need be, and by means of these signs a few English words get to be known. After the establishment of the Supreme Court, increased attention was paid to English: this was chiefly due to the influence of the law courts. By that time Ram Ram Mistori and Ananda Ram Dass, who were representative men in Calcutta, had learned many English expressions: Ram Narayan Mistori, a pupil of Ram Ram Mistori, was engaged as clerk to an attorney and used to write out petitions for a great many people; he also kept a school, his pupils paying from fourteen to sixteen rupees a month. Following his example, others, as for instance Ram Lochan Napit and Krisha Mohun Basu, adopted the profession of schoolmaster: their pupils used to read some English book and learn the meaning of words by heart. At marriage ceremonies and festivals, everybody would contemplate with awe and astonishment, and loudly applaud, any boy who could utter a few English expressions. Following the example set by others, Mr. Sherborn had opened his school at a somewhat late period, and the children of people belonging to the upper grades of society were being educated at his establishment.

Now boys with a real desire to learn may pick up something or other, by dint of their own exertions, at any school they may be attending. All schools have their good and bad points, and there are a large number of lads so peculiarly constituted that they keep wandering about from school to school, under pretence of being dissatisfied with each one they go to, and think, by passing their time in this unsettled way, to deceive their parents into the belief that they are learning something. So Matilall, after attending Mr. Sherborn's school for a few days, had himself entered anew at the school of a Mr. Charles.

The chief end in view in all education is the development of a good disposition and a high character, the growth of a right understanding, and the attainment of a thorough mastery of any work that may have to be attended to in the practical business of life. If the education of children is conducted on these lines, they may become in every way respectable members of society, competent to understand and duly execute all their business both at home and abroad. But to ensure that such a training shall be given, both parents and teachers have need to exert themselves. The young will naturally follow in the footsteps of their elders. Goodness in the parents is a necessary condition of the growth of goodness in the children. If a drunken father forbids his child liquor, why should the child listen to him? If a father, himself addicted to immorality, attempts to instruct a son in morals, he will at once recall the mousing cat that professed asceticism, and will only mock at his hypocrisy. The son whose father lives a virtuous life has no great need of advice and counsel: mere observation of his father will generate a good disposition. The mother too must keep her attention constantly fixed on her child: there is nothing so potent in its humanising effect on a child's mind as a mother's sweet conversation, kindness and caresses. A child's good behaviour is assured when he distinctly realises that if he does certain things, his mother will not take him into her lap and caress him. Again, it is the teacher's duty to guard against making a mere parrot of his pupil, when he is teaching him by book. If a boy has to get all he reads by heart, his faculty of memory may be strengthened, it is true; but if his intelligence is not promoted, and he gets no practical knowledge, then his education is all a sham. Whether the pupil be old or young, the matter should be explained to him in such a way that his mind may grasp what he is learning. By a good system of education, and judicious tact in teaching, an intelligent comprehension of a subject may be effected such as no amount of mere chiding will bring about.

Matilall had learned nothing of morality or good conduct in his Vaidyabati home, and now his residence in Bow Bazar proved a curse rather than a blessing. Becharam Babu had two nephews, whose names were Haladhar and Gadadhar. These boys had never known what it was to have a father; and though they occasionally went to school out of fear of their mother and uncle, it was more of a sham than anything else. They mostly wandered at their pleasure, unchecked, about the streets, the river ghâts, the terraced roofs of houses and the open common; and they utterly refused to listen to anybody who tried to restrain them. When their mother remonstrated, they would just retort: "If you do this we will both of us run away"; so they were left to do pretty much as they pleased. They found Matilall one of their own sort, and within a very short time a close intimacy sprang up between them; they became quite inseparable; would sit together, eat together, and sleep together; would put their hands on each other's shoulders, and go about both in doors and out of doors hand in hand, or with their arms round each other's necks. Whenever Becharam's wife saw them, she would say: "They are three brothers, sons of one mother."

Neither children nor youths nor old men can remain for any length of time passive or engaged in one kind of occupation: they must have some way of dividing the twenty-four hours of the day and night between a variety of occupations. In the case of children, special arrangements will have to be made to ensure their having a combination of amusement with instruction. Neither continuous play nor continuous work is a good thing. The chief object of all recreation is to enable a man to pay greater attention to his labour afterwards, his body refreshed by relaxation. The mind only becomes enfeebled by unbroken exertion, and anything learnt in that condition simply floats about on the surface without sinking into it. But in all games there is this to be considered, that those only are beneficial in which there is a certain amount of bodily exertion; no benefit is to be derived from cards or dice or any pastimes of that kind: the only effect of such amusements is to increase the natural tendency to idleness, which is the source of such a variety of evils. Just as there is no good to be derived from unceasing work, so by continuous play the intelligence is apt to get blunted, for thereby the body only is strengthened, the mind is not disciplined at all; and as the latter must be engaged in something or other, is it to be wondered at that in such a condition it should adopt an evil rather than a good course? It is thus that many boys come to grief.

Matilall and his companions Haladhar and Gadadhar roamed about everywhere like so many Brahmini bulls, doing just as they pleased and paying no attention to anyone. They were constantly amusing themselves either with cards and dice or else with kites and pigeon-flying. They could find no time either for regular meals or for sleep. If a servant came to call them into the house, they would only abuse him, and refuse to go in. If ever the maid came to tell them that her mistress could not retire to rest until they had had their supper, they would abuse her in a disgraceful manner. The maid-servant would sometimes retort: "What courteous language you have learned!" All the most worthless boys of the neighbourhood gradually collected together and formed a band. Noise and confusion reigned supreme in the house all day and night, and people in the reception-room could not hear each other's voices: the only sounds were those of uproarious merriment. So much tobacco and ganja was consumed that the whole place was darkened with smoke: no one dared pass by that way when this company was assembled, and there was not a man who would venture to forbid such conduct. Becharam Babu indeed was disgusted when the smell of the tobacco reached him, as it occasionally did; but he would only give vent to his favourite exclamation of disgust and impatience.

Most terrible of all evils are the evils that spring from association with others. Even where there is unremitting attention on the part of parents and teachers, evil company may bring ruin; but where no such effort is made, the extent of corruption that association with others brings about cannot be estimated in language. Matilall's character, far from improving, was, by the aid of his present associates, deteriorating day by day. He might attend school for one or two days in the week, but would merely remain seated there like a dummy, treating the whole thing as a supreme bore. He was continually joking with the other boys or drawing on his slate; would scarce attend for five minutes together to his lessons; and could think of nothing but the fine time he would have with his companions out of school. There are teachers possessed of sufficient skill and tact to draw to the acquisition of knowledge the mind of even such a boy as Matilall: being acquainted with various methods of imparting instruction, they adopt that which is likely to prove most efficacious in each particular case. Now the teaching in Mr. Charles' school was as indifferent as the teaching in Government schools often is at the present day. Equal attention was not paid to all the classes and all the boys, and no pains were taken to ascertain whether they thoroughly understood the easy books they had to read before they proceeded to more difficult ones. A good many people are firmly convinced that a school derives its importance from the number of books prescribed, and the amount read. It was considered quite sufficient for the boys to repeat their lessons by heart: it was not supposed to be necessary to know whether they understood or not; and it was never taken into consideration at all whether the education they were receiving was one that would fit them for the practical business of afterlife. Unless influences are very strong in their favour, boys attending such schools have not much chance of receiving any education at all. Take into account Matilall's father, the companions he had collected about him, the place he was living in, the school he was attending, and some idea may be formed of the extent of his intellectual training.

Teachers vary as much as schools do. One man will take immense pains, while another will simply trifle away his times, fidgetting about and pulling his moustache. Mr. Charles' factotum was Bakreswar Babu, of Batalata; and he could do nothing without him. This man made it his practice to visit his pupils' rich parents, and say to them all alike: "Ah sir, I always pay special attention to your boy! he is the true son of his father: he is no ordinary boy, that: he is a perfect model of a boy." Bakreswar Babu had charge of the education of the higher classes in the school, but it was exceedingly doubtful whether he himself understood what he taught. If this had got generally known he would have been disgraced for life, so he kept very quiet on the subject. His sole work was to make the boys read; and if any boy asked him for the meaning of a word, he would bid him look in the dictionary. He was bound of course to make a few corrections here and there in the translation exercises the boys did for him; for if he were to pass them all as correct, where would be his occupation as a school-master? So he would make corrections, even when there was no necessity for doing so, and when by doing so he actually made mistakes which did not exist before: then if the boys asked him what he was about, he would tell them they were very insolent and had no business to contradict him. He generally paid most attention to rich men's sons, and would question them at length about the rents and value of their property. In a very short time, Matilall became a great favourite with Bakreswar Babu: the boy would bring him presents of flowers or fruit or books, or handkerchiefs. Bakreswar Babu's idea was that he ought not to let boys like Matilall slip out of his hands, for when they reached man's estate, they might become as a "field of beguns" to him,—a perpetual source of profit. What benefit too, he thought, would he derive in the next world from looking after the affairs of this school!

The time of the great autumn festival, the Durga Pujah, had now arrived. In the bazaars and everywhere there was a great stir, and the general bustle and confusion gave additional zest to Matilall's passion for amusement. He suffered agonies so long as he had to remain in school: his attention was perpetually distracted; at one moment sitting at his desk, at the next playing on it; never still for a single moment. One Saturday he had been attending school as usual, and having got a half-holiday out of Bakreswar Babu, had left for home. On his way he purchased some betel and pán, and was proceeding merrily along, his whole attention fixed on the pigeon and kite shops that lined the road, and taking no note of the passers-by, when suddenly a sergeant of police and some constables came up and caught him by the arm, the sergeant telling him that he held a warrant for his arrest, and that he must go quietly along with him. Matilall did his best to get his arm free, but the sergeant was a powerful man and kept a firm grasp as he dragged him along. Matilall next threw himself on the ground and, bruised all over and covered with dust as he was, made repeated efforts to escape: the sergeant thereupon hit him with his fist several times. At last, as he lay overpowered on the ground, the thought of his father caused the boy to burst into tears, and there rose forcibly in his mind the question: "Why have I acted as I have done? Association with others has been my ruin." A crowd now began to collect in the road, and people asked each other what was the matter. Some old women discussing the affair inquired: "Whose child is this that they are beating so?—the child with the moon-face? ah, it makes one's heart bleed to hear him cry!" The sun had not set when Matilall was brought to the police-station: there he found Haladhar, Gadadhar, Ramgovinda and Dolgovinda, with other boys from his neighbourhood, all standing aside, looking extremely woe-begone. Mr. Blaquiere was police magistrate at that time, and it would have been his business to examine the prisoners; but he had gone home, so they had to remain for the night in the lock-up.

V

Baburam in Calcutta

Singing snatches of a popular love-song:—

> *"For my lost love's sake I am dying:*
> *"And my heart is faint with sighing."*

and varying his song with whistling, Meeah Jan, a cart- man, was urging his bullocks along the road, abusing them roundly for their slowness, twisting their tails, and whacking them with his whip. A few clouds were overhead, and a little rain was falling. The bullocks as they went lumbering along, succeeded in overtaking the hired gharry in which Premnarayan Mozoomdar was travelling. It was swaying from side to side in the wind: the two horses were wretched specimens of their kind, and must surely have belonged to the far-famed race of the Pakshi-raj, king of birds. They were doing their best to get along, poor beasts, but notwithstanding the blows that rained down on their backs from the driver's whip, their pace did not mend very considerably. Before starting on his journey, Premnarayan had eaten a very hearty meal, and at each jolt of the gharry his heart was in his mouth. His disgust however increased as the bullock cart drew ahead of his vehicle. Premnarayan need not be blamed for this. Every man has some self-respect which he does not care to lose. The majority have a high opinion of themselves, and while some lose their tempers if there is the slightest failing in the respect they think due to them, others feel humiliated and depressed.

Premnarayan, in his passion, expressed his thoughts thus to himself:—"Ah! what a hateful thing is service. The servant is regarded as no better than a dog! he must run to execute any order that is given. How long has my soul been vexed by the rude behaviour of Haladhar, Gadadhar, and the other boys! They would never let me eat or sleep in peace: they have even composed songs in derision of me: their jests have been as irritating to me as ant-bites; they have signalled to other boys in the street to annoy me: they have gone so far as to clap their hands at me behind my back. Can anyone submit tamely to such treatment as this? It is enough to drive a sane man out of his senses. I must have a good stock of courage not to have run away from Calcutta long ago: it is due to my good genius only that so far I have not lost my employment. At last the scoundrels have met with their deserts: may they now rot in jail, never to get out again! Yet after all these are idle words; is not my journey being made with the express object of effecting their release? has not this duty been imposed upon me by my employer? Alas, I have no voice in the matter! if men are not to starve, they must do and bear all this."

Baburam Babu of Vaidyabati was seated in all a Babu's state; his servant, Hari, was rubbing his master's feet. Seated on one side of him the pandits were discussing some trivial points relating to certain observances enjoined by the Shastras, such as:—"Pumpkins may be eaten today, beguns should not be eaten tomorrow; to take milk with salt is quite as bad as eating the flesh of cows." On the other side of him, some friends were engaged in a game of chess: one of them was in deep thought, his head supported on his hand: evidently his game was up, he was checkmated. Some musicians in the room were mingling their harmonies, their instruments twanging noisily. Near him were his mohurrirs writing up their ledgers, and before him stood sundry creditors, tenants of his, and tradesmen from the bazaar, some of whose accounts were passed, and others refused. People kept thronging into the reception-room. Certain of his tradespeople were explaining how they had been supplying him for years with one thing and another, and now were in great distress, having hitherto received nothing by way of payment; how, moreover, from their constant journeyings to and fro, their business was being utterly neglected and ruined. Retail shopkeepers too, such as oilmen, timber-merchants and sweetmeat-sellers, were complaining bitterly that they were ruined, and that their lives were not worth a pin's head: if he continued to treat them as he was doing, they could not possibly live: they had worn out the muscles of their legs in their constant journeyings to and fro to get payment: their shops were all shut, their wives and children starving. The whole time of the Babu's dewan was taken up in answering these people. "Go away for the present," he was saying, "you will receive payment all right; why do you jabber so much?" Did any of them venture to remonstrate, Baburam Babu would scowl, abuse him roundly, and have him forcibly ejected from the room.

A great many of the wealthy Babus of Bengal take the goods of the simple country-folk on credit: it would give them an attack of fever to have to pay ready-money for anything. They have the cash in their chests, but if they were not to keep putting their creditors off, how could they keep their reception-rooms crowded? Whether a poor tradesman lives or dies is no concern of theirs; only let them play the magnifico, and their fathers' and grandfathers' names be kept before the public! Many there are who thus make a false show of being rich; they present a splendid figure before the outside world, while within they are but men of straw after all.

"Out of doors you flaunt it bravely, wealth is in your very air:

"In the house the rats are squealing, and the cupboard's mostly bare."

It would be death to them to be obliged to regulate their expenditure by their income, for then they could not be the owners of gardens or live the luxurious life of the rich Babu. By keeping up a fine exterior they hope to throw dust in the eyes of their tradesmen. When they take money or goods from others, they practically borrow twice over; for when pressure is brought to bear upon them to make them pay, they borrow from one man only to pay what they owe someone else; and when at last a summons is issued against them, they register their property under another person's name, and are off somewhere out of the way for the time being.

Baburam Babu was devoted to his money and very close-fisted: it was always a great grief to him to be obliged to take cash out of his chest. He was engaged in wrangling with his tradespeople when Premnarayan arrived, and whispered in his ear the news from Calcutta. Baburam was thunderstruck for a time. When shortly after he recovered himself, he had Mokajan Meeah summoned to his presence. Now Mokajan was skilled in all matters of law. Zemindars, indigo planters, and others were continually going to him for advice; for a man like this, gifted with such ability for making up cases, for suborning witnesses, for getting police and other officers of the court under his thumb, for disposing secretly of stolen property, for collecting witnesses in cases of disputes, and generally for making right appear wrong and wrong right, was not to be found everyday. Out of compliment to him, people all called him Thakchacha: this was a great gratification to him, and his thoughts often shaped themselves thus: "Ah, my birth must have taken place at an auspicious moment! my observances of the seasons of Ramjan and Eed have answered well; and if I am only properly attentive to my patron saint, I fancy my importance will increase still further." Though engaged in his ablutions at the time that Baburara Babu's peremptory summons reached him, he came away at one and listened, in private, to all Baburam had to say. After a few minutes' reflection, he said : "Why be alarmed, Babu? How many hundred cases of a similar kind have I disposed of! Is there any great difficulty in the way this time? I have some very clever fellows in my employ; I have only to take them with me, and will win the case on their testimony: you need be under no apprehension. I am going away just now, but I will return the first thing in the morning."

Baburam, though somewhat encouraged by these words, was still not at all comfortable in his mind. He was much attached to his wife, and everything she said was always, in his view, shrewdly to the point: were she to say to him, "This is not water, it is milk," with the evidence of his own eyes against him, he would reply: "Ah, you are quite right! this is not water, it is milk. If the mistress of the house says so, it must be so." Most men, whatever the affection they have for their wives, are at least able to exercise some discretion as to the matters in which those ladies are to be consulted and to what extent they should be listened to. Good men love their wives with heartfelt affection; but if they are to accept everything their wives say they may just as well dress in saris, and sit at home. Now Baburam Babu was entirely under his wife's thumb: if she bade him get up, he would get up; if she bade him sit down, he would sit down.

Some months before this, she had presented her husband with a son, and she was busy nursing the infant on her lap, her two daughters seated by her. Their conversation was running on household affairs and other matters, when suddenly the master of the house came into the room and sitting down with a very sad countenance, said: "My dear wife, I am most unlucky! The one idea of my life has been to hand over the charge of all my property to Matilall on his reaching man's estate, and to go and live with you at Benares; but all my hopes have, I fear, been dashed to the ground."

The Mistress of the House.—O my dear husband, what is the matter? Quick, tell me! my breast is heaving with emotion. Is all well with my darling Matilall?

The Master.—O yes, so far as his health goes he is well enough, but I have just received news that the police have apprehended him and put him in jail.

The Mistress.—What was that you said? They have dragged away Matilall to prison? And why, why, my husband, have they imprisoned him? Alas, alas! The poor boy must be a mass of bruises! I expect, too, he has had nothing to eat and not been able to get any sleep. O my husband, what is to be done? Do bring my darling Matilall back to me again!

With this, the mistress of the house began to weep: her two daughters wiped away the tears from her eyes, and tried their best to console their mother. The infant too seeing its mother crying, began to howl lustily.

In the course of his enquiries, made under pretence of conversation, her husband got to know that Matilall had been in the habit, under one pretext or another, of getting money out of her. She had not mentioned the matter to her husband for fear of his displeasure: the boy had been unfortunate, and she could not tell what might have happened if he had got angry. Wives ought to tell all that concerns their children to their husbands, for a disease that is concealed from the surgeon can never be cured. After a long consultation with his wife, the master sent off a letter by night, to arrange for some of his relatives to meet him in Calcutta at his lodgings.

A night of happiness passes away in the twinkling of an eye, but how slowly drag the hours when the mind is sunk in an abyss of painful thought! It may be close to dawn, and the day may be every moment drawing nearer, but yet it seems to tarry. Ways and means occupied the whole of Baburam Babu's thoughts throughout the night: he could no longer remain quietly in the house, and long before the morning came was in a boat with Thakchacha and his companions. As the tide was running strong, the boat soon reached the Bagbazaar Ghât.

Night had nearly come to an end: oil-dealers were busy putting their mills in order, ready to work: cart-men were leading their bullocks off to their day's toil: the washermen's donkeys were labouring with their loads upon the road: men were hurrying along at a swing-trot with loads of fish and vegetables. The pandits of the place were all off with their sacred vessels to the river for their morning bathe; the women were collecting at the different ghâts and exchanging confidences with each other. "I am suffering agonies from my sister-in-law's cruelty," said one. "Ah, my spiteful mother-in-law!" exclaimed another. "Oh, my friends!" cried another, "I have no wish to live any longer, my daughter-in-law tyrannises over me so, and my son says nothing to her; in fact, she has made my son like a sheep with her charms." "Alas!" said another, "I have such a wretch of a sister-in-law! she tyrannises over me day and night."

Another lamented, "My darling child is now ten years old; my life is so uncertain, it is high time for me to think of getting him married."

There had been rain in the night, and patches of cloud were still to be seen in the sky; the roads and the steps of the ghâts were all slippery in consequence. Baburam Babu puffed away at his hooka and looked out for a hired gharry or a palki, but he would not agree to the fare demanded: it was a great deal too much to his mind. When the boys who had collected in the road saw how Baburam Babu was chaffering, some of them said to him: "Had you not better, sir, be carried in a coolie's basket? The charge for that will be only two pice." As Baburam Babu ran after them and tried to hit them, roundly abusing them the while, he fell heavily to the ground. The boys only laughed at this and clapped their hands at him from a safe distance. Baburam with a woebegone countenance then got into a gharry with Thakchacha and his companions. The gharry went creaking along, and eventually pulled up at the house of Bancharam Babu, of Outer Simla.

Bancharam Babu was the principal agent of a Mr. Butler, an attorney living in Boitakhana; he had had a good deal of experience in the law-courts and in cases-at-law: though his pay was only fifty rupees a month, there was no limit to his gains, and festivals were always in full swing in his house.

Beni Babu of Bally, Becharam Babu of Bow Bazar, and Bakreswar Babu of Batalata, were all seated in his sitting-room, waiting for Baburam Babu. With the arrival of that worthy the business of the day commenced.

Becharam.—Oh Baburam, what a venomous reptile have you been nourishing all this time! You would never listen to me, though time after time I sent word to you. Your boy Matilall has pretty well done for his chances in this world and in the next: he drinks his fill, he gambles, he eats things forbidden: caught in the very act of gambling, he struck a policeman: Haladhar, Gadadhar, and other boys were with him at the time. Having no children of my own, I had fondly thought that Haladhar and Gadadhar would be as sons to me, to offer the customary libation to my spirit when I was no more, but my hopes are as goor into which sand has fallen. I really have no words to express my disgust at the boy's behaviour.

Baburam.—Which of them has corrupted the other it may be very difficult to say with any certainty; but just now please tell me how I am to proceed with reference to the investigation.

Becharam.—So far as I am concerned, you may do exactly as you think fit. I have been put to very great annoyance. The boys have been going into the temple at night and drinking heavily there: they have made the beams black with the smoke from tobacco and ganja: they have stolen my gold and silver ornaments and sold them; and one day they even went so far as to threaten to grind the holy shalgram to powder and eat it with their betel in lieu of lime. Can you expect me then to subscribe towards their release? Ugh! certainly not.

Bakreswar.—Matilall is not so bad as all that: I have seen a good deal of him at school: he has naturally a good disposition. He was no ordinary boy; he was a perfect model of behaviour: how then he can have become what you describe is beyond me.

Thakchacha.—May I ask what need there is of all this irrelevant talk? We are not likely to get our stomachs filled by simply chatting of oil and straw: let a case be thoroughly well got up for the trial.

Bancharam (highly delighted at the prospect of making a good thing out of the case.)—Matters of business require a man of business. Thakchacha's words are shrewdly to the point: we must get a few good witnesses together and have them thoroughly instructed in their role betimes; we must also engage our friend Mr. Butler the attorney. If after all that we do not win our case, I will take it up to the High Court. Then if the High Court can do nothing, I will go up to the Council with the case; and if the Council can do nothing, we must carry it to England for appeal. You may put implicit confidence in me: I am not a man to be trifled with. But nothing can be done unless we secure the services of Mr. Butler. He is a thoroughly practical man: knows all manner of contrivances for upsetting cases, and trains his witnesses as carefully as a man trains birds.

Bakreswar.—A keen intelligence is needed in time of misfortune. A very careful preparation for the trial is required: why be jeered at for want of it?

Bancharam.—So clever an attorney as Mr. Butler it has never fallen to my lot to see. I have no language capable of expressing his astuteness: three words will suffice for him to have all these cases dismissed. Come, gentlemen, rise and let us go to him.

Beni.—Pardon me, sir, I could not do what I know to be wrong, even were my life at stake! I am prepared to follow your advice in most matters, but I cannot risk my chances of happiness in the next world. It is best to acknowledge a fault if one has really been committed: there is no danger in truth, whereas to take refuge in a lie only intensifies an evil.

Thakchacha.—Ha! ha! what business have bookworms with law? The very mention of the word sets them all atremble! If we take the course this gentleman advises, we may as well at once prepare our graves! Sage counsels indeed to listen to!

Bancharam.—At this rate, gentlemen, it will be the case of the old proverb over again,—"The festival is over, and your preparations still progressing." I have no doubt that Beni Babu is a man of very solid parts; why, in the Niti Shastras, he is a second Jagannath Tarkapanchanan! I shall have to go some day to Bally to hold an argument with him, but we have no time for that just now; we must be up and doing.

Becharam.—Ah, Beni my friend, I am quite of your mind! I am getting an old man now: already three periods of my life have passed away and one only is left to me. I too will do no wrong, even if my life be at stake. Who are these boys that I should do what is wrong for them? They have made my life a perfect burden to me. Shall I be put to any expense for them? Certainly not: they may go to jail for all I care, and then perhaps I may contrive to live in peace. Why should I trouble myself anymore about them? The very sight of their faces makes my blood boil. Ugh! the young wretches!

VI

Matilall's Mother and Sisters

The Vaidyabati house was all astir with preparations for a religious ceremonial. The sun had not risen when Shridhar Bhattacharjea, Ram Gopal Charamani and other Brahman priests, set to work repeating mantras. All were employed upon something: one was offering the sacred basil to the deity: some were busy picking the leaves of the jessamine: others humming and beating time on their cheeks. One was remarking: "I am no Brahman if good fortune does not attend the sacrifices"; and another, "If things turn out inauspiciously, I will abandon my sacred thread." The whole household was busily engaged, but not a member of it was happy in mind. The mistress of the house was sitting at an open window and calling in her distress upon her guardian deity: her infant boy lay near her, playing with a toy and tossing his little limbs in the air. Every now and again she glanced in the direction of the child, and said to herself: "Ah my darling, I cannot say what kind of destiny awaits you! To be childless is a single sorrow and anxiety: multiplied a hundredfold is the misery that comes with children. How is a mother's mind distracted if her child has the slightest complaint! she will cheerfully sacrifice her life in order to get him well again: so long as her babe is ill, all capacity for food and sleep deserts her: day and night to her are alike. If a child who has caused her so much sorrow grows up good, she feels her work accomplished; but if the contrary be the case, a living death is hers: she takes no interest in anything in the world and cares not to show herself in the neighbourhood. The haughty face grows wan and pinched: in her inmost heart, like Sita, she gives expression to this wish: 'Oh, Earth, Earth, open, and let me hide myself within thy bosom!' The good God knows what trouble I have taken to make Matilall a man: my young one has now learned to fly, and heavy is my chastisement. How it grieves me to hear of such evil conduct: I am almost heartbroken with sorrow and chagrin. I have not told my husband all: he might have gone mad had he heard all. Away with these thoughts! I can endure them no longer: I am but a weak woman. What will such laments avail me now? what must be, must be."

A maid-servant came in at that moment and took the child away, and the mistress of the house engaged in her daily religious duties.

Man's mind is so constituted that it cannot readily forget any particular matter it may be absorbed in, to attend to other affairs in hand. When therefore she tried to perform her usual devotions, she found herself unable to do so. Again and again she set herself to fix her attention on the mantras she had to repeat, but her mind kept wandering: the thought of Matilall surged up like a strong and irresistible flood. At one time she fancied that the orders for his imprisonment had been passed, and her imagination depicted him as already in fetters, and being led off to jail: she even thought she saw his father standing near him, his head bowed down in woe, weeping bitterly; and again she almost fancied that her son was come to see her, and was saying to her: "Mother, forgive me: what is past cannot now be mended, but I will never again cause you such trouble and sorrow." She then began to dream of some great calamity as about to befall Matilall,—that he would be transported perhaps for life. When these phantoms of her imagination had left her, she began to say to herself: "Why, it is now high noon! can I have been dreaming? No, surely this is no dream! I must have seen a vision. I wish I could tell why my mind is so distracted today!" With these words she laid herself silently down on the ground, and wept bitterly.

Her two daughters, Mokshada and Pramada, were busy drying their hair on the roof, and Mokshada was saying to her sister: "Why sister Pramada, you have not half combed your hair, and how dry it is too! But it must be so, for it is ages since a drop of oil fell upon it. It is just the use of oil and water that keeps people in good health: to bathe once a month, and without using oil, would be bad for anyone. But why are you so wrapped in thought? anxiety and trouble are making you as thin as a string."

Pramada.—Ah, my sister, how can I help thinking? Cannot you understand it all? Our father brought the son of a Kulin Brahmin here when I was a mere child and married me to him. I only heard about this when I was grown up. Considering the number of the different places where he has contracted marriage, and considering his personal character too, I have no wish to see his face: I would rather not have a husband at all than such a one.

Mokshada.—Hush, my dear! you must not say that. It is an advantage to a woman to have a husband alive, whether his character be bad or good.

Pramada.—Listen then to what I have to tell you. Last year, when I was suffering from intermittent fever and had been lying long days and nights on my bed, too weak to rise, my husband came one day to the house. From the time of my earliest impressions, I had never seen what a husband was like: my idea was that there was no treasure a woman could possess like a husband, and I thought that if he only came and sat with me for a few moments and spoke to me, my pain would be alleviated. But, my sister, you will not believe me when I say it! he came to my bedside, and said: "You are my lawful wife, I married you sixteen years ago: I have come to see you now because I am in need of money, and will go away again directly: I have told your father that he has cheated me: come, give me that bracelet off your wrist!" I told him that I would first ask my mother, and would do what she bade me. Thereupon he pulled the bracelet off my wrist by brute force; and when I struggled to prevent his doing so, he gave me a kick and left me. I fainted away, and did not recover till mother came and fanned me.

Mokshada.—Oh my dear sister Pramada, your story brings tears into my eyes. But consider, you still have a husband living: I have not even that.

Pramada.—A fine husband indeed, my sister! Happily for me, I once spent sometime with my uncle, and learned to read and write and to do a little fancy work with my needle; so by constant work during the day and by a little occasional reading, writing or sewing, I keep my trouble hidden. If I sit idle for anytime, and begin to think, my heart burns with indignation.

Mokshada.—"What else can it do? Ah, it is because of the many sins committed by us in previous births that we are suffering as we are! It is by plenty of hard work that our bodies and minds retain their vigour: idleness only causes evil thoughts and evil imaginations and even disease to get a stronger hold upon us: it was uncle that told me that. I have done all I can to soften the pains of widowhood. I always reflect that everything is in God's hands: reliance upon Him is the real secret of life. My dear sister, if you so constantly ponder on your grief, you will be overwhelmed in the ocean of anxiety: it is an ocean that has no shore. What good can possibly result from so much brooding? Just do all your religious and secular duties as well as you can: honour our father and mother in everything: attend to the welfare of our two brothers: nourish and cherish any children they may have, and they will be as your own.

Pramada.—Ah my sister, what you say is indeed true, but then our elder brother has gone altogether astray. He is given over to vicious ways and vicious companions; and as his disposition has changed for the worse, so his affection for his parents and for us has lessened. Ah, the affection that brothers have for their sisters is not one-hundredth part of the affection that sisters have for their brothers! In their devotion to their brothers, sisters will even risk their lives; but brothers always think that they will get on much better if they can only be rid of their sisters! We are Matilall's elder sisters: if he comes near us at all, he may perhaps make himself agreeable for a short time, and we may congratulate ourselves upon it; but then have we any influence whatever upon his conduct?

Mokshada.—All brothers are not like that. There are brothers who regard their elder sisters as they would their mother, and their younger sisters as they would a daughter. I am speaking the truth: there are brothers who look upon their sisters in the same light as they do their brothers: they are unhappy unless they are free to converse with them; and if they fall into any danger, they risk their lives to save them.

Pramada.—That is very true, but it is our lot to have a brother just in keeping with our unhappy destiny. Alas, there is no such thing as happiness in this world! At this moment, a maid-servant came to tell them her mistress was crying: the two sisters rushed downstairs as soon as they heard it.

It was a fine moonlight evening, the moon shedding her radiance over the breadth of the Ganges. A gentle breeze was diffusing the sweet fragrance of the wild jungle flowers; the waves danced merrily in the moonlight: the birds in a neighbouring grove were calling to each other in their varied notes. Beni Babu was seated at the Deonagaji Ghât, looking about him and singing snatches of some up-country song on the loves of Krishna and Radha. He was completely absorbed in his music and was beating time to it, when suddenly he heard somebody behind him calling his name and echoing his song. Turning round, he saw Becharam Babu of Bow Bazar: he at once rose, and invited his guest to take a seat.

Becharam opened the conversation. "Ah! Beni, my friend! those were home truths you told Baburam Babu today. I have been invited to your village: and as I was so pleased with what I saw of you the other day, I wanted to come and call on you just once before leaving."

Beni.—Ah, my friend Becharam, we are poor sort of folk here! We have to work for our living: we prefer to visit places where the secrets of knowledge or virtue are investigated. We have a good many rich relatives and acquaintances, but we feel embarrassed in their presence; we visit them very occasionally, when we have fallen into any trouble, or have any very particular business on hand. It is never a pleasure to call on upon them, and when we do go we derive no intellectual benefit from the visit; for whatever respect rich men may show to other rich men, they have not much to say to us; they just remark "It is very hot today. How is your business getting on? Is it flourishing? Have a smoke?" If only they speak cheerfully and pleasantly to us, we are fully satisfied. Ah, learning and worth have nothing like the respect shown to them that is shown to wealth! Paying court to rich men is a very dangerous thing: there is a popular saying:—"The friendship of the rich is an embankment made of sand." Their moods are capricious: a trifle will offend them just as a trifle will please them. People do not consider this: wealth has such magic in it that they will put up with any humiliation, any indignity from a rich man; they will even submit to a thrashing, and say to the rich man after it:—"It is your honour's good pleasure." However this be, it is a hard thing to live with the rich and not forfeit one's chances of happiness in the next world. In that affair of today, for instance, we had a hard struggle for the right.

Becharam.—From observation of Baburam Babu's general behaviour, I am inclined to think that his affairs are not prospering. Alas, alas, what counsellors he has got! That wretched Mahomedan, Thakchacha, a prince of rogues! there is an evil magic in him. Then Bancharam, the attorney's clerk! he is like a fine mango, fair outside but rotten at the core. Well-practised in all the arts of chicanery, like a cat treading stealthily along in the wet, he simulates innocence while all the while exercising his wiles to entrap his prey. Anybody falling under the influence of that sorcery would be utterly, and forever, ruined. Then there is Bakreswar the schoolmaster, a teacher of ethics forsooth! A passed master indeed in the art of cajolery, a very prince of flatterers! Ugh! But tell me, is it your English education that has given you this high moral standard?

Beni.—Have I this high moral standard you attribute to me? It is only your kindness to say so. The slight acquaintance I have with morality is entirely due to the kind favour of Barada Babu, of Badaragan: I lived with him for sometime, and he very kindly gave me some excellent advice.

Becharam.—Who is this Barada Babu? Please tell me some

particulars about him. It is always a pleasure to me to hear anything of this kind.

Beni.—Barada Babu's home is in Eastern Bengal, in Pergunnah Etai Kagamari. On the death of his father he moved to Calcutta, and found great difficulty at first in providing himself with food and clothing: he had not even the wherewithal to buy his daily meal. But from his boyhood he had always engaged in meditation upon divine things, and so it was that when trouble befell him it did not affect him so much. At this time he used to live in a common tiled hut, his only means of subsistence being the two rupees a month which he received from a younger brother of his father's. He was on terms of intimacy with a few good men and would associate with none but these: he was very independent, and refused to be under obligations to anybody. Not having the means to keep either a man-servant or a maid-servant, he did all his own marketing, cooking for himself as well; and he did not neglect his studies even when he was cooking. Morning noon and night, he calmly and peacefully meditated on God. The clothes in which he attended school were torn and dirty, and excited the derision of rich men's sons: he pretended not to hear them when they laughed and jeered at him, and eventually succeeded by his pleasant and courteous address in winning them completely over. With very many, pride is the only result of English learning: they scorn the very earth they live on. This however found no place in the mind of Barada Babu: his disposition was too calm and mild. When he had completed his education he left school, and at once obtained employment as a teacher, on thirty rupees a month. He then took his mother, his wife and his two nephews to live with him, and did his very utmost to make them comfortable. He would also look after the wants of the many poor people living in his immediate neighbourhood, helping them, as far as his means allowed, with money, visiting them when they were sick, and supplying them with medicine. As none of these poor people could afford to send their children to school, he held a class for them himself every morning. One of his cousins who had fallen dangerously ill after his father's death, recovered entirely, thanks to the unremitting attention of Barada Babu, who sat by his bedside for days and nights together. He was deeply devoted to his aunt, and regarded her quite as a mother. Some men appear to have a contempt for the things of this world in comparison with things of eternity, like the contempt for death that is characteristic of those who are in constant attendance at burning-ghâts. Does death or calamity befall any of their friends or kinsfolk, the world, they feel, is nothing, and God all. This idea is constantly present to the mind of Barada Babu: conversation with him and observation of his conduct soon make it apparent; but he never parades his opinions before the world. He is in no sense ostentatious: he never does anything for mere appearance sake. All his good deeds are done in secret: numbers of people meet with kindness from him, but only the person actually benefited by him is aware of it; and he is much annoyed if others get any inkling of it. Though a man of varied accomplishments, he is without a particle of vanity. It is the man who has only a smattering of learning who is puffed up with pride and self-importance. "Aha!" says such a one to himself, "what a very learned man I am! Who can write as I do? Who is so erudite as I? How I always do speak to the point!" Barada Babu is a different sort of man altogether: though his learning is so profound, he never treats the thoughts of others as beneath his attention. It does not annoy him to hear an opinion expressed opposite to his own: on the contrary, he listens with pleasure, and reviews his own beliefs. To describe in detail all his good qualities would be a long affair, but they may be summed up in the remark that so gentle and god-fearing a man has rarely been seen: he could not do wrong even if his life were at stake. Yes, the amount of instruction to be had from personal intercourse with Barada Babu far exceeds any to be got from books!

Becharam.—Ah, how it charms one to hear of a man like that! But now, as it is getting very late, and I have to cross the river, I will, with your permission, return home. Let me see you for a moment at the police, court tomorrow.

VII

THE TRIAL OF MATILALL

Very strange is this world's course, and past man's comprehension. How hard it is to determine the causes of things! When we remember for instance the account of the origin of Calcutta, it will appear almost miraculous; for even in a dream none could have imagined that Calcutta as it was could ever have become Calcutta as it is. The East India Company first had a factory at Hooghly, their factor being Mr. Job Charnock. On one occasion he quarrelled with the leading police official of the place; and as the East India Company did not in those days possess the power and dignity which they afterwards acquired, their agent was maltreated and forced to have recourse to flight. Job Charnock had a house and a bazaar of his own at Barrackpur, which in consequence has been known as Chanak, even down to the present time. He had married a woman whom he had rescued from the funeral pile just as she was about to become a suttee; but whether the marriage contributed to the mutual happiness of each, there is no evidence to show. Job Charnock was constantly journeying to and fro between Barrackpur and Uluberia, where he was building a new factory: it was the wish of his heart to have a factory there, but how many undertakings fall just short of completion! As he journeyed to and fro, he used often to pass by Boitakhana, and would halt for a rest and a smoke under a large tree there. This tree was the favourite resort of many men of business, and Job Charnock was so enamoured of the shade of it that he decided upon building his factory there. The three villages of Sutanati, Govindpur and Calcutta, which he had purchased, soon filled up, and it was not long before people of all classes took up their abode there for trade, and so Calcutta soon became a city, and populous. The first beginnings of Calcutta as a city date from the year 1689 of the Christian era. Job Charnock died some three years after that. In those days the great plain where the Fort and Chowringhee now are was all jungle. The Fort itself formerly stood where the Custom House now stands, and Clive Street was the chief business quarter of the city. So fatal to health was Calcutta at one time considered, that the English gentlemen who had escaped with their lives during the year, would annually meet together on the 15th of November and offer their congratulations to each other. One prominent characteristic of Englishmen is to have everything about them scrupulously clean, and disease gradually diminished as sanitary precautions came more and more into vogue. But the people of Bengal do not take this lesson to heart: to the present day there are tanks near the houses of our wealthiest citizens, which smell so bad that one can hardly approach them.

In former days the duties connected with the Revenue and Criminal Courts and the Police Administration of Calcutta devolved upon a single Englishman: he had a Bengali official as his subordinate, and he himself was called the Jemadar. Later on, there came to be other Courts; and with the view of checking the high-handedness of the English in the country, the Supreme Court was established. The administration of the Police was made an independent charge, and was very ably conducted. In the year 1798 of the Christian era, Sir John Richardson and others were employed as Justices of the Peace; and afterwards, in the year 1800, Mr. Blaquiere and others were appointed to hold this office. The jurisdiction of the Justices extended to every part of the country. When it became necessary for the jurisdiction of those who were simply Magistrates to extend beyond their head districts, the assistance of the Judge's Court of the particular district had to be sought, and consequently many Magistrates in the Mofussil have now been made Justices of the Peace. Mr. Blaquiere has been dead some four years; it was currently reported that his father was an Englishman and his mother a Brahman woman, and that he had received his earliest education in India, but had afterwards gone to England and been well educated there. During his tenure of office as head of the Police Department, Calcutta trembled at his stern severity, and all were afraid of him. After sometime he gave up the detective part of his work and the apprehension of criminals, to confine his attention to the trial of prisoners brought before him. He made an excellent judge, being well versed in the language of the country, its customs, manners, and all the inner details of the life of the people. He had the Criminal Law too at his fingers' ends; and having for sometime acted as interpreter to the Supreme Court, was thoroughly well acquainted with the proper method of conducting trials.

Time and water run apace. Monday came. Ten o'clock had just struck by the church clock: the police court was crowded with police officers, sergeants, constables, darogahs, naibs, sub-inspectors, chowkidars, and with all sorts and conditions of people. Some of these were keepers of low lodging-houses and women of loose character, who sat about the Court chewing betel and pán: some, as their bloodstained clothes sufficiently showed were victims of assaults: some were thieves, who sat apart dejected and sad: some, conspicuous by their turbans, were engaged in writing out petitions in English. Some were complainants in the different cases, who tramped noisily about the court; others, who were to be witnesses, were busily whispering to each other: the men who make it their business to provide bail were sitting about as thick as crows at a ghât. Here were pleaders' touts, using all their arts to get clients for their masters: there were pleaders engaged in coaching their witnesses: and here the amlahs were writing out cases that had been sent up by the Police. The sergeants of police looked very important as they marched up and down with proud and pompous port. The chief clerks were discussing different English magistrates: this one was declared to be a great fool, that one a very cunning man, a third too mild and easily imposed upon, a fourth too harsh and rough; they pronounced also an unfavourable criticism on the orders passed the previous day in a particular case. The police court was so crowded, indeed, that it seemed the very Hall of Yama, and all looked forward with fear and trembling to their fate.

Baburam Babu came bustling up to the court, accompanied by his pleader, his counsellor Thakchacha, and some of his relatives. Thakchacha was wearing a conical cap, fine muslin clothes, and the peculiar turned-up shoes of his class. His crystal beads in hand, he was invoking the names of his special guardian genius and his Prophet, and muttering his prayers with repeated shakings of the head; but this was all mere ostentation. A man so full of tricks as Thakchacha is not met with everyday. At the police court he spun about hither and thither, for all the world like a peg-top. At one moment he was coaching his witnesses in a whisper; the next, walking about hand in hand with Baburam Babu; the next, consulting with Mr. Butler: in this way he attracted everybody's attention. Now it is a failing with many people to imagine their fathers and grandfathers (who may have been great rogues in reality) to have been celebrated people, well known to all; and the consequence is that when they have to introduce themselves to others they will do so, saying: "I am the son of so-and-so, and the grandson of so-and-so." To anybody who came up to converse with Thakchacha, he would introduce himself as the son of Abdul Rahman Gul, and the grandson of Ampak Ghulam Hosain. A sircar in the court, who was fond of his joke, remarked to him: "Come, tell me what is your special business? A few low-class Mahomedans in your own neighbourhood may perhaps know the names of your father and grandfather, but who is likely to know them in this city of Calcutta? perhaps however they carried on the profession of syces." Thakchacha, his eyes inflamed with passion, replied: "I can say nothing here, as this is the police court: in any other place, I would fall upon you and tear you to pieces." As he said this, he grasped Baburam Babu's hand in his, to make the sircar imagine him a man of much importance, held in high honour.

Meanwhile there was a stir near the steps of the police court: a carriage had just driven up: the door was opened, and a withered old gentleman alighted from it. The sergeants of police raised their hats in salute, and called out, "Mr. Blaquiere has arrived." The magistrate, having taken his seat on the bench, disposed first of some cases of assault. Matilall's case was then called. The complainants, Kale Khan and Phate Khan, took up their position on one side, while on the other side stood Baburam Babu of Vaidyabati, Beni Babu of Bally, Bakreswar Babu of Batalata, Becharam Babu of Bow Bazar, and Mr. Butler of Boitakhana. Baburam Babu was wearing a fine shawl, and had a gorgeous turban on his head: his sacred caste mark, with the sign of the Hom offering over it, was conspicuous on his forehead. With tears in his eyes, and his hands folded humbly in supplication, he gazed at the magistrate, who, he fondly imagined, would be sure to commiserate him if he saw his tears. Matilall, Haladhar, Gadadhar, and the other accused, were brought before the magistrate: Matilall stood there, with his head bowed low in shame. When Baburam Babu saw the boy's face pinched from want of food, his heart was pierced. The complainants charged the accused with gambling in a place of ill-fame, and with having effected their escape when arrested by grievously assaulting them; and they stripped and showed the marks of the assault upon their persons. Mr. Butler cross-examined the complainants and their witness at some length, and conclusively showed that there was no case made out against Matilall. This was not at all surprising, considering that for one thing he had all a pleader's art exercised in his favour, and for another that there was collusion between the complainants and the counsel of the accused. What will not money do? An old proverb runs:—

"Gold for the dotard a fair bride will win."

Mr. Butler afterwards produced his witnesses, who all declared that on the day the assault was said to have been committed, Matilall was at home at Vaidyabati; but on cross-examination by Mr. Blaquiere, they were not so clear. Thakchacha saw that things were not going well: a slight slip might ruin everything. Most people, reduced to the necessity of having recourse to law, give up all ideas of right and wrong: they sever themselves from all connection with truth, once they have to enter the Law Courts: their sole idea must be to win their case somehow or other. Thakchacha then went forward himself, and gave evidence that on the day and at the time mentioned by the prosecution he was engaged teaching Matilall Persian at his home in Vaidyabati. Though the magistrate subjected him to severe cross-examination, Thakchacha was not a man to be easily confused: he was well up in lawsuits, and his original evidence was not shaken in anyway. Then Mr. Butler addressed the Court, and after some deliberation the magistrate passed orders that Matilall should be released, but that the other accused should be imprisoned for one calendar month, and pay a fine of thirty rupees each.

Loud were the cries of Hori Bol on the passing of this order, and Baburam Babu shouted: "Oh Incarnation of Justice, most acute is your judgment! soon may you be made Governor of the land!"

When they were all in the courtyard of the police court, Haladhar and Gadadhar caught sight of Premnaryan Mozoomdar, and at once commenced singing in his ear with the intention of annoying him;—

"Hasten homeward, hasten homeward, Premnarayan Mozoomdar,
"Hop into your native jungle, black-faced monkey that you are!"

Premnarayan only replied: "What wicked boys you are! Here you are going to jail, but you cannot cease your tricks." While he was still speaking, they were led away to jail. When Beni Babu, who was a very worthy god-fearing man, saw virtue thus defeated and vice triumphant, he was perfectly astounded. Thakchacha, shaking his head and smiling sardonically, said to him: "How now, sir, what does the man of books say now? Why, if we had acted in accordance with you suggestions, it would have been all up with us." At this moment Bancharam Babu came running up in haste, gesticulating and saying: "Ha! ha! see what comes of trusting me! I told you I was no fool." Bakreswar too had his say. "Ah, he is no ordinary boy is Matilall! he is a very model of what a boy should be." "Ugh!" exclaimed Becharam Babu: "It was not I that wished this wrong done: I did'nt want to see this case won, far from it." Saying this, he took Beni Babu's hand and went off with him. Baburam Babu having made his offerings at Kali's shrine at Kalighat, embarked on a boat to return home.

Though the Bengalees have always great pride of caste, it may sometimes fall out that even a Mahomedan may be regarded as worthy of equal honour with the ancestral deity, and Baburam Babu began now to regard Thakchacha as a veritable Bhishna Deva: he put his arms round his neck and forgot everything else in the joy of victory: food and devotions were alike neglected. Again and again they repeated that Mr. Butler had no equal, that there was no one like Bancharam Babu, that Becharam Babu and Beni Babu were utter idiots. Matilall gazed all about him, at one moment standing on the edge of the boat, at another pulling an oar, at another sitting on the roof of the cabin or hard at work with the rudder. "What are you doing, boy?" said Baburam to him, "Do sit quiet for a moment, if you can." One of Baburam Babu's gardeners, Shankur Mali, of Kashijora, prepared the Babu's tobacco for him: his heart expanded with joy, when he saw his master looking so happy, and he asked him: "Will you have many nautches at the Durga Pujah this year, sir? Isn't that a cotton factory over there? How many cotton factories have these unbelievers set up?"

Change is the order of things in this world. Anger cannot long remain latent in the mind, but must reveal itself sooner or later; and so with a storm in nature, when there is great heat, and a calm atmosphere, a squall may suddenly rise. The sun was just setting, the evening coming on, when suddenly, in the twinkling of an eye, a small black cloud rose in the west: in a few minutes deep darkness had overspread the sky, and then with a rushing roar of wind the storm was on them. No one could see his neighbour: the boatmen shouted to each other to look out: the lightning flashed, and all were terrified at the loud and repeated thunder claps: down came the rain like a waterspout, and they were driven to take shelter in the cabin. The waters rose and dashed against the boats, several of which were swamped. Seeing this, the men in the remaining boats struggled hard to get to shore, but the violence of the wind drove them in the opposite direction. Thakchacha's chattering ceased: frightened out of his senses, and clasping his bead chaplet in his hands, he gabbled aloud his prayers, calling on his Prophet and Patron,—Saint Mahomed Ali, and Satya Pir.

Baburam Babu too was in great anxiety. It seemed to be the

beginning of the punishment of his misdeeds: who can remain calm in mind when he is conscious of wrong? Cunning and craft may suffice to conceal a crime from the eye of the world, but nothing can escape the conscience. The sinner is ever at the mercy of its sting: he is always in a state of alarm and dread, never at ease: he may occasionally indulge in laughter, but it is unnatural and forced. Baburam Babu wept from sheer fright, and said to Thakchacha: "Oh, Thakchacha, what is going to happen? I seem to see an untimely death before me! surely this is Nemesis. Alas, alas! to have just effected the release of my son, and yet to be unable to get him safe home and deliver him to his mother: my wife will die of grief if I perish. Ah, now I call to mind the words of my friend Beni Babu: all would have been well had I not turned aside out of the path of rectitude." Thakchacha too was in a high state of alarm, but the old sinner was a great boaster, and so he answered: "Why be so alarmed, Babu? Even if the boat is swamped, I will take you to shore on my shoulders: it is misfortune that shows what a brave man really is." The storm increased in violence, and the boat was soon in a sinking condition: all were in an extremity of terror, shouting for help, and Thakchacha's only thought was his own safety.

VIII

Baburam and Matilall return Home

M r. Butler had just arrived at his office and was overhauling his books to see what business was doing during the current month: his dog was asleep near him. Every now and again the Saheb would whistle, and take a pinch of snuff; then he would examine his account book or stand up and stretch his legs. He thought anxiously of the large sums he would have to pay as fees in the different offices of the Court: though by no means possessed of large resources, he knew very well that business would be at a standstill if he did not pay his money down before Term opened. He was thus engaged when the *sircar* of Mr. Howard, another attorney, entered his office, and put two papers into his hand. The Saheb's face beamed with delight, and he called out to Bancharam to come to him at once. Bancharam, throwing his shawl over a chair and sticking his pen behind his ear, attended at once to the summons. "Ha, Bancharam!" said Mr. Butler, "I am in luck indeed: there are two cases against Baburam Babu—an action in ejectment for non-payment of revenue, and a suit in equity. Mr. Howard has served me with a notice, and a *subpœna* to attend." On hearing this news Bancharam clapped his elbows against his sides with delight and said: "Aha, Saheb, see what a fine headman I am! all sorts of good things will come to us by my introduction of Baburam. Give me the two papers quick and let me go in person to Vaidyabati. These are not matters to be entrusted to another: I shall have to employ a good deal of coaxing and wheedling, and all my arts of persuasion will have to be called into requisition. If I can only once climb to the top of the Tree of Fortune, I will simply shower rupees down: just now we are very short of cash, and we cannot afford that in a business like ours; by a sudden dash like this we may safely reckon on getting something."

Meanwhile in the Vaidyabati house, propitiatory sacrifices were being offered: musical instruments of all kinds were braying and jangling. The crash of drums, the blare of brass trumpets, the clashing of cymbals, astonished the dawn. In the great hall of worship offerings for Matilall's welfare were in progress. The Brahmans were variously occupied in reciting the hymn to Durga, working up Ganges clay into representations of Siva, or offering leaves of the sacred basil to the holy *shalgram* in the centre of the hall. Others, deep in thought, their heads resting on their hands, were saying to each other: "How about our divine Brahmanhood now? so far from having saved Matilall, our master too must now have perished with him. If he was aboard yesterday, the boat must have been lost in the storm last night: there can be no doubt about that. Anyhow the family are ruined: the young Babu will now be proclaimed master, and what kind of man he is likely to turn out no one can say: our prospects of gain appear now to be very remote." One of the Brahmans present said very quietly: "Why are you so anxious? nobody is depriving us of our gains. Apply to our own case the simile of the saw cutting the shell. The saw will cut chips off the shell whether it moves forward or whether it moves backwards: even if the master be no more, there will have to be a gorgeous *shraddha*. The master is not a young man, and if the old lady objects to spending much on his *shraddha*, everybody will abuse her." Another remarked: "Ah, my friend, that may be all very true, but in case of his death our gains will become very precarious: I prefer the supply to be as constant as the Vasudhara: let us be ever getting, ever eating, say I: one shower will not suffice a long-continued thirst."

Baburam Babu's wife was a most devoted partner: ever since her lord's departure she had been very restless and had neglected her daily food. She had been sitting all night at one of the windows of the house from which the Ganges was visible. As the wind blew in strong gusts every now and again, she shuddered with fright: she kept gazing out into the storm, but her heart trembled as she looked: the continual rumbling of the thunder made her anxious, and she called upon the Almighty in her distress. Time went by: hardly a boat passed up or down the Ganges: whenever she heard a sound she would get up and look: occasionally she saw a light glimmering faintly in the distance and at once concluded it came from some vessel. At last a boat did come in sight, and she waited for it to come and tie up at the *ghât;* but when it passed on, only skirting the shore without coming to land, the agony of despair pierced her heart like a dart.

The night had almost come to an end and the storm had gradually lulled. How beautiful is the calm of creation that succeeds tumult and confusion! The stars again shone in the sky: the moon's light seemed to dance sportively on the waters of the river: so still had the earth become that even the rustle of the leaves could be heard.

Baburam Babu's wife, as she anxiously gazed about her, exclaimed in her impatience: "Oh Lord of Creation! to my knowledge I have done no wrong to anyone: I have committed no sin that I am aware of. Must I now after so long a time endure all the pangs of widowhood? Wealth I care nothing for: ornaments I have no use for: to be poor would be no hardship to me, I should not grieve: but this one boon I pray for, that I may be able to look upon the faces of my husband and my son when I die." Indeed her mental anguish was extreme, but being a cautious woman, as well as naturally reserved, she restrained herself lest her tears should distress her daughters. So the night passed away, and music in the house ushered in the dawn. The sound of melody, ordinarily so attractive, in the case of one afflicted in mind only serves to open the floodgates of grief; and the sorrow of the mistress of the house was but intensified by the sweet sounds.

Just then a fisherman came to the Vaidyabati house to sell fish: in answer to their enquiries, he said: "During the storm there was a boat in a more or less sinking condition on the sandbank known as the Bansberia Chur: I rather think it must have been swamped: there was a stout gentleman in it, a Mahomedan, a young gentleman, and others." This news was as if a thunderbolt had fallen amongst them: the music at once ceased, and all the members of the household lifted up their voices and wept.

Later in the day, towards evening, Bancharam Babu arrived with his usual bustle at the reception-room of the Vaidyabati house, and enquired for the master: on hearing the news from one of the servants, he fell into deep thought, resting his head on his hand, and then exclaimed: "Alas, alas, a great man has departed!" Having given way for sometime to loud lamentation, he finally called for a pipe of tobacco, and thus reflected, as he puffed away:—"Ah! Baburam Babu is now dead, would that I also were so! Where now are all those hopes with which I came? They have vanished, and here am I with the great Durga Festival coming off at home, the image not yet decorated, or even coloured, and without the wherewithal to pay for it: I am quite at a loss to know what to do. A few rupees just now would have been exceedingly serviceable, no matter how they might have been got. I could have given some to my master, some I would have kept for myself: it would have been a very simple thing to cook the accounts by making a false entry or two. Who could have anticipated that the heavens would have burst asunder and fallen upon my head like this?" Then, just for the look of the thing, he shed a few tears before the servants, weeping really for the loss of his dear rupees. The officiating Brahmans, seeing him there, came and sat down by him. The wearers of the sacred thread are, as a rule, a very astute sort of people: it is hard to get at their thoughts. Some began to recount the good qualities of Baburam Babu: others complained that they were now orphans, bereft of their father: others, unable to restrain their greed of gain, remarked: "There is no time now for mourning: we must bestir ourselves to ensure Baburam Babu's happiness in the next world: he was a man of no ordinary importance." Without paying much attention to what they were saying, Bancharam Babu smoked away, and nodded his head: he knew the old proverb: "What advantage does the crow get, even if the *bael* is ripe?" It seemed as if he had got to the end of all things, so thoroughly broken-hearted was he: he could only sigh as he listened to what was being said: he had no plans, nor, alas, could he think of anybody to fleece! The idea once occurred to him that he might make something by informing the family that some fine portions of their property might be lost to them unless they held a very careful enquiry, but then he considered that his words would be only wasted if he spoke when their grief was so fresh. While he was thus musing, a sudden stir arose at the door, where a messenger had just arrived with a letter: the address was in the handwriting of Baburam Babu, but the messenger could give no particulars. The mistress of the house snatched at the letter, carried it into the house, opened it hurriedly, and devoured its contents. The letter was as follows:—

"Last night I was in terrible danger: the boat I was in was carried away in the darkness, at the mercy of the storm, and the boatmen lost all control over it: finally, it capsized with the violence of the waves. I was in extreme terror as it was sinking, but at the next moment I remembered you: I imagined you standing near me and saying: 'Be not afraid in the time of adversity: call on the Almighty with body, mind, and soul: He is merciful, and will rescue you out of your danger.' I acted accordingly, and when I fell into the water I found myself upon a sandbank, where the water was only knee deep. The boat was soon dashed to pieces by the violence of the storm. I remained on the sandbank the entire night and reached Bansberia next morning. Matilall fell ill from exposure, but he has been under medical treatment and is now again convalescent. I expect to reach home by nightfall."

The moment that she had read the letter, the heat of her grief was extinguished: she pondered long, and then exclaimed: "Can such a joyful destiny indeed befall so sorrowful a wretch as myself?" Even while she spoke, Baburam Babu arrived with his son and Thakchacha. Everywhere there was a great stir. The minds of all the members of the household had been shrouded in a mist of grief, and now the sun of joy had risen. As she gazed upon her husband and her son, holding her two daughters by the hand, the mistress of the house wept tears of joy. She had been intending to upbraid Matilall for his conduct, but now all was forgotten: the two girls, holding their brother's hands, fell at their father's feet and wept. When the infant boy saw his father, it was as though he had found a treasure: he kept his arms tight round his neck, and for long refused to slacken his embrace: the women of the household too offered loud prayers for the welfare of their master, as though with *pán* and betel in hand, they were praying for the welfare of a bridegroom. Baburam Babu was for sometime like a man in a trance, unable to utter a word. Matilall reflected to himself: "The sinking of the boat has been a piece of good luck for me: it has saved me from a good scolding from my mother." As soon as the Brahmans in the outer apartments of the house saw Baburam Babu, they greeted him with vociferous blessings, saying in the Sanskrit tongue "Supreme over all is the might of the gods," and adding: "How could any calamity befall you, sir, with your own merits on the one hand, and on the other the divine rites that have been performed on your behalf? If such can befall, then are we no Brahmans."

Thakchacha rose up in great wrath when he heard this language, and said: "Sir, if it is by the influence of these men that calamity has been averted from you, is all my trouble on your behalf to go for nothing? do my prayers count for nothing?" The Brahmans at once humbly acquiesced saying: "Ah sir, just as the divine Krishna was once Arjuna's charioteer, so you have been the master's! all has happened by the might of your intelligence: you are a special incarnation: calamity flies far away from any place where you are, as from any place where we are."

Bancharam Babu had been all this time like a serpent with its crest-jewel lost, depressed and sad. He shed a few sham tears, to show off before Baburam Babu (his eyes were always rather watery), and his breast heaved with emotion. Fish would fall to his bait, he was firmly persuaded, if now he only threw in sufficient. When he heard the Brahmans' talk, he came up to them and with his favourite gesture, said: "I am no fool I can tell you: calamity could not possibly befall the master with me. Am I merely a Calcutta grasscutter that I could not have helped him?"

IX

MATILALL AND HIS FRIENDS

When a child is once corrupted, it is hard to effect any improvement. Every means should be tried to instil good principles into the mind from childhood: the character may then ripen for good and the mind become more strongly bent towards the right than towards evil; but if a boy gets hold of bad companions or receives ill advice in his early boyhood, then, such is the unsteadiness natural to his age, all will probably go wrong with him thereafter. So long then as he remains still a boy, with the mind of a boy, he must be assiduously employed in a variety of good pursuits. If boys were to receive an education like this up to the age of twenty-five, there would be no probability of their following evil courses: their minds would by that time have become so elevated that the mere mention of evil would excite anger and loathing. But it is very difficult for children in this country to receive such a training, owing, in the first place, to the lack of good teachers, and in the second to the lack of good books. There is urgent need of works that will promote the growth of high principles and of sound judgment, but ordinary people are persuaded that a solid education consists in teaching the meaning of a number of sounds: then again, very few people seem to have any idea of the methods whereby good principles are implanted in the mind; and finally the nature of the home surroundings of children in this country is strongly against the implanting of such principles. One boy may have a drunkard or a gambler as his father, another may have as his uncles men of immoral life; the mother herself too, being unable to read or write, may not exert herself for her children's education. A great deal of evil moreover is learnt from association with the different members of the household, the men and women servants; it may be also that from consorting with all kinds of boys in the village or at the village-school, children get to learn their evil ways and vicious habits, and so are ruined for life. Even where but one of the causes mentioned exists, the obstacle in the way of good education is grievous enough, but where they all exist in combination, there the drawbacks are simply terrible. It is like setting fire to straw: let a man only pour *ghee* where the fire is beginning to blaze, and within a very short space the flame is everywhere, and reduces to ashes whatever it finds in its way.

Many people thought that Matilall would have reformed after the affair of the police court; but the boy who is devoid of good qualities and high principles, and without any regard for honour or dishonour, has no particular feeling of abhorrence for punishments. Evil thoughts and good thoughts alike have their origin in the mind, and are therefore intimately bound up with the character: a mere physical affliction or trouble then cannot be expected to change the wind's direction. Doubtless, when the sergeant of police was dragging Matilall along through the streets, he may have thought it at the actual time a trouble and a disgrace, but the feeling was only momentary: once in the guard-room, he seemed to have lost all anxiety or fear or sense of dishonour and he was such a nuisance all that night and the whole of the next day to his neighbours, as he sang and imitated the cries of dogs and jackals, that they put their hands to their ears, and exclaiming "*Ram, Ram!*" said to each other: "Why, we are far worse off with this boy in our neighbourhood than if he were in prison." When he stood before the magistrate next day, he kept his head bent down like Shishu Pal, of *Mahabharata* renown, but it was done to deceive his father. In reality he recked little whether he went to jail and was put in fetters, or what happened to him.

Boys absolutely devoid of respect, of fear, and of shame, and addicted to purely evil courses, are afflicted with no ordinary disease: their complaint is really mental, and if only the proper remedies are applied, a cure may in process of time be effected. But Baburam Babu had no ideas on the subject at all: he was firmly convinced that Matilall was a very good boy, and used at first to wax very wrath if he heard him abused. Though all sorts of people were continually telling him about his son, he was as one who heard not; and if afterwards from his own observations a doubt did arise in his mind, he kept his misgivings to himself, and for fear of being mortified before others, refrained from expressing them, but simply gave secret orders to the door-keeper not to let Matilall leave the house. This was no remedy: the disease had obtained too strong a hold upon the boy, and no possible good could result from simply keeping him a prisoner and constantly in his sight. You may put a bar of iron on a mind once corrupted, without making any impression: on the contrary, mere repression may only have the effect of intensifying the evil in the mind. At first Matilall used to get out of the house by jumping over the wall. On the release of his old companions of Bow Bazar from jail, they came to live at Vaidyabati, and some of the boys of the place having joined them, they formed themselves into a band. Matilall's sense of respect and fear was soon destroyed altogether by his association with these young scamps, and he ended by paying no attention at all to his father.

Boys who have not been accustomed from their childhood to innocent and harmless amusements, are apt to take to diversions of a low kind. The children of Englishmen are instructed by their parents in a variety of innocent pastimes, in order that they may have sound minds and sound bodies: some draw and paint: some cultivate a taste for botany: some learn music: some devote themselves to sport and gymnastics: each takes up the form of harmless enjoyment most congenial to him. Boys in this country follow the example that is set them: their one wish is to be dressed in gorgeous attire, with a profusion of gold embroidery and jewels: to make up picnic parties of their chums and gay companions, and to live luxuriously in all a Babu's style. Fondness for display and extravagance naturally characterizes the season of youth: if care is not very early exercised in this matter, the desire grows in intensity, and a variety of evils result, by which eventually body and mind alike may be irretrievably ruined.

Matilall gradually threw off all restraint: he became so depraved that, continuing to throw dust in his father's eyes, he now openly spoke of him in the most unfilial and atrocious manner. The constant burden of his talks with his companions was: "Ah, if my old father would but die, I could then enjoy myself to my heart's content!" Any money he demanded from his parents they gave him: if there was any hesitation on their part, he would at once say: "Very well, then, I will go hang myself, or else take poison." His parents in their alarm thought: "Ah, what must be, must! Our life is bound up with the boy's life, he is our *Shivratri* lamp: let him live and we shall have our libations when we are gone." Matilall spent his whole time in riotous living: he hardly spent a minute of his day at home: at one time he would be engaged at a picnic, taking part in a theatrical entertainment, or making one of a party of amateur musicians: at another, he would be running about getting up a procession in honour of some local deity, or else absorbed in contemplating a nautch: or again, he would be creating a disturbance, and making unprovoked assaults upon other people. His appetite for stimulants, whether it were *ganja*, opium or even wine, never failed him, and tobacco of course was in constant demand.

They carried foppery to an extreme, these young Babus, wearing their hair in curls and using powder for their teeth. Their dress was of fine Dacca muslin embroidered with gold lace: on their heads they wore embroidered caps; carried in their hands silk handkerchiefs perfumed with attar of roses, and light canes; and smart English dress shoes with silver buckles adorned their feet. As, moreover, they had no spare time for their regular meals, they carried about with them all sorts of dainty sweetmeats.

Unless an evil disposition is checked at the very outset, it grows worse everyday, and in time becomes quite brute-like in its nature: just as when a man has once become enslaved to opium, the quantity he takes tends constantly to increase, so when a man has become addicted to evil habits, the craving for still more grievous courses comes naturally of itself. Matilall and his companions soon began to think the amusements they had hitherto been indulging in too tame: they no longer gave them any special pleasure; so they set to work to devise means for more solid pleasures. They now started sallying forth in a band late in the evenings, setting fire to and plundering houses, setting the thatch of poor people's huts alight, visiting the houses of loose women and creating a disturbance, pulling their hair about, burning their mosquito curtains, and plundering their dresses and ornaments. Sometimes, they would even insult a respectable girl. The people of the place were terribly annoyed at all this, but the young men only snapped their fingers at them in derision, and consigned them all to perdition.

Baburam Babu had been for sometime in Calcutta on business. One day towards evening, a zenana *palki* was passing the Vaidyabati house. As soon as the young scoundrels saw it, they at once ran out, surrounded it, and commenced beating the *palki*-bearers, who thereupon set the *palki* down and ran for their lives. Opening the *palki*, they saw a beautiful young girl inside. Matilall ran forward, seized the girl's hand, and dragged her out of the *palki* trembling all over with confusion and fear. In vain she looked around her for help: she saw only pitiless dark space. Then weeping bitterly she called on the Almighty: "Oh Lord, protect the helpless young orphan! I am content to die, only grant that I may not lose my honour." As the young Babus were all struggling together to get possession of her, she fell to the ground; they then tried to drag her by main force into the house. Matilall's mother hastened outside in some trepidation when she heard the sound of the girl's weeping, and the miscreants thereupon took to their heels. Seeing the mistress of the house, the young girl fell at her feet and said in her distress: "Oh dear lady, protect my honour! You must be a devoted wife yourself." None but a faithful and virtuous wife can understand the danger of a virtuous woman. Baburam Babu's wife at once lifted the girl off the ground and wiped away her tears with the border of her *sari*, saying as she did so: "My dear child, do not weep, you have no further cause for fear: I will cherish you as my own dear child: the Lord Almighty always protects the honour of the woman who is faithful to her vows." With these words she dispelled the girl's fears, and when she had soothed and consoled her, accompanied her to her home, and left her there.

X

THE MARRIAGE CONTRACT

The waving of lamps and the loud clanging of bells showed the worship of the goddess Nistarini to be in full swing in Sheoraphuli. Becharam Babu looked into the shrine of the goddess as he went by on foot: lining both sides of the road were shops: in some of them heaps of potatoes, grown at Bandipore and Gopalpore, were exposed for sale: in others, the shopkeepers were hard at work selling parched rice and sweetmeats, grain and *dál*. Here in one part were oil-merchants sitting near their mills, (which were simply the hollowed out trunks of trees,) and reading the *Ramayan* in the vulgar tongue: now and then they would urge on their cattle, as they went circling round, with a click of the tongue, and when the circle was completed, would shriek out the passage: "Oh Ram! we are monkeys, Ram, we are monkeys!" Women were busily engaged in cutting up fish for sale by the light of their lamps, and calling out: "Buy our fish, buy our fish!" while cloth merchants, reciting some passage from the *Mahabharat*, were murdering its unhappy author. All this, as he passed through the Bazaar, Becharam Babu was closely observing. When a man is taking a solitary walk, anything that has recently occupied his attention keeps recurring to his mind. Now, Becharam Babu was very fond in those days of processional singing; and as he went along an unfrequented path, after leaving his dwelling, one of his favourite songs came into his mind. The night was dark and there was hardly a soul about: only a few bullock-carts, their wheels creaking as they lumbered along, were on their way home: dogs were barking here and there. So Becharam Babu began to put all his lung-power into the song he was chanting in the monotone peculiar to processional music. The village women hearing his nasal twang, screamed aloud in their terror, for it is the rooted conviction of the country folk that only ghosts adopt this peculiar vocal style. Hearing the commotion Becharam was somewhat disconcerted, so he took to his heels and soon reached the Vaidyabati house.

Baburam Babu had a big gathering. Beni Babu of Bally, Bakreswar Babu of Batalata, Bancharam Babu of Outer Simla and many others were present. Thakchacha sat on a chair near the master. Several pandits were there discussing the *Shastras*; some had taken up passages of the treatises concerning logic and metaphysics for discussion: others were hotly discussing the dates that would be auspicious or otherwise for the annual festivals: others were giving their interpretation of the *slokas* out of a particular portion of the *Bhagavad Gita:* others were holding a great argument on grammatical niceties. One of the pandits, a man with an Assamese designation and a resident of Kamikhya, who was sitting near the master, said to him as he pulled away at his pipe: "You are a very fortunate man, sir, to possess two sons and two daughters. This year is a somewhat unpropitious one, but if you offer up a sacrifice, the stars may all be favourable again, and you can use their influence on your behalf." In the midst of the discussion Becharam Babu arrived, and the whole company rose to their feet as he entered, and welcomed him most cordially. The visitor had been more or less in a bad temper since the affair of the police court, but a courteous and kind address has a great effect in turning a man's wrath away; and Becharam Babu, mollified by the courteous welcome so unanimously accorded him, sat down with a smile close to Beni Babu. Baburam Babu thereupon said to him: "Sir, the seat you have taken is not a good one: come and sit with me on my couch." Men after each other's hearts are as inseparable as cranes, and notwithstanding the pressing invitation of Baburam Babu, Becharam Babu would not give up his seat near Beni Babu.

After sometime spent in conversation on different topics, Becharam Babu asked: "What about Matilall's marriage contract? Where has it been arranged?"

Baburam.—A good many proposals for a contract of marriage have come in: Haridas Babu of Guptipara, Shyma Charan Babu of Nakashipur, Ram Hari Babu of Kanchrapara, and many others belonging to differents districts have sent in proposals. These have all been passed over, and a marriage has been arranged with the daughter of Madhav Babu of Manirampur. He is a man possessed of considerable property; we shall, moreover, make a good deal out of the connection.

Becharam.—Beni, my friend, what do you think about this? Come, tell me plainly and openly your opinion.

Beni.—Becharam, my dear friend, it is no easy matter to tell you plainly: you know the proverb: "A dumb man makes no enemies." Besides what is the use of discussing a thing that has been settled?

Becharam.—Oh, but you must tell me: I like to know the ins and outs of every marriage.

Beni.—Listen then: Madhav Babu of Manirampur is a very quarrelsome sort of person,—has not even the manners of a gentleman. He has a reputation amongst Brahmans for orthodoxy, only gained by making presents to them, but he is an utterly unscrupulous man. True, he may be able to make handsome presents of money and other things on the occasion of his daughter's marriage; but is money the only thing worth taking into consideration when a marriage is in question? Surely the first requisite is a respectable family, and the next a good girl; and then if there is wealth as well, so much the better, but it does not very much matter. Now Ram Hari Babu of Kanchrapara is a very excellent person: he lives cheerfully and contentedly on the income he derives from his own exertions, and never casts a longing eye on another man's wealth. He may not be in very good circumstances, I allow, but he has always been very careful to have his children well educated, and the one object of his thoughts has been the happiness and moral well-being of his family. To be connected with such a man as this would be a source of entire happiness.

Becharam.—Baburam Babu, who is the intelligent person who has recommended this match to you? Avarice will be your ruin yet. But what right have I to speak? It is after all our social system that is at fault: whenever the topic of marriage comes to the front, people always say: "How sir! will you give me a pot of silver? will you give me a necklace of pearls?" It is only an idiot who would think of saying: "Look first to see whether your proposed relation be respectable or not: enquire whether the girl be a good girl or otherwise." This is a mere trifle: if only wealth is to be got, that is everything.

Bancharam.—We want family, we want beauty, and we want wealth as well: how can a family possibly get on if it professes to despise wealth?

Bakreswar.—True enough: we must keep up a proper respect for wealth. What do we get by intercourse with a poor man? Are our stomachs filled by it?

Thakchacha (*bending down from his chair*).—All this talk is a reflection upon me: it was I that counselled this match. I would have been ashamed to show my face in the world if I had not succeeded in getting a girl of noble parentage. I took immense pains to ascertain that Madhav Babu of Manirampur was a good man. Why, he is a man at whose name the tiger and cow might drink at the same pool together! besides, look at the advantage of being able to get his *lathials* whenever we need them in cases of dispute. Then too everybody connected with the Law-Courts is under his thumb: there are a thousand ways in which he can be of assistance to us in any strait. Ram Hari Babu of Kanchrapara on the other hand, is a feeble sort of person: he makes a very precarious living: what would have been the good of an arrangement with him?

Becharam.—A fine counsellor you have got Baburam! If you listen to all such a counsellor has to advise, you are bound to get to heaven, body and all. And what a son, too, you have! And so he is actually about to be married? What do you think about it all, Beni Babu!

Beni.—I think that the man who will first thoroughly educate his son, and who will take special pains that he shall grow up thoroughly moral, will be best able to be of assistance to his son when the time comes that he should marry. Many evils are likely to arise if a boy is married at an unreasonable age.

On hearing all this, Baburam Babu rose in much irritation and hurriedly retreated into the inner apartments of the house, where his wife was engaged in discussing the match with some of the women of the village. Going up to her, he informed her of all that had been said outside, and as he stood there in some perplexity, inquired: "Cannot we put off Matilall's marriage for a few days?" His wife replied: "What is this that you are saying? Plague take our enemies! By divine favour Matilall is now sixteen: would it look well not to marry him now? If you upset the arrangements now, the proper season for marriage will slip away. You surely do not know what you are doing: is the caste of a good man to be destroyed in this way? Go at once, and take the bridegroom off with you."

At this advice from his wife, all the master's indecision disappeared. He at once went outside and gave the order for the lamps to be lit: the musical instruments all struck up at the same time, and the English bands began to play. Baburam lifted the bridegroom into his palanquin, and taking Thakchacha by the hand, walked by the side, with heavy gait, accompanied by his kinsmen and near friends. From the roof of the house the boy's mother gazed down upon her son's face, and the women of the household called out, "Ah, mother of Mati! Ah, how beautiful is your child!" The friends of the bridegroom were all with him: they amused themselves by taking torches to the rear of the crowd and setting people alight, and by letting off squibs and fireworks near the houses and in the thick of the crowd. None of the poor people ventured to remonstrate, though they were sadly annoyed.

The bridegroom soon reached Manirampur, and got down from the palanquin. Both sides of the road were crowded with people gazing at the bridegroom. The women chattered away to each other about him. "The boy has a certain amount of beauty," said one, "but if his nose were a bit straighter, he would look better." Another remarked, "His complexion, fair as it is, would look better even fairer."

The marriage was to take place at a late hour, but it had not struck ten when Madhav Babu, taking a *durwan* with a lantern, came out to meet the bridegroom and his guests. After he had joined the marriage procession in the street, nearly half an hour was wasted in the exchange of compliments, each man wishing to give precedence to the other. While one said: "Pray sir! precede me!" the other politely declined: "Nay sir! do you please go first." At last, Beni Babu of Bally went forward and said: "Please one of you gentlemen go on ahead. I cannot stand here in the street and catch cold." An amicable arrangement being at last come to, the whole company arrived at the house of the bride's father and entered.

The bridegroom took his seat in the assembly. Numbers of roughs were standing about, ripe for mischief. The distribution of money to the village, and other subjects, then came up for discussion. Thakchacha was doing his best, but apparently without avail, to effect some arrangement for his own profit. A rough blustering sort of fellow came up to him and said: "Who is this low Mahomedan? Get out of this! what has a Mahomedan to do with Hindu concerns?" Thakchacha was furious, and shaking his head fiercely, his eyes inflamed with passion, abused the man roundly.

This was the very opportunity Matilall's young friends, Haladhar, Gadadhar, and the other young Babus, had been longing for. They saw from the clouds that were gathering that a storm was imminent. One set to work to tear the carpet into pieces, another to extinguish the lamps: some set the chandeliers clashing and jingling, while others threw missiles among the assembled company. Some of the people of the bride's father, seeing the confusion they were creating, began to abuse them and strike them with their fists, and Matilall seeing the quarrel in progress, thought to himself: "I fancy I am not destined to get married. I may have to return home after all, with the thread only on my wrist."

XI

THE POETASTER

The pandits of Agurpara were enjoying their usual evening lounge beneath their favourite tree: they were all either taking snuff or smoking, coughing and sneezing, chaffing each other and joking. One of them asked: "How is Vidyaratna? The good Brahman, in his zeal for gain, has lamed himself going to Manirampur in response to an invitation. I was concerned to see him leaping on a stick yesterday as he went to bathe." Vidyabhushan replied: "Oh! Vidyaratna is all right again: the pain in his foot has been considerably alleviated, what with warm lime and turmeric, and dry fomentations. Come, gentlemen, listen to the poetry which our friend the great poet Konkan has composed with special reference to the Manirampur entertainment."

> Let the drum beat in triumph, uplift the glad song,
> For the guests are assembled, a glittering throng;
> In the gay halls of Madhub, as radiantly bright,
> As the heaven of Indra, entrancing the sight.
> How dazzling the glow that illuminates all,
> How brilliant the flowers that engarland the wall!
> See, apart sit the friends of the bridegroom and bride,
> Retainers in scarlet on every side.
> What ravishing melody floats on the air
> With perfume of blossoms surpassingly rare!
> Be sure, so celestial a scene to array
> In Hymen's sweet honour, took many a day.
> But the ground is just soaking here under the tent
> Where the rain is descending through many a rent.
> And these up-country durwans, offensively loud,
> What business have they to be hustling the crowd?
> Discordant the noises that deafen the ear,
> And the shouts and the hubbub are awful to hear.
> Yet in view of the sweets and the dainties in store,
> You'd put up with annoyances double or more.
> See those figures in paste on the walls stuck about!

How the pedigree-poets their rhapsodies shout!
Now list to these verses, and publish the fame
Of Konkan,—the paragon verse-maker's name!
The bridegroom is coming! A silence profound
Is felt for a moment, and plaudits resound.
But the juvenile Babus are eager for fun,
And lo! in a minute the row has begun.
His schemes are miscarrying, Thakchacha fears,
As he listens aghast to the shouts and the jeers.
We too are astounded;—this banging and crashing!
This rending of carpets and clanging and clashing!
Why, the glass chandeliers they are wantonly smashing!
We'd better be off, we are in for a thrashing!
In wonder sits Mati, revolving the thought,
"It seems my investiture's profiting nought!"
"The scoundrel Bakreshwar!" uprises a shout,
"Give him a caning and hustle him out!"
And Bancharam also, the schemer profound,
Is wriggling in torture and howls on the ground.
Says Becharam hastily, "Here, come aside;
Thing do not look promising: where shall we hide?"
And carries off Beni, bereft of resource.
While ever the tumult increases in force.
"Help, help!" holloas Baburam, much in alarm,
For support round a pillar entwining his arm.
Ho, speed to the rescue Thakchacha the brave!
But to keep a whole skin's the one thought of the knave!
Whom, with head muffled up as he gingerly goes,
They arrest as chief culprit, and hurl on his nose,
And roll in the dust till his eyes are of sand full,
And tear out the hair of his head by the handful.
Bear "Tauba!" and "Tauba!" the Mussulman yell!
"Of my sins I repent, on the border of hell!
"But I'd nothing whatever to do with it, no!
Al innocent Moslem,—why badger him so?
"Bismillah! alack! To appear on the scene
"Such an outrage to suffer, was folly I ween!
"Among the mild Hindus I guilelessly came
"From the purest of motives; and this is their game!

"Ah fool! the advice of thy friends to despise,
"At the cost of thy beauty, thy beard, and thine eyes!"
Now enter the durians *athirst for the fray,*
And round them their lathis *impartially lay;*
Then howls of excitement and terror and pain,
The crack of the truncheon and swish of the cane!
The friends of the bridegroom and those of the bride
Are scuttling in terror on every side:
Within flies the bridegroom, the company's scattered,
And all the gay trappings of Hymen are shattered.
"Thakchacha still here?" some enthusiast shouts,
"Pour mud on his turban and tear off his clouts!"
In dishonour poor Baburam slinks from the hall
And all his brave show goes for nothing at all.
His costume's in tatters within and without,
And shawlless and shoeless he stumbles about,
Distractedly moaning:—"How hard is my case
"Whom death from exposure now stares in the face!
"The oncoming tempest I hear from afar:
"'Tis the progress triumphal of Death on his car!
"Thus helpless and sole, not a creature to aid,
"Can his dire visitation be longer delayed?
"I am bruised and exhausted, and breath I have none:
"The Fates are against me! O what have I done?
"And my pitiful lot, if it reaches the ear
"Of the wife of my bosom, will kill her, I fear.
"Did the marriage come off? I'm unable to tell!
"From a blow on the cranium unconscious I fell.
"These schemes matrimonial dictated by vanity
"Have landed me here on the verge of insanity!"
Thus loudly bewailing, a cottage he spies.
Where no cruel warder an access denies.
And there in a corner, alone, on a mat,
Monumental in misery,—Thakchacha sat!
"Ah traitor and craven, 'twas cruelly done,
"Thy comrade deserting, thou treacherous one!
"O frailty of mortals! how faileth the best,
"When the touchstone of peril puts love to the test!"
"Hush, check your emotion!" his champion replies,

"For where are we safe from our enemies spies?
"You'll own, when you've heard me,—my confident trust is—
"You've done your protector a grievous injustice!"
'Tis daybreak, as homeward they ruefully wend,
And Konkan his epic thus brings to an end.

On hearing this lampoon upon Baburam Babu, Tarkavagish was furious, and exclaimed: "Ha, ha! this is poetry indeed! Sarasvati in the flesh! Kalidas come to life again! What profound learning too has the great poet Konkan displayed! So precocious a boy cannot possibly live long. The metre too,—astounding,—never heard anything like it,—it runs like a nursery rhyme! Now a man who is a Brahman and a pandit to boot will always speak good of a rich man: there is nothing gentlemanly in mere abuse." With these words, he got up in a rage, and would have left the place, but the assembled pandits expressed their full approval of his words, and urging him to stop and be calm, got him at last by sheer force to sit down again. Another pandit then skilfully introduced other topics, and ignoring what had passed began to sing the praises of Baburam Babu and Madhab Babu. A Brahman, being generally father dense, cannot easily see when a joke is intended: through constant study of the *Shastras*, his mind moves solely in the region of the *Shastras* and has no practice in worldly matters. Tarkavagish however was soon mollified and amused himself with the subject in hand.

XII

Barada Babu

Becharam Babu of Bow Bazar was sitting in his reception-hall, and with him were a few persons singing snatches of songs. The Babu was himself selecting the different subjects, and his selection was a sufficiently varied one: the verses were being sung to the most popular tunes. Many people in the exuberance of their enthusiasm would have rolled about on the floor on hearing such ravishing strains, but Becharam Babu sat there as stolid as a painted marionette. Beni Babu of Bally arrived while the music was still in progress, and Becharam Babu at once stopped it, and said to his guest: "Ah! Beni, my friend! what, are you still alive? Baburam is still nursing his wrath; it is like fire smouldering amid burnt rags. He absolutely refuses to be pacified. Some unpleasantness was bound to arise out of the affair of Manirampur: it has been an experience for us. It is commonly reported that the family has a bitter enemy, and that he went as one of the bridegroom's party."

Beni.—Speak to me no more on the subject of Baburam Babu: the whole affair has annoyed me extremely. I should like to get away altogether and give up my house at Bally: the old Sanscrit saying occurs to me, "What else may not destiny have in store for me?"

Becharam.—Well, such is the way things are going with Baburam: what else can you expect from such a man, with such a counsellor, such companions, and such a son? Yet his younger son is a good boy: how is that? He is the lotus flower on the dung-heap.

Beni.—You may well ask that: it is indeed extraordinary, but there is a reason for it. You may perhaps remember my having told you sometime back about Babu Barada Prosad Biswas. Well, for sometime past that gentleman has been living at Vaidyabati. I had been thinking a good deal on the subject, and I saw that if Baburam Babu's youngest son, Ramlall, grew up like Matilall, the family would very soon become extinct, but that here was an excellent opportunity for the boy to learn to grow up a good man. I considered the matter well, and went to the gentleman I have mentioned, taking Ramlall with me. The boy has ever since then exhibited such an extraordinary affection for Biswas Babu that he is constantly at his side: he is very rarely at home, for he regards Biswas Babu as a father.

Becharam. You did, it is true, once relate to me all the virtues of this Biswas Babu, but, to tell you the truth, I have never heard of a single individual possessed of so many virtues before: how is it, that now he has attained to so good a position, he is so modest, and unpretending?

Beni.—It is generally very difficult for a man to be humble and unassuming who has been accustomed to wealth from his boyhood, and who has never encountered adversity, but gone on steadily piling up riches. A man like this has, as a rule, no perception of the feelings of others: I mean by that, he has no idea what is pleasing or what is distasteful to others, for his thoughts are centred in himself: he considers himself a great man, and his people all encourage him in the idea by extolling his magnificence. Under these conditions pride reaches a fearful height: modesty and kindliness can never take firm root in such soil. It is on this account that in Calcutta the sons of rich men so rarely turn out well. Puffed up by their father's wealth on the one hand or their own position on the other, they swagger through life, treating all men with contempt and derision. It is calamity and misfortune that alone avail to strengthen man's mind. The first requisite of man is humility: that quality absent, a man has no chance of either discerning aright or correcting his faults, and without humility he cannot advance in virtue and in worth.

Becharam.—How was it that Barada Babu became so good?

Beni.—Barada Babu fell into trouble in his earliest boyhood, and from that time he used to meditate unceasingly on the Almighty: the result of this constant meditation was that he became firmly convinced that it was his bounden duty to do everything that was pleasing to God, and to avoid what was displeasing to Him even though life were at stake: this conviction he proceeded to carry into practice.

Becharam.—How did he settle with himself what was pleasing and what displeasing to the Almighty?

Beni.—There are two ways of attaining to knowledge on this subject. First, the mind must be brought under control: to effect this, constant meditation and the steady growth of good principles are necessary. A searching self-examination, a course of severe and steady meditation, may develop the faculty of discrimination between right and wrong; and in proportion as that faculty is developed, a man will become averse to conduct that is displeasing to the Almighty, and attached to a course that is pleasing to Him. In the second place that faculty may be steadily exercised by reading and reflecting on what good men have written. Barada Babu has left nothing undone that can help to make him good. He has never wandered aimlessly about like ordinary people. When he rises in the morning, he always offers up his prayers to God, and the tears in his eyes show the feelings that rise up in his mind at the time. He then calmly examines his conduct most searchingly, to see whether it has been good or bad. He never prides himself upon his good qualities, but is exceedingly distressed if he detects the very slightest fault in himself. He takes great delight in hearing of the good qualities of others, but he only expresses his sorrow after a brotherly manner when he hears of their faults. By such assiduous practice it is that his mind has become pure and serene. Is there anything astonishing in the fact that a man should thus grow in virtue who so subdues his mind?

Becharam.—Ah, Beni my friend, it is most refreshing to hear of such people as Barada Babu! I must have an interview with a man like this, if only for once. How does he spend his days?

Beni.—He is engaged in business most of the day, but he is not like other people. Most men who are engaged in business think solely of position or wealth: he does not think so much of these things: he knows well that wealth and position are but as a drop of water: they may be pleasant to see, pleasant to hear of, but they do not accompany a man beyond the grave: nay, unless a man walks with great circumspection, they may both generate in him an evil disposition. His chief object in engaging in business is to get the means of exercising and putting to the test his own virtues. In a business career, bad qualities such as avarice, ill-will, and want of principle, are brought into prominence, and it is by the onslaught of such enemies that men are ruined. On the other hand, the truly virtuous man is the man who proceeds with circumspection. To talk of virtue in the abstract is an easy thing enough, but unless a man gives an illustration of it in his own conduct, his words are a sham. Barada Babu is always saying that the world resembles a school. Genuine virtue is the outcome of a thorough discipline of the mind in the business of life.

Becharam.—Surely Barada Babu does not regard wealth as a thing of no account?

Beni.—No, not at all; he by no means considers wealth despicable, but virtue comes first in his estimation. Wealth is only of secondary importance; that is to say, in the acquisition of wealth, due regard must be paid to the maintenance of virtue.

Becharam.—What does Barada Babu do with himself in the evenings?

Beni.—When once the evening has set in, he spends his time in profitable conversation with his family, and in reading or listening to their talk. The members of his family all try to follow his example, observing the excellence of his character. He is so attached to his family that the heartfelt prayer of his wife is that she may have such another husband in all her births: if they lose sight of him even for a moment, his children fret with impatience. Barada Babu's daughters are as good as his sons. While in many homes brothers and sisters are continually grumbling and quarrelling with each other, Barada Babu's children never exchange high words: always, whether at their lessons, or at their meals, they converse affectionately together; and they are very unhappy if their parents are at all ailing.

Becharam.—I have heard that Barada Babu is always about in the village.

Beni.—That is quite true. Whenever he hears of anyone being in trouble, or in misfortune, or sick, he cannot remain quiet at home. He assists many of his neighbours in manifold ways, but he never even hints it to anyone: when he has done a kindness to another, he considers himself the person benefited.

Becharam.—Ah, friend Beni, my eyes have never looked on such a man, much less have I ever heard him with my ears! Why, association with such a character would make even an old man good, much more help a young boy to grow up virtuous. Ah, my friend! it will indeed be a gratifying thing if the younger son of Baburam manages to grow up a good man.

XIII

BARADA BABU'S PUPIL

B arada Babu had an extraordinary and unusual knowledge of educational methods. He had special acquaintance with all the different faculties and emotions of the mind, and with the methods whereby men may become intelligent and virtuous by the proper exercise of them. A teacher's work is no light one: there are many who have but a mere smattering of knowledge, and take up teaching just from want of other occupation; good instruction cannot be expected from men of this type. To be a genuine teacher, a man must be thoroughly acquainted with the whole tendency of the mind and all its energies; and he must by calm and patient observation discover and learn the best way to become a really practical guide of youth. To teach in a haphazard fashion, without doing something of this kind, is like striking a stone with a *kodáli*; it may fall on the stone a hundred times, but not a handful of soil will it cut. Now Barada Babu was a man of great acuteness and shrewd observation: he had so long paid special attention to the subject of education that he was well versed in the best methods of instruction: and the learning that was imparted according his system was really solid. As education is now in Government schools, its real end is not attained, for the reason that nothing is done for the harmonious development of the faculties of the mind and the emotions. The scholars learn everything by heart, and consequently memory alone is awakened: the faculty of thought and reflection generally lies dormant, and the idea of bringing the different activities of the mind into play seems not to exist. The chief end of education being to develop all the mental powers and qualities harmoniously with the gradual growth of the scholar, one faculty should not be abnormally exerted at the expense of another. Just as the body gets compact and grows well-knit by an harmonious exercise of all the limbs, so the mind is strengthened and the intelligence developed by an harmonious exercise of the sum total of their energies. All the moral qualities likewise should be simultaneously elicited: because one may be brought into play it does not follow that all will be. Reverence for truth, for instance, may be developed, without a single particle of kindliness: a man may have a large element of kindliness in his nature, but no practical knowledge of the business of life. Again, he may be perfectly honest in his business relations, and yet display indifference or absolute want of affection for his father, mother, wife and children; or he may be all that is proper in his domestic relations, but wanting in uprightness in his business affairs. Barada Babu was well aware in fact, that faith in God was the foundation of the due development and exercise of the qualities of the mind, and that they could only be duly developed in proportion as that faith increased; for otherwise the task was as futile as trying to write on water.

Most fortunately for him, Ramlall had become Barada Babu's pupil, and all his faculties were being harmoniously developed and exercised. Association with a good man is a far more potent factor in developing moral qualities than mere instruction; indeed by such intercourse a mind may be as completely transformed as a branch of the wild plum grafted on to a mango tree. So great is the majesty of a really noble character that even its shadow falling on one that is base and corrupt raises it in time to its own image. By association with Barada Babu the mind of Ramlall became almost a complete reflection of his. With the object of making himself strong, as soon as he rose in the morning, he would take a stroll in the open air; for strength of mind he knew could not exist without strength of body: after his walk, he would return home and engage in prayer and meditation. The only books he read were those the perusal of which promoted the growth of intelligence and good character, and the only persons he conversed with were those whose conversation had the same effect. On merely hearing the name of any good person, he would go and visit him, making no enquiries about his caste or condition in life. So keen was his intelligence that in conversation with anyone he would speak only on matters of real moment: he had no taste for gossip. If anybody spoke on subjects of but trifling importance, he succeeded by force of his intelligence in extracting the pith of the matter, as a fruit-extractor the pulp of the fruit. The steady growth of faith in God, of morality, and of a good understanding formed the burden of his meditations. By such consistent conduct as this, his disposition, his character and his whole conduct became more and more worthy of commendation.

Goodness can never be hid. The people in the village would say to each other: "Ah, Ramlall is the Prahlad of a family of Daityas." In all their griefs and misfortunes he was ever to the front with his help. He did all he could think of to assist any in need of help, by his personal exertions on their behalf, whether with his purse or with his understanding. Old and young, they were all known to Ramlall, and were all his friends. If they heard him abused, it was as though a dart had pierced their ears; if they heard him praised, great was the rejoicing. The old women of the village would say to each other: "If we had such a child we should never let him out of our sight. Oh, what a store of merit must his mother have laid up to have got a son like this!" The young women, observing Ramlall's beauty and good qualities, exclaimed in their hearts: "God grant that such a husband may fall to our lot!"

Ramlall's good disposition and character were manifested in manifold ways, both at home and abroad. He never failed in any single particular of his duty towards each member of his home circle. His father, observing him, thought to himself;—"Ah, my younger son is becoming lax in his observances of Hindu religious customs! he does not keep the sacred mark on his forehead, nor use the customary vessels at his prayers, nor even the beads for the repetition of the sacred name of *Hori:* and yet he does perform his devotions after his own manner, and is not addicted to vice. We may tell any number of lies: the boy, on the contrary, knows nothing but the truth. He is most devoted to his parents, yet never consents to what he thinks wrong, even at our urgent request. Now I find a good deal of duplicity necessary in my business: both truth and falsehood are requisite. How otherwise could I keep up the great festivals that I have constantly to be celebrating in my house, the Dol Jatra, the Durga Pujah and others? Now Matilall may be a wicked boy, but he keeps up his Hindu observances; besides, after all, I do not think he is so very bad; he is young yet, he must sow his wild oats." Ramlall's mother and sisters were deeply affected by his many good qualities: they rejoiced with the joy of those who out of dense darkness see light. Matilall's evil behaviour had had a most distressing effect upon them *i* bowed down as they had been in shame at the evil reports they heard of him, they had known little ease of mind. Now again there was in their hearts, because of Ramlall's good qualities, and their faces were lighted up with joy. At one time all the men-servants and maid-servants of the house, getting only abuse or blows from Matilall, had been in terror of their lives: now, softened by Ramlall's gentle address and kind treatment, they paid all the greater attention to their work.

When Matilall and his companions, Haladhar and Gadadhar, saw this behaviour of Ramlall, they remarked to each other that the boy had gone silly,—must be cracked,—and said to the master of the house: "This brat should certainly be sent to a lunatic asylum: he is a mere child, yet his sole talk day and night is of virtue: it is disgusting to hear an old man's words in the mouth of a child." Others of Matilall's companions would occasionally say:—"Mati Babu, you are in luck's way: things don't look promising for Ramlall: he will soon come to grief if he makes a parade of virtue like this: you will then get all the property, and there will be no obstacle to your complete enjoyment. Even if he does live, he will be little better than an idiot. But what can you expect? what says the proverb? 'As the teacher so the taught.' Could he find no other master in this wide world that he must get hold of some *mantras* from an Eastern Bengalee, and go wandering about parading his virtue before the world? If he does this much more, we will send him and his teacher about their business. The canting humbug! he goes about saying: 'Ah, how happy I should be if my elder brother were to give up the society of his evil companions!' 'Ah, if my elder brother were only to frequent the society of Barada Babu, what a good thing it would be!' Ha ha! Barada Babu indeed,—the dismal old blockhead, a very prince of prigs. Look out, Mati Babu: take care that you do not after all get under his influence and go to him? What, are we to go to school again? If he wishes, let him come to us and be taught: we are very hard up for a little amusement."

Thakchacha was always hearing about Ramlall, and he began to think the matter over: the one aim of his life was to find a favourable opportunity for making a successful swoop or two on Baburam Babu's property. So far, most of the suits-at-law had ended disastrously, and he had had no opportunity for such a stroke: yet he never failed to keep on baiting his ground before casting his nets. Ramlall however having become what he was, he could not expect any fish to fall into his net, for however skilfully it might be cast the boy would advise his father not to enter it. Thakchacha saw then that a great obstacle had presented itself in his way and he thus reflected: "The moon of hope must have sunk behind a cloud of despair, for it is no longer visible." After profound deliberation, he observed one day to his employer;—"Babu Saheb, your youngest son's behaviour has made me very anxious: I do not think he can be quite right in his mind. He is always angry with me and tells everybody that I have corrupted you: my heart is wounded when I hear this. Ah, Babu Saheb! this is not as it should be: if he speaks like this to me, he may one day speak harshly to you. The boy will doubtless become good and gentle in time, but now he is boorish and rude, and must be corrected; besides, so far as I can judge, you may lose all your property if this course is allowed." A casual remark may very easily disturb the mind of a man who is naturally rather dense. As a boat in the hands of an unskilful steersman is tossed about in a storm, unable to make the shore, so a dull-witted man is in almost constant perplexity, seeing only chaos around him: he can himself come to no decision on the merits of any subject. For one thing, poor Baburam Babu was naturally rather thick-headed, and for another, Thakchacha's words were to him as the sacred *Vedas*: so he stood stupidly gazing about like a man in a maze, and after a while asked Thakchacha what plan he could suggest. That astute individual replied: "Your boy, sir, is not a wicked boy: it is Barada Babu that is the origin of all the mischief. Only get him out of the way, and the boy will be all right. Ah, Babu Saheb! the son of a Hindu should observe all the ordinances of his religion as a Hindu. A man has need of both good and bad qualities if he is to engage in the business of this life: the world is not all honest: what use would it be to me if I were the only upright man in it?"

Men always regard with approval, as the opinion of a really great mind, language that is in keeping with their own convictions. Thakchacha was well aware that he had only to talk about the observance of Hindu ceremonial, and the preservation of property, and his aim would be accomplished; and, as a matter of fact, it was by such talk that he achieved his end. When Baburam heard the advice Thakchacha gave, he acquiesced at once in it, remarking: "If this is your opinion, finish the matter off at once: I will supply you with any money you may want, but you must work out the plan yourself."

There was a good deal of discussion of this kind about Ramlall. "Many sages, many saws," says the proverb. Some said: "The boy is good in this respect": others would reply: "But not good in this." One critic complained: "He is deficient in one important quality, which makes all his other excellences go for nothing, just as when a speck of cow-dung has fallen into a vessel of milk, the whole is tainted." Another retorted: "The boy is perfect."

Thus time went on. At last it chanced that Baburam Babu's eldest daughter fell dangerously ill. Her parents called in a number of physicians to see her. Matilall, needless to say, never once came near his sister, but went about saying that a speedy death was preferable to the life of a widow in a rich man's house; and during the time of her illness, he only indulged himself the more. Ramlall on the other hand was unremitting in his attention: foregoing both food and sleep, and full of anxious thought, he exerted himself to the utmost for the girl's recovery. But she did not recover, and as she was dying she put her hand on her younger brother's head, saying: "Ah, brother Ram! if I die, and am born a girl in my next birth, God grant that I may have a brother like you. I cannot tell you what you have done for me. God make you as happy as you wish." With these words, his sister breathed her last.

XIV

THE FALSE CHARGE

Boys who are at all wild are not to be satisfied with ordinary amusements: they constantly require new and fresh sources of pleasure, and if they do not find what they want abroad, they will return and sit in melancholy brooding at home. Those that have uncles at home perhaps recover their lost spirits, for they can chaff and joke with them to their heart's content: they will at least go so far as to jest about making arrangements for their last journey to the Ganges, on the ground that they are a burden to the family. But when such is not the case, they are bored to death, and regard the world with the eyes of a man who is sick of life. Passionately devoted as they were to practical joking of all kinds, Matilall and his companions invented ever new pranks, and it was hard to foretell what would be their next. Their thirst for some form of amusement became more intense everyday: one kind might occupy them for a day or two, but it soon palled upon them, and they suffered torments of *ennui* if nothing else turned up. Such was the way in which Matilall and his companions spent their days. In course of time, it became incumbent on each of them in turn to devise something new in the way of amusement.

So one day Haladhar wrapped Dolgovinda up in a quilt and, after instructing all his chums in their different parts, repaired to the house of Brojonath, the *kabiraj*. It was thick with smoke from the preparation of drugs: different operations were in progress: powders were being prepared, made up of a number of different ingredients; essential oils were being refined, and gold ground into powder. The *kabiraj* himself was just on the point of leaving his house, with a box of his drugs in one hand and a bottle of oil in the other, when Haladhar arrived and said to him: "Oh, sir, please come as quick as you can: a boy is very ill of fever in the house of a zemindar, and he seems to be in a very critical state: his life and your fame, you see, are both at stake: you will get undying honour if you restore him to health again. It is thought that he may get all right by the administration of some very powerful drug: if you can succeed in curing him, you will be richly rewarded." Upon this, the *kabiraj* made all haste, and was soon at the bedside of the patient.

The young Babus, who were all present, called out: "Welcome, welcome, sir *kabiraj,* may you revive us all! Dolgovinda has been lying on his bed some fifteen days with this fever: his temperature is very high, and he suffers from terrible thirst: he gets no sleep at night, only tosses restlessly about. Please examine his pulse carefully, sir, and meanwhile refresh yourself by having a smoke." Brojonath was a very old man, without much education: he was not very skilful even at his own trade, had no opinions of his own, and could do nothing on his own responsibility. In person he was emaciated, with no teeth, a harsh voice, and a heavy grey moustache, of which he was so enamoured that he was always stroking it. He sighed as he looked at the patient's hand, and sat perfectly motionless. Haladhar then said to him: "Honoured sir, have you nothing to say?" The *kabiraj* without replying gazed intently on the face of the patient, who was glaring wildly about him, lolling his tongue out, and grinding his teeth. He also gave a tug at the *kabiraj's* moustache: and as he moved away a little, the boy rolled about and struggled to get hold of the bottle of oil in his hand. The Babus then said: "Come tell us, sir, what is the matter?" The *kabiraj* replied: "The attack is a very severe one: there seems to be high fever and delirium. If I had only had news a little earlier, I might have managed to cure him: as it is, it would be impossible even for Shiva to do so." As he spoke, the patient got hold of his bottle of oil, and rubbed a good handful of it over his body. The *kabiraj* seeing the visit was likely to cost him dear, hurriedly took the bottle away, corked it well, and got up to go. "Where are you going, sir?" They all cried. The *kabiraj* replied: "The delirium is gradually increasing: I do not think there is any further necessity for keeping the patient in the house: you should now exert yourselves to make his end a happy one by taking him to the Ganges to die."

As soon as he heard this, the patient jumped up, and the *kabiraj* started back at the sight. The young Babus of Vaidyabati ran after him, and as the *kabiraj,* who had gone on a short distance, stopped dumbfounded and amazed, they began to hustle him, with shouts of "*Hori Bol: Hori Bol!*" and one of them threw him over his shoulders, and started for the Ganges. Dolgovinda then came up to him, and said: "Aha my dear sir, you gave orders to have the patient taken to the Ganges: the doctor himself it is who is now being carried thither! I will myself perform the ceremony of putting you into the water, and of then throwing you on to the funeral pyre." The views of the fickle are ever changing, and so a little later he said: "Will you send me to the Ganges again? Go, my dear friend! go to your home, and to your children, but before you go, you must give me that bottle of oil. With these words, he snatched the bottle from the *kabiraj*, and all the young lunatics, smearing themselves over with the oil, leaped into the Ganges. The *kabiraj* became as one bereft of his senses when he saw all this, and thinking that he might breathe again if he could only get away, he increased his pace. Thereupon Haladhar, as he was swimming about, screamed out: "Ho there, respected *kabiraj!* I am gething more and more bilious everyday: you must give me some of your powders to take: do not run away: if you do, your wife will have to remove her bracelet and be a widow." The *kabiraj* threw down his box of drugs, and hurried home crying, "Alas! alas!"

In the month of Phalgun, as spring comes in, all the trees are coming out in new leaf, and the sweet odour of flowers is diffused around. Barada Babu's dwelling-house was on the banks of the Ganges: some little distance in front of it was his favourite garden-house, and all round it a garden. Barada Babu used to sit every evening in the garden-house, to enjoy the fresh air and his own meditations, or to converse with any friends who might visit him there. Ramlall was always with him, and was made the confidant of his most secret thoughts, whereby he obtained much good advice. At every opportunity, he would question his preceptor minutely on the means of attaining to a knowledge of the Supreme Being, and to perfect purity of mind.

One day Ramlall remarked to Barada Babu: "Sir, I have a great longing to travel: staying here, it is a constant grief to me to listen to the bad language of my elder brother and the evil counsel of Thakchacha, but my love for my parents and for my sister makes me disinclined to stir from home. I cannot decide what to do." Barada Babu replied;— "Much benefit is to be derived from travel: breadth of vision is not to be had without it: the mind is enlarged by the sight of different countries, and different people. Much knowledge too is acquired by a minute enquiry into the different customs of the people of different countries, into their habits, and the causes determining their condition, whether good or bad. Association moreover with all sorts of people, causes bitter prejudices to disappear and induces good feeling. If a man is educated only at home, his knowledge is derived from books only. Now education, association with good men, practical employment, and intercourse with all sorts of people, are all necessary to a man: it is by agencies such as this that the understanding becomes clear, and an impetus is given towards the moulding of a good character. But before he sets out on his travels, it is all important that a man should know the different matters he will require to investigate, for without this, travel will prove a mere aimless wandering about, like the circling round and round of an ox when threshing out the grain. I do not go so far as to say that no benefit is to be had from such travelling, that is not my meaning: some benefit or other there must be. But when a man on his travels is ignorant of the kind of enquiries he ought to make, and cannot make them, he does not derive the full benefit of his labour. Many Bengalees are fond of travelling about, but if you ask them for facts about the places they visit, how many of them can give you a sensible answer? This is not altogether their own fault, it is the result of their bringing-up. A good understanding is not to be had all at once from the sky, without some training in the art of observation, enquiry and reflection. In the education of children it is requisite that an opportunity should be given them of seeing models of a great variety of objects: as they look at all the pictures, they will compare one with another: that is to say, they will see that one object has a hand, another has no foot, that one has a peculiar mouth, another no tail; and by such comparison the faculties of observation and reflection will be brought into play and developed. After a time such comparisons will come easy to them; they will be able to reflect on the causes for the peculiarities of different objects, and will have no difficulty in perceiving the various classes into which they naturally fall. By instruction of this kind, assiduity in research is encouraged and the faculty of reasoning exercised. But in our country an education like this is hardly ever given, and as a natural consequence, our wits are muddled and run to waste: we have no instinctive perception of the essential and unessential features of any enquiry. When a question is under consideration, many of us have not even the requisite intelligence to know what kind of enquiries should be made in order that a conclusion may be arrived at; and it is no falsehood to say that the travels of a good many people are but idle and profitless. But considering the education you have had, I should imagine that travel would be of great advantage to you."

"Now if I do go abroad" said Ramlall, "I shall have to stay for sometime in places where there is society: and with what classes, and with what kinds of people, should I chiefly associate?"

"That is no easy question," Barada Babu replied: "I must contrive though to give you some kind of an answer. In every rank in life there are people good and bad: any good people you may come across you may associate with; but you know by now how to recognise such: I need not tell you again. Association with Englishmen may make a man courageous, for they worship courage, and any Englishman committing a cowardly act, is not admitted into good society. But it does not at all follow that a man is therefore virtuous because he happens to be courageous. Courage is very essential to everybody, I admit; but real courage is that which is the outcome of virtue. I have told you already and now tell you again, that you must always meditate on the Supreme Being, otherwise all that you see, or hear, or learn, will only have the effect of increasing your pride. One thing more: men often wish to do what they see others doing; the Bengalees especially, from association with Englishmen, have acquired a false superficial kind of Anglicism, and are filled with self-conceit in consequence; pride is the motive force in all they do. It will do you no harm to remember this."

They were conversing together in this way when suddenly some police-officers rushed in from the west side of the garden and surrounded Barada Babu. He looked at them sharply, and asked them who they were and what their business with him was. They replied: "We are officers connected with the police: there is a warrant out against you on the charge of illegal confinement and assault, and you will have to appear before the Court of the English Magistrate of Hooghly; we shall have moreover to search your premises for proofs of the charge." Ramlall rose up at these words, and when he had read the warrant, he shook with rage at the falsity of the charge, Barada Babu took his hand and made him sit down again, saying: "Do not put yourself out: let the matter be thoroughly well sifted. All sorts of strange accidents befall us on earth, but there is no need to be disturbed in mind at all when calamity comes: to be agitated in the presence of misfortune is the mark of an ignorant mind. Besides, I am conscious of my entire innocence of the crime I am accused of: what cause then have I for fear? Still the order of the court must be attended to, so I shall put in an immediate appearance. Let the officers search my house, and see with their own eyes that there is no one concealed there." The police-officers having received this order, searched everywhere but found nothing. Barada Babu then had a boat fetched, and made all his arrangements for his journey to Hooghly. Meanwhile by some good chance Beni Babu arrived at his house, so he set out on his journey to Hooghly, taking Beni and Ramlall with him. Both were somewhat anxious, but by his cheerful conversation on a variety of topics, he soon put them at their ease.

XV

TRIAL OF BARADA BABU

The court of the magistrate of Hooghly was crowded. The defendants in the different suits pending, the complainants, witnesses, prisoners, pleaders and officers were all present. The majority were restless and impatient, anxiously awaiting the arrival of the magistrate, but he was not yet even in sight. Barada Babu, taking Beni Babu and Ramlall with him, spread a blanket underneath a tree, and sat down. Some of the clerks of the court who were near, came up to him and began to talk significantly about coming to an arrangement, but Barada Babu refused to pay any heed to them. Then, with the view of exciting his fears, they observed: "The magistrate's orders are very severe; but everything is left to us, and we can do exactly what we think fit: it is our business to draw up the depositions, so we can upset everything by a mere stroke of the pen; but we must have money. An investigation will have to be made, and this is the time it should be done: our best efforts will be useless when the orders in the case have once been passed." Ramlall on hearing all this was a little alarmed, but Barada Babu replied quite fearlessly: "Gentlemen, you must do whatever is your duty. I will never consent to give a bribe. I am perfectly innocent and have no fears." The clerks of the court went off to their places in high wrath.

Presently some pleaders came up and said to him: "We perceive, sir, that you are a very respectable man, and have evidently fallen into some trouble; but you must take care that your case is not lost for want of proper investigation. If you wish to have witnesses prepared, we can supply you with some on the spot: we have every facility for doing so at a trifling expense. The magistrate will be here directly, so seize this opportunity to do what is necessary." Barada Babu answered: "Gentlemen, you are extremely kind; but even should I have to wear fetters, I will wear them. I shall not be much troubled in mind at that: it will be a disgrace, I know,—I am ready to acknowledge it as such; but I will not walk in the way of falsehood even to save my life." "Good heavens!" they exclaimed ironically, "here is a man belonging to the Golden Age. Surely King Yudhishthira come to life again!" and they went away laughing quietly to themselves.

It was now past two o'clock and still there was no sign of the magistrate: all were looking out for him as intently as crows on a sacred *ghât*. Some among them said to a Brahman astrologer who was present: "Pray sir, calculate for us whether the magistrate will come today or not" The astrologer at once replied: "Come, tell me the name of some flower." Somebody mentioned an *hibiscus*. The astrologer, calculating on his fingers, said, "No, the magistrate will not come today: he has business at home." Believing the charlatan's words implicitly, they all made preparations to tie up their bundles of records, and got up, saying to each other: "Ah, *Ram, Ram!* now we breathe freely again, let us go home and sleep."

Thakchacha had been sitting with four others within the court enclosure, with a bundle of papers under his arm and a cloth over his face: he was now walking about, his eyes blinking restlessly, his beard waving in the breeze and his head bent low. Just then Ramlall's gaze fell on him and he remarked to Barada Babu and Beni Babu: "See, see! Thakchacha is here! I fancy he is at the bottom of all this, otherwise why should he turn away his head when he saw me?" Barada Babu, raising his head, saw him and said, "I think so too; he is looking sideways in our direction, and moreover whenever his gaze falls on my face he turns and says something to his companions: it seems to me that Thakchacha is our evil genius; as the proverb has it, "he is the spirit in the *sirish* seed."

Beni Babu was never seen without a smile on his face: his pleasantry was of great service to him in his search for information. He could not refrain from shouting out the name of Thakchacha, but none of his shouts were attended to. Thakchacha had drawn a paper from under his arm and was to all appearance busily examining it: he pretended not to hear and did not even raise his head. Thereupon Beni Babu went up to him, and with his characteristic gesture said to him: "Hallo, what is the matter? What has brought you here?" Thakchacha said nothing, only examined his paper minutely; indeed he seemed to be seized with a sudden fit of modesty. But as he must, he thought, put Beni Babu off somehow or other without answering his question, he replied: "Ha, Babu! The river has risen a good deal today, how will you get back? I might as well ask you too why you are here, and why you keep on asking me the same thing. I have a good deal of business on hand just now and my time is short: I will speak with you later on: I will return directly." With these words, Thakchacha slipped away, and was soon apparently engrossed in some trifling conversation with his companions.

PEARY CHAND MITRA

Three o'clock struck: everybody was walking about impatiently. There is no chance of getting business promptly attended to in the Mofussil, and people get utterly weary of hanging about the courts. They were just breaking up when suddenly the magistrate's carriage was heard approaching. Shouts were at once raised: "The Saheb is coming! The Saheb is coming!" The astrologer looked utterly crestfallen, and people began to say to him: "Your honour's calculations are somewhat amazing." "Ah!" replied he, "it must be owing to something pungent that I have eaten today that my calculations have been so upset." The clerks of the court were all standing in their places, and directly the magistrate entered they all bent their heads low to the ground and salaamed to him.

The magistrate took his seat on the bench whistling casually. His *hooka* bearer brought him his *hooka:* he put his feet up on the table, and lying back in his chair, pulled away contentedly, now and then drawing out his handkerchief, which was scented with lavender-water, to mop his face. The office of the court interpreter was crowded. Men were hard at work writing out depositions, but as the old proverb has it: "He wins who pays." The head clerk of the court, the *sheristadar,* with a shawl over his shoulders and a fine turban on his head, took a number of records of cases and read them out in a sing-song before the magistrate, who all the while was glancing at a newspaper, or writing some of his own private letters: as each case was read out he asked: "Well, what is all this about?" The *sheristadar* gave him the information that suited his own wishes on the subject, and the opinion of the *sheristadar* was practically the opinion of the magistrate.

Barada Babu was standing on one side with Beni Babu and Ramlall, and was perfectly amazed when he heard the kind of judgments that were being delivered. Considering the depositions that had been made in his own case, he began to think that there was very little chance of matters turning out auspiciously for him. That the *sheristadar* would show him any favour was in the highest degree improbable, but he knew the old proverb: "Destiny is the friend of the helpless." As he thus reflected, his case was called on for hearing. Thakchacha had been sitting inside the court: he at once took his witnesses with him, and stood before the magistrate, proud and confident. When the papers in the case had been read, the *sheristadar* said: "My lord, this is a clear case of illegal confinement and assault." Thakchacha thereupon ceased stroking his moustache and glared atrBarada Babu, thinking that at last his end was achieved. In the other cases no questions had been put to the defendants when the records had been read: they had been treated as summarily as goats for the sacrifice; but the magistrate's glance, as luck would have it, falling upon Barada Babu before he passed his orders, the latter respectfully explained to him in English, all the circumstances of the case, saying: "I have never even seen the person who has been put forward as having been confined and assaulted by me, nor did the police-officers when they searched my premises find anybody there. Beni Babu and Ramlall were with me at the time; if you will be good enough to take their evidence, my declaration will be substantiated."

Remarking the gentlemanly appearance of Barada Babu and the good judgment that had distinguished his language, the magistrate was anxious to make an enquiry. Thakchacha gave many significant hints to the *sheristadar,* and he for his own part, seeing the turn things were taking, reflected that he might after all have to disgorge the rupees he had taken, so laying aside all his fears before the magistrate, he said: "My lord, there is really no necessity for hearing this case over again." Upon this the magistrate pursed his lips in some perplexity and turned the matter over in his mind, cutting his nails the while. Barada Babu seeing his opportunity again explained to him, quietly and in detail, the real facts of the case. As soon as the magistrate had heard him, he took the evidence of Beni Babu and Ramlall, and the charge appearing upon their statements to be manifestly a false one, was dismissed.

The final orders had not been passed before Thakchacha was off as hard as he could run. Barada Babu saluted the magistrate respectfully and went out. When the court was closed, everybody began to compliment him: he paid little heed however to them and manifested no particular pleasure at winning his case, but quietly got into his boat, accompanied by Beni Babu and Ramlall.

XVI

THAKCHACHA AT HOME

Thakchacha's house was on the outskirts of the city: on either side of it were filthy tanks, and in front the shrine of some guardian saint. Inside the enclosure was a store-house for grain, and ducks and fowls were running about the yard. Rogues of every description were in the habit of assembling at the house early every morning.

Thakchacha could assume many characters in the conduct of his business: he could be gentle or passionate: he could laugh or frown: he could make a parade of virtue or a show of force, with equal facility. When the business of the day was over, he would take his bath and his food, and then sit by his wife and smoke: and as he smoked the tobacco would gurgle and hiss in its well-chased bowl of Bidri ware. Their conversation was generally on their mutual joys and sorrows.

Thakchacha's wife was held in great repute amongst the women of the district. They were firmly convinced that she was well versed in religious ritual and incantations, in the art of making bad qualities good, in mesmerising, in causing even death or timely disappearances, in magic and sorcery, and in fact in every variety of the black art. For this reason women of all classes of life came constantly to her to hold secret converse. An old proverb has it: "As the god, so the goddess," and Thakchacha and his wife were a well-matched pair: the husband got his living by his wits, and the wife by her reputed learning.

A woman who earns her own living is apt to become somewhat imperious, and her husband rarely receives from her unfeigned respect and attention. Thakchacha had consequently to put up occasionally with his wife's reproaches. She was now sitting upon a low cane stool, saying to her husband: "You are always roaming about, everywhere but at home. What good does it all do to me or the children? You are always saying that you have such a lot of business on hand; is our hunger appeased by such talk as that? Now it is the desire of my heart to dress well and to mix in the society of women of good position, but I never get a glimpse of any money. You go wandering about like a lunatic; do remain quietly at home for a change." Thakchacha replied somewhat testily: "How can I possibly tell you all the trouble I have had to undergo. Look at my great anxieties, look at all the artifices, intrigues and trickery I have to employ: I have no language to express it all. Then just as the game is on the point of falling into my hands, off it flies again. Never mind, sooner or later it will be caught." Just at this moment, a servant came to tell them that a messenger was arrived from Baburam Babu's house to summon Thakchacha, who thereupon looked at his wife and said: "You see, the Babu is continually sending for me: he will do nothing without consulting me. I will strike when the hour is come."

Baburam Babu was seated in his reception-hall: with him were Bancharam Babu of Outer Simla, Beni Babu of Bally, and Becharam Babu of Bow Bazar: they were all chatting hard. Thakchacha sat down among them as a monkey chief might sit amidst his subjects. Baburam at once greeted him: "Ha, Thakchacha, your arrival is most opportune: my difficulties are as great as ever: I am more involved than ever in these law-suits. Come and tell me some way of preserving my property."

Thakchacka.—Litigation is natural to a man who is a man. Your misfortunes will all be at an end when your cases are won: why then should you feel alarmed?

Becharam.—Mercy! what advice is this you are giving? Baburam Babu will be completely ruined by your instrumentality: of that there is not the slightest doubt. What do you say, Beni, my dear friend?

Beni.—Some portions of the estate should be sold, I think, to clear off the debts, and some arrangements made for reducing the expenditure: the suits-at-law also should be looked into and cleared off. But our words are wasted, like one crying in a bamboo jungle. Thakchacha's are the only words attended to.

Thakchacha.—I pledge my word of honour that all the suits that have been instituted at my instigation will be gained: I will clear all the difficulties away. Fighting is one of the necessities of man's existence: what cause then is there for alarm?

Becharam.—Ah, Thakchacha, how grand is the heroism you have always exhibited! What a magnificent display of courage you made when the boat was swamped! Why it was all on your account that we suffered so on the occasion of the marriage. You displayed great bravery, I must say, in getting up that false charge against Barada Babu. Not one of the affairs of Baburam Babu in which you have meddled but has turned out most prosperously! All hail to you: I humbly salute you! But ugh! my gorge rises at the mere recollection of you and all your works! what more can I say to you? Come, friend Beni, get up and come away: it is no pleasure to me to sit here any longer.

XVII

BABURAM'S SECOND MARRIAGE

There had been heavy rain in the night: the roads and *ghâts* was all muddy and wet: the sky was still overcast, and there were occasional distant rumblings of thunder: frogs croaked everywhere in loud chorus. The shopkeepers in the bazaar had opened out their awnings, and were now engaged in smoking. Owing to the rainy weather very few people were moving about: only a few *gariwans* passed along the road, singing at the top of their voices, and some coolies bearing loads on their heads, absorbed in their favourite melody, of which the refrain ran:—

> *"Oh yes, my darling Bisakha!*
> *"Your friend's just off to Mathura."*

A number of barbers lived on the west side of the Vaidyabati Bazar. One of them was sitting in his verandah on account of the rain, and as he sat there, every now and then looking up at the sky or humming softly to himself, his wife brought her infant child to him and said, "I have not yet got through all my house work: just nurse this child for me a bit! the pots and pans have not yet been scoured, and the floor has not been rubbed down with cowdung; and besides, I have a lot of cooking to do. I am the only woman in the house: how can I possibly do all this myself?—have I four hands or four feet?"

The barber straightway tucked his shaving instruments under his arm and got up to go, saying, "I have no time just now to nurse the child. Baburam Babu is to be married tomorrow: I must be off at once." His wife started back, saying: "Good heavens! what next? what, that fat unwieldy old man going to marry again! Alas, alas! And such an excellent housewife as he has already, a chaste divinity, as pure as Lakshmi! What, he must go and tie a co-wife to her neck! It is a crying shame! Why, there is a really nothing that men will not do!" The barber was dumbfounded by this eloquent outburst, but taking no notice of what his wife was saying, stuck his hat of plaited leaves on his head and went off.

That day was a very cloudy one, but early next morning the sun shone brightly. The trees and plants seemed all to have received new life, and the joyous sounds of beast and bird, in field and garden, were redoubled. Baburam Babu, Thakchacha, Bakreswar Babu, and Bancharam Babu were just getting into one of the numerous boats at the Vaidyabati Ghât, when suddenly Beni Babu and Becharam Babu appeared. Thakchacha pretended not to see them, and shouted to the boatmen to let the boat loose, while they remonstrated: "But master, the ebb tide is still running! how shall we be able to get along against it even if we punt with poles or haul with ropes?" Baburam Babu received his two friends very courteously, saying: "Your arrival is most opportune: come, let us all be off." Becharam Babu then remonstrated: "Ah Baburam, who in the world advised you to go and marry at your age?"

Baburam.—Ah Becharam, my dear friend, am I so old as all that? I am a good deal younger than you are: besides, if you say that my hair is quite gray and that I have lost all my teeth, that is the case with a good many others even at an early age: it is not such a very great drawback. I have a good many things to think of; one of my sons has gone to the bad, another has become a lunatic: one of my daughters is no more, another is as good as a widow. If I have children by this marriage, my family will be preserved from extinction: I am, moreover, under an obligation to marry: if I do not do so the girl's father will lose caste, for they have no other family they can marry her into.

Bakreswar.—That is indeed true: do you suppose that the master has entered upon a matter of this importance without taking everything into consideration? I know no one of a better understanding.

Bancharam.—We are Kulins: we must maintain the traditions of our family at any cost, and where wealth is a recommendation as well, why, there is nothing more to be said!

Becharam.—Confound your family traditions and bad luck to your wealth! Alas, how many persons have combined to overthrow one house! What do you say, friend Beni?

Beni.—What shall I say? our remonstrances are but as idle words, as the tears of one weeping in a wilderness. But really this matter is a cause of great grief to me. To marry again when you already have one wife, is a grievous sin: no man who wished to maintain his virtue could ever do such a thing. There may be a *Shastra* of an opposite opinion, it is true; but there is never any necessity for following it: that such a *Shastra* is not a genuine one there can be no reasonable doubt, and should it be taken as a guide in actual practice, the bonds of marriage would thereby become much weakened. The feelings of the wife towards her husband cannot remain as before, and the feelings of the husband towards his wife will also be constantly changing. If such a calamity as this befalls a family, it cannot possibly prosper or be happy. If there is such a rule in the *Shastras*, that rule should not be regarded as binding. Be that as it may, it is very base of Baburam Babu to marry a second time, considering what a wife he has still living. I know nothing about the details of the matter: it has only just come to my ears.

Thakchacha.—Ah, the man of books picks a hole in everything! he seems to me to have nothing else to do. I am getting an old man now, and my beard is gray. Must I be always arguing with such children? Does the learned Babu know how much wealth this marriage will bring to the family?

Becharam.—Mercenary wretch that you are! do you recognise money only? Have you no regard for anything else? You are a low unprincipled scoundrel, that is all I can say. Ugh! friend Beni, come, let us be off.

Thakchacha.—I will have a talk with you someother day: we cannot waste anymore time now. You will have to hurry if you want to reach the house in time.

Thereupon, Becharam caught hold of Beni Babu by the hand and got up, saying: "We will never, as long as we live, go to such a marriage; and if there be such a thing as virtue in the world, may you not return in peace! Only ruin can attend your counsel: you who are now enjoying yourself at Baburam Babu's expense! I have nothing more to say to you. Ugh!"

XVIII

MOZOOMDAR ON THE MARRIAGE

The sun was just setting: gloriously beautiful was the western sky with its many and varied tints. On land and water the sun's tremulous light seemed gently smiling, while a soft breeze blew: everything was calm and inviting. On such an evening as this, a number of young men were thronging with loud and boisterous shouts down the main street of Vaidyabati. They knocked against the passers-by, smashing the things they were carrying, hustling them, throwing their baskets away and robbing them of their supplies of food. They sang continuously at the top of their voices, imitating the howls of dogs at the same time. On either side of the road people fled, calling for assistance and protection, trembling, and bewildered with fear. Like a storm sweeping down from all four quarters of the compass at once, with the roar of heavy rain, this whirlwind came tearing and raging past. And who are these mighty men? Who indeed but those models of virtue, Matilall and his companions?—King Nala and Yudhishthira over again! They are far too great personages to pay heed to anyone: so full of self-importance and of pride are their heads that they are as unsteady in their gait as men drunk with much wine. They have it all their own way as they come swaggering along.

Just then an old man from the village, one Mozoomdar, his solitary lock waving in the breeze, a stick in one hand and some vegetables in the other, approached them, leaning heavily on his stick. They all surrounded him and began to amuse themselves at his expense. Mozoomdar was a little hard of hearing, and when they said to him: "Come, tell us, how is your wife?" he replied: "I shall have to roast them before I can eat them." They laughed heartily, and Mozoomdar would have liked to slip away, but there was no escape for him. The young Babus seized him, and making him sit on the bank of the river, gave him a pipe of tobacco, saying to him: 'Come, Mozoomdar, tell us all about the row at the marriage of the master of Vaidyabati: you are bit of a poet: it is a pleasure to us to listen to you. If you do not tell us, we shall not let you off, and we shall go and tell your wife that you have met with an untimely death." Mozoomdar saw that he was in a bad way, and that there was no getting out of it unless he complied; so, making the best of a bad job, he set his stick and vegetables on the ground and commenced his narrative.

"It is a pitiable tale that I have to tell. What an experience has it been to me, accompanying the master! It was close on evening when the boat drew up at the Barnagore *ghât*. Some women had come to the riverside to draw water: as soon as they saw the master, they veiled their faces slightly and began to chatter hard to each other, laughing quietly the while. 'Ha what a lovely bridegroom!' they cried, 'what a sweet *champac* flower for a lucky girl to fondle in her braided hair!' Said one of them: 'Old or young, whichever he may be, the girl will have no difficulty in seeing him with her eyes: that of itself is something. May the wretched lot that has befallen me befal no one else: married at the age of six, I have never even set eyes on my husband. I have heard that he has married some fifty wives, and is over eighty years of age; and though he is such a wretched tottering old man, he never makes any objection to marry if he is only well paid for it. Surely some great crimes must have been committed in former births, or else daughters would never be born into a Kulin's family!' 'My dear,' said another woman to her, 'you have finished drawing water now: come along, you ought not to gossip like this when you come to the riverside. Why, your husband is alive, whereas the man I was married to was actually dying, with his feet in the Ganges, when the ceremony of marriage was performed! What possible good will it do to discuss the religious duties of Kulin Brahmans? The secrets of the heart are best kept locked up in the breast.'"

"It grieved me to listen to the talk of the women, and the words of Beni Babu, which he spoke at the time of our departure, recurred to my mind. Then on landing at the Barnagore *ghât*, there was a good deal of trouble in trying to get a *palki*, but not a single bearer was to be had, and the time for the ceremony was fast slipping away. We had to proceed as best we could. After a good deal of floundering about in the mud, we reached the house of the bride's father. How can I describe to you the figure that the master presented after he had tumbled down in the road? we had only to put him upon an ox, for him to have appeared a veritable Mahadeva, and we might have presented Thakchacha and Bakreswar as Nandi and Bhringi in attendance upon him. I had heard rumours that there would be a large distribution of presents, but on getting up to the great hall, I saw that there was to be nothing of the sort: it was all a delusion, and another illustration of the old proverb,—"Sand has fallen into the *goor*." Thakchacha, seeing his hopes destroyed, was glaring around him everywhere, and strutting insolently about. I could not help smiling to myself, but I thought it would be safer not to express my real sentiments. The bridegroom had meanwhile withdrawn for the ceremonies performed by the women of the family. The women, old and young, all surrounded him, their ornaments jingling as they moved about. They were horrified when they saw the bridegroom. During the performance of the ceremony, when bride and bridegroom gaze into each other's eyes, he was obliged to put his spectacles on: the women all burst out laughing and began to make fun of him. He flew into a passion and called out, 'Thakchacha! Thakchacha!' Thakchacha was just on the point of running into the women's apartments, when the people belonging to the party of the bride's father got him on the ground. Bancharam Babu was pugnacious, and got well thrashed. Bakreswar Babu was hustled about so that he resembled a pigeon with swollen neck. When I saw the disturbance, I left the bridegroom's party and joined that of the bride. What became of everybody in the end I cannot say, but Thakchacha had to return home in a *dooly*. You all know the saying—"In avarice is sin, and in sin death." Now listen to the poetry I have composed:—

> *Any counsel his parasite pours in his ears,*
> *Baburam, the old dotard, as gospel reveres.*
> *Still dreaming of riches by day and by night,*
> *No thought ever stirs him of wrong or of right.*
> *In saving and getting he squanders his life,*
> *And lately it struck him, "I'll marry a wife!"*
> *"Fie! you're old," cry his friends, "and what can you noed more?*
> *"You've your wife and your children, with grandsons in store?"*
> *But their kindly advice for themselves they may keep"*
> *At a trifle like bigamy, fortunes go cheap!*
> *So all in a flurry he orders a boat,*
> *And with kinsmen and servants is shortly afloat.*
> *Good Beni's remonstrance he haughtily spurns,*
> *Who home to his rice unrewarded returns.*
> *Becharam is disgusted, and toddles away:*
> *"Thakchacha, you scoundrel!" was all he could say.*
> *But the Barnagore women such volleys of jeers*
> *Exchange through their chudders where'er he appears,*
> *That the bridegroom gets nervous, and asks in affright,*

"Can I really be such a ridiculous sight?
"Is some further expenditure needed, alas?"
And anxiously studies his face in the glass.
Reassured of his beauty, and freed from alarm
He swaggers along, upon Thakchacha's arm.
But scarce is he rid of that terrible doubt,
When in mud like a pumpkin he's tumbling about;
And his friends in the mire as they flounder half-dead,
See the Halls, not of Hymen but Pluto. ahead.
And indeed it turns out, when he's taken the yoke,
That his vision connubial has vanished in smoke;
For the cluster of pearls he was hoping to claim,
And the gold and the silver, were nought but a name!
Thakchacha, outwitted, with furious scowl
Glares round him, scarce able to stifle a howl.
And oh, when its time for the bridegroom to enter
The ladies' domain, of what mirth he's the centre!
Every bangle a-jangle, around him they flutter,
And flout him and scout him till scarce he can stutter.
"This pot-bellied dotard to wed with a baby!
"This bloated old octogenarian gaby!
"With a head like a gourd, not a tooth to his gum!
"'Tis an overgrown ogre in spectacles come!
"And the child, the sweet blossom, our jewel so rare!
"Ah, shame on the Kulins, such deeds who can dare!"
While, shrinking and blinking and all of a shiver,
The bridegroom, a captive whom none will deliver,
Cries feebly as one in the direst of pain,
"To the rescue, Thakchacha!" again and again.
That hero leaps in at the piteous sound,
But is seized by the durwans and hurled to the ground.
The remains of his beard he may rescue today,
But a terrible hiding's his share of the prey.
The guests, who consider it risky to stay,
Have other engagements, and hasten away.
Your servant, the tumult increasing still more,
Not without some temerity, made for the door,
And retired, with a fortitude second to none.
All hail to you, masters! my story is done.

XIX

Death of Baburam Babu

Having just come in from his morning walk, Beni Babu was sitting in his garden-house. He was gazing about him, and had just caught up a refrain of Ram Prasad's

"Swift to its goal life ebbs away."

—when suddenly from a bower of creepers to the west of him, he heard a voice: "Ha! friend Beni! True indeed it is that 'swift to its goal life ebbs away.'" Starting up from his seat, Beni Babu saw Becharam Babu of Bow Bazar hurrying towards him, and going to meet him, said: "Becharam, my dear friend, what has happened?" Becharam Babu replied: "Throw your shawl over your shoulders and come with me at once: Baburam Babu is very ill: you must see him just once."

The two friends soon reached Vaidyabati, and saw that Baburam Babu had a very severe attack of fever: his temperature was very high, and he was suffering from intense thirst, tossing restlessly about on his bed. Some slices of cucumber and a cloth steeped in rose-water lay beside him, but he could retain no nourishment. The villagers all thronged around, loudly discussing the nature of his illness: one of them was saying: "Our pulse is the pulse of vegetarians and fish-eaters: nothing but harm can arise from the use of leeches, purgatives, and blisters. The best kind of treatment for us is that of the old village doctor; and then, if no relief is obtained, and grave symptoms occur, a doctor using the English methods might be called in." Another remarked: "It would be a good thing to have the opinion of a Mahomedan *hakim:* they often effect wonderful cures, and their drugs are all as pleasant to take as that delicious sweetmeat the *mohanbhog.*" Another said: "You may say what you will, but doctors who treat on English methods give instantaneous relief in all such cases of sickness, as if by the repetition of a *mantra*: a cure will be very difficult without proper medical treatment." The sick man kept repeatedly asking for water. Brojonath Raya, the old *kabiraj*, who was sitting by him at the time, said: "The case is a very serious one: it is not a good thing to be constantly giving him water:

we must give him a little of the juice of the *bael*. We are none of us his enemies, I should imagine, that we should be giving him just now as much water as he wants." All this wrangling was going on by Baburam Babu's bedside. The next room was filled with a number of pandits, who, of course, regarded as of chief importance the performance of sacrifices to Shiva, the worship of the sun, the offering of a million of *hibiscus* flowers at Kali's shrine at Kalighat, and all such religious ceremonials. Beni Babu had been standing listening to the discussion going on round Baburam Babu, but everybody was talking at once and nobody listening to anybody else. "Many sages many Opinions" says the old proverb, and each man thought his words as infallible as the mystic *mantra* possessed by Druva. Though Beni Babu attempted once or twice to express his own opinion, his words were lost almost before he had opened his lips, and being unable to get a word in edgewise, he took Becharam Babu outside with him.

Just then Thakchacha approached them, limping painfully along: he was exceedingly anxious on account of Baburam Babu's illness, reflecting that all his chances of gain had slipped away. Beni Babu, seeing him, said: "Thakchacha, what is the matter with your leg?" Becharam burst in with the remark: "What, my friend, have you never heard of the affair of Barnagore? The pain he is suffering is only the punishment for his evil advice: have you forgotten what I said in the boat?" Thakchacha tried to slip away when he heard this, but Beni Babu caught him by the arm and said: "Never mind that now! is anything being devised for the recovery of the master? There is great confusion in the house." Thakchacha replied: "When the fever commenced, I took Ekramaddi the *hakim* with me: by the administration of purgatives and other drugs he reduced the fever, and allowed his patient to eat spiced rice; but the fever returned again the other day, and since then Brojonath the *kabiraj* has been looking after the case. The fever seems to me to be steadily increasing: I cannot imagine what to do." Beni Babu said: "Thakchacha, do not be angry at what I am going to say: you should have sent us news of this before. However, that cannot be helped now: we must call in a skilled English doctor at once."

At this moment, Ramlall and Barada Prasad Babu approached. Ramlall's face was quite worn from night-watching, from the labour and toil of nursing, and from anxiety of mind; his daily anxiety was to devise means for restoring his father to convalescence and health. Seeing Beni Babu he said to him: "Sir, I am in grievous trouble:

with all this confusion in the house no good advice is to be had from anyone. Barada Babu comes every morning and evening to look after my father, but none of the people here will allow me to carry out his instructions. Your arrival is most opportune: please adopt any steps you think necessary."

Becharam Babu gazed steadily at Barada Babu for sometime, and then with tears in his eyes caught hold of his hand and cried: "Ah, Barada Babu, why is it that everybody does you reverence, except on account of the many good qualities you possess? Why, it was Thakchacha here who advised Baburam Babu to have that charge of illegal confinement and assault brought against you, and all kinds of violence and knavery have been practised on you without rhyme or reason, at their instigation; and yet, when Thakchacha fell sick, you cured him, treating him and even nursing him yourself, and now too, when Baburam is ill, you spare no effort to give good advice, and to look after his welfare. Now generally speaking, if one man but speaks harshly against another, enmity at once springs up between them, and though a thousand apologies may be made, the feeling does not pass away; but though you have been grievously insulted and injured, you have no difficulty in forgetting the insult and injuries you have suffered. No feeling towards another but brotherly kindness arises in your mind. Ah, Barada Babu, many may talk of virtue, but never have I found any possessing such as you possess. Men are naturally base and corrupt; how then can they judge of your qualities? But as day and night are true, your qualities will be judged above."

Somewhat vexed by these remarks of Becharam Babu, Barada Babu bowed his head and said humbly: "Sir, pray do not address me like this. I am but a very insignificant person: what is my knowledge or what my virtue after all?"

"We had better postpone this conversation" Beni Babu said, "tell me now what to devise for the master's illness."

Barada Babu replied: "If you gentlemen think the idea a good one, I can go to Calcutta and bring a doctor back with me by the evening: no further confidence, I think, should be placed in Brojonath Raya."

Premnarayan Mozoomdar, who was standing near, remarked: "Doctors do not properly understand the pulse, and they let their patients die in their houses. We ought not to dismiss the *kabiraj* altogether: on the contrary, let the *kabiraj* and the doctor each take up a special feature of the case."

"We can take that matter into consideration afterwards" Beni Babu said, "go now, Barada Babu, and fetch a doctor."

Barada Babu started off for Calcutta at once, without taking either his bath or his food, though they all remonstrated: "Sir, you have the whole day before you, take a mouthful of food before you start." He only replied: "If I stop to do that there will be delay, and all my trouble may go for nought."

Baburam Babu, as he lay on his bed, kept asking where Matilall was, but it was hard to get a glimpse of even the top tuft of his hair: he was always out on picnics with his boon companions, and paid no heed to his father's illness. Beni Babu observing this conduct sent a servant out to Matilall in the garden, but he only sent back some feigned excuse; he had a very bad headache, and would come home later on. As the fever left Baburam Babu about two o'clock in the afternoon, his pulse became exceedingly weak: the *kabiraj* examining it, said: "The master must be removed from the house at once. He is a man of long experience, an old man, and a man highly respected; and we ought certainly to ensure that his end be a happy one." On hearing this the whole household broke out into loud lamentations, and all his kinsmen and neighbours assisted in carrying him into the great hall of the house. Just then Barada Babu arrived with the English doctor. The latter, observing the state of his pulse, remarked. "You have called me in at the last moment: how can a doctor possibly be of any use if you only summon him just before taking a patient to the Ganges?" With these words he departed.

All the inhabitants of Vaidyabati stood round Baburam Babu, each asking some question or other, such as: "Honoured sir, can you recognise me?" "Come, sir, say who I am?" Beni Babu remonstrated: "Please do not vex the sick man in this way? What is the good of all this questioning?" The officiating priests had now completed their sacrifices, and approached with the sacred flowers of blessing; but they saw at once that their ceremonial had all been in vain. Seeing that Baburam Babu's breathing was becoming heavier, they all took him to the Vaidyabati Ghât. After tasting of the Ganges water and breathing the fresher air, he revived a little: the crowd too had diminished in numbers. Ramlall sat beside his father while Barada Prasad Babu came and stood in front of him. After a short pause, the latter said very quietly: "Pray meditate for this once with all your mind upon the Supreme God: without His favour we are utterly helpless." Baburam Babu hearing these words, gazed intently for a few seconds at Barada Prasad Babu, and began to shed tears. Ramlall wiped away his tears and gave him a few drops off milk to drink. Baburam Babu then grew more composed and said in a low tone: "Ah, my friend Barada Babu, I now know that I have no other friend in the world but you! Through the evil counsel of a certain individual, I have committed many and grievous crimes: these are continually recurring to my memory, and my soul seems to be on fire. I am a grievous sinner: how shall I make answer for it? Can you possibly forgive me?" As he uttered these words Baburam Babu took hold of the hand of Barada Babu, and closed his eyes. His friends and neighbours who were near began repeating the name of God. Thus, in full possession of his faculties Baburam Babu passed away.

XX

THE SHRADDHA CEREMONY

On the death of his father, Matilall succeeded to the *guddee*, and became the head of the house. His former companions never left his side for a moment, and he grew as proud as a turkey-cock, rejoicing in the thought that at last after so long a time he might give his extravagance its full bent. When Matilall displayed a little grief on his father's account, his companions said to him: "Why are you so depressed? who expects to live forever with his father and mother? You are now lord and master." A fool's grief is a mere empty name. How can true sorrow possibly affect the mind of the man who has never given any happiness to those whom he should hold most sacred—his father and his mother—but on the contrary untold pain and misery? The feeling, if it does arise, passes away like a shadow, and the natural consequence is that such a man can never have any veneration for the memory of his father, and his mind is never inclined to do anything to keep him in remembrance. Matilall's eager desire to know the extent of the property which his father had left, very soon overshadowed his grief. Acting on the advice of his companions, he put double locks on the house-door and on the money-chest, and became more easy in his mind when he had done so. He was in a perpetual state of alarm lest his money should somehow or other fall into the hands of his mother, stepmother, brother or sister, and be altogether lost to him in consequence. His companions were continually saying to him: "Money is a very important thing, sir! Where it is in question, no confidence is to be reposed even in one's own father. Now there is your younger brother always carrying a big bag of virtue about with him wherever he goes, and with truth always on his tongue; yet even his preceptor never shows indulgence to anyone, but whenever he has the opportunity enforces his full claims. We have seen a good many shams of that kind. Anyhow, Barada Babu must know something of witchcraft: he must have lived sometime at Kamrup. How otherwise is it possible to account for the great influence he had over Baburam Babu at the time of his death?"

Not very long after this conversation, Matilall proceeded to visit his relatives and kinsmen, to signify his accession to his new position as master of the house. Busybodies are at all times to be found, ready to interfere in other people's concerns. Like the twists and turns of the *jelabhi* sweetmeat, their conversation touches on a variety of topics, but never goes straight to the point: like air it wanders where it will, and it is as difficult to get hold of, for it will generally be found on close examination to have a double meaning. Some of those he visited said: "The master was a most worthy person: had it not been for his great store of merit, he could not have had the children he did. His death too,—why, it was characteristic of the man! it was marvellous! Ah, sir, all this time you have been under the shelter of a mountain, shielded and protected! You will now have your own discretion to depend upon: the family all look to you: you have the whole number of religious festivals to keep up: you have, moreover, to perpetuate the name of your father and your grandfather. First, of course you must perform the *shraddha* with due regard to your property: you need not in this matter dance to the tune of the world's opinion. Why Ram Chandra himself offered a funeral cake of sand to his father's shade, and if you have to abridge your expenditure in this respect, it is idle to mourn over that: but to do nothing at all is not good. Ah, sir, you must know that your father's name resounds far and wide! by virtue of his name the tiger and the cow drink at the same pool! can his *shraddha* then be like the *shraddha* of a poor and insignificant man? Even those encumbered with debt must avoid the world's reproach." Matilall could not comprehend the drift of all this talk. These men, while nominally manifesting their bosom friendship as kinsmen for a kinsman, were really in their inmost hearts eager to have a gorgeous *shraddha* ceremony, and themselves to get the management of it, so that they might gain importance thereby; but they would never give a plain answer to a plain question. One of them said: "It will never do not to have the *shorash*, with the usual display of silver and other presents." Another remarked: "You will find it very hard to keep the world's respect, if you do not have a *dan-sagar*, with costly presents of every kind for all comers." Another said: "It will be a very poor sort of *shraddha*, if there is no *dampati-baran* for poor Brahmans." And another said: "It will be a great disgrace if pandits are not invited to attend, and a distribution of alms not made to the poor." There was a good deal of wrangling over the affair. "Who wants your advice?"—"Who told you to argue?"—"Who listens to your conclusions?"—"Nobody respects you in the village: it is only in your own opinion that you are the head man," such remarks were freely bandied about from one to the other. Each of those present indeed was in his own estimation the most important man there, and each man thought what he had to say the conclusion of the whole matter.

Three days after this discussion, Beni Babu, Becharam Babu, Bancharam Babu, and Bakreswar Babu, arrived at Matilall's house. Thakchacha was sitting near Matilall, as melancholy and spiritless as a snake with its jewelled crest lost: with bead-rosary in his hand and with trembling lips, he was muttering his prayers. His attention was not directed to the brisk conversation that was going on around him: his eyes were rolling about, their glance chiefly directed at the wall. When he saw Beni Babu and the others, he rose hurriedly and saluted them. Such humility on Thakchacha's part had never been witnessed before, but the old proverb has it:—"With the venom, goes the glamour."

Beni Babu took hold of Thakchacha's hand, and said to him: "Why, what are you doing? How is it that you, a venerable old Moulvi as you are, honour us like this?"

Bancharam Babu said: "We must waste no more time: our leisure is very limited. Nothing is as yet arranged; come, tell us what should be done."

Becharam.—Baburam's affairs are in great confusion: some of the property will have to be sold to clear off debts. It would not be right to celebrate the *shraddha* on a magnificent scale and incur more debt by so doing.

Bancharam.—What is this I hear? Surely the very first requisite is to avoid the censure of the world: the property may be looked after later on. Shall honour and reputation be allowed to float away on the waters of this flood?

Becharam.—That is very bad advice, and I will never assent to it myself. How now, friend Beni, what do you say?

Beni.—To incur debt again in any case where there is already a good deal, and where it is doubtful whether it can be cleared off even by a sale of property, is really a species of theft; for how can the new debt incurred be cleared off?

Bancharam.—Bah! that is only an English idea. As a matter of fact the rich always live on credit: they incur debts here only to pay them off there. A respectable man like you should not be a marplot, or put obstacles in the way of a good action. I have no property to give away myself, but if anyone else is prepared to make presents to all the pandits, am I bound to offer any opposition? We all of us have pandits more or less dependent upon us, and they will all want to receive invitations. It is only natural they should: they must live.

Bakreswar.—Very well said, sir! There is an old saying: "Death before dishonour."

Becharam.—Baburam Babu's family are in the centre of a conflagration: as far as I can see they will soon be utterly ruined. We must try and find a remedy to prevent this. A curse on this method of purchasing renown at the expense of debt! I do not consider Brahman followers to have such a claim upon me that I should sacrifice others to fill their maws: a pretty business that would be! Come, my friend Beni, let us be off.

As soon as Beni Babu and Becharam Babu had gone, Bancharam said: "A good riddance! these two gentlemen understand nothing about the matter: they only talk. How refreshing it is to speak with a man of real intelligence. Thakchacha, come and sit by me: what is your opinion in this matter?"

"It is a great pleasure to me also," Thakchacha replied, "to have a talk with a man like you: those two gentlemen are daft: I am afraid to go near them. All that you have said is very true: a man's life is practically thrown away if his honour and power are lost. You and I will look well after the particulars and get rid of all the difficulties. Is there any cause for alarm then?"

Matilall was naturally very extravagant, and fond of display: he had no knowledge of money matters at all, and knew nothing of business. He put full confidence in Bancharam and Thakchacha: for apart from the fact that they were always frequenting the courts and had the law at their fingers' ends, they had managed to win an influence over him, exactly hitting off his wishes by their clever ingenuity.

"Do you undertake the entire management of this business," said he, "I will sign my name to anything you require."

"Let me have the master's will out of the box," Bancharam Babu said. "Under the terms of the will, you are the only heir: your brother is a lunatic, consequently his name has been omitted. If you take the will and hand it into court, you will have letters of administration granted you, and the property may then be mortgaged, or sold upon your signature only." Matilall at once opened the box, and took the will out.

When Bancharam had done all that was necessary in the courts, he made arrangements with a money-lender, and returned to the Vaidyabati house with the papers and the money. Matilall signed the papers the moment he caught sight of the money, and putting his hands on the bag of rupees was on the point of placing it in the box, when Bancharam and Thakchacka said to him, "Ah, sir! if the money remains with you, it will soon be all spent: it will be safer, we think, in our charge. You are so good-natured you know, so tender-hearted, that you cannot deny anything even to a look: we, knowing people better, will be able to drive all suppliants away."

Matilall thought to himself: "This is very excellent advice: besides, how am I to get any money to spend after the *shraddha*? I have no father now to get money from by a mere look." So he agreed to their proposal.

Great were the preparations for the *shraddha* ceremony of Baburam Babu. What with the noise of arranging the *shorash* and the silver presents to be given to the pandits, the smell of the sweetmeats, the buzzing of hornets, the pungent smoke from wet wood, and the continual stream of things arriving for use on the occasion, the whole house was full of confusion and bustle. Brahmans of the poorer classes, whether connected with family worship, or with shop or bazar accounts, all wearing silk clothes, and with Ganges clay on their foreheads, were continually crowding in for invitations to the *shraddha* ceremony. Of the Tarkavagishas, Vidyaratnas, Nyayalankars, Bachaspatis, and Vidyasagars, all learned and celebrated pandits, there was no end. Sages and *gurus* were continually arriving. It was like the festival of the village leather-seller, on the death of a cow.

The day of the ceremony arrived. Pandits from all parts of the country had come for the assembly usual on such occasions, and seated near them were their relatives, kinsmen and friends. Before them were arranged presents of every description and for all comers; horses, *palkis*, brass dishes, broadcloth, oil vessels, and hard cash. On one side of them the processional singing was in progress, and in the midst of the singers was Becharam Babu enthusiastically absorbed in the music. Outside the house were collected together Brahmans of lesser degree, pedigree reciters, mendicants, *sannyasis* and beggars. Thakchacha, not having sufficient effrontery to sit down in the assembly, was roaming about in the crowd.

The venerable Pandits were taking snuff and conversing together on subjects connected with the *shastras*. One of their characteristics is the difficulty they find in carrying on a discussion at their great meetings calmly and composedly: some element of discord is always sure to arise. One of the pandits introduced a portion of the *Nyaya shastras* for discussion:—"Smoke is the effect of fire, and this is a different substance from a water-jar." A pandit from Orissa thereupon remarked, "The water-jar is itself distinct from a mountain." "What is this, my friend, that you are saying?" asked a pandit from Kashigoya, "you surely have not paid proper attention to the sentence: he who regards a water-jar, clothes, and a mountain as the same as smoke from a fire, simply murders the famous Siromani." A pandit from Eastern Bengal said: "Smoke is an entirely different substance from a water-jar: smoke is the effect of fire: how then can there be smoke when there is no fire?" And so the dispute went on, and at last, from simply glaring at each other, they got to a hand-to-hand scrimmage.

Thakchacha thought matters were looking serious and that he had better calm things down before they went any further; so going quietly up to them, he said: "I say, gentlemen, why are you making such minute enquiries about such trifles as a water-pot or a lamp? I will make you a much more valuable present; I will give you two waterpots apiece." A very sharp Brahman amongst the pandits at once got up and said, "Who are you, you low fellow? An infidel outcast present at the *shraddha* of a Hindu? This is not the *shraddha* of a she-ghost, that an apparition like you should be the superintendent of it." As he said this, everybody present began abusing Thakchacha, thumping him with their fists, pushing him about and beating him with sticks. Thereupon Bancharam Babu hurried up and said: "If you make a disturbance and interfere with the *shraddha* in this way, I will know the reason why: I will get a summons out against you at once from the High Court. I am not a man to be trifled with I can tell you." Bakreswar Babu too had his say. "That is right: besides, the boy who is performing the *shraddha* is no common boy, he is the very model of a boy." Becharam Babu observed: "It is becoming a matter of notoriety that nothing ever goes right where Thakchacha and Bancharam have the management. Ugh! Ugh." The disturbance did not cease. The rowdy vagrants who were present, and others, kept adding to the confusion, and as blows from the canes continually rained on them, they shouted out, "A fine *shraddha* indeed you have celebrated." At length all the respectable gentlemen present, seeing the state of affairs, exclaimed:—

"Friends! Call this a shraddha? *Whose* shraddha *I pray?*
"'Tis death to a Brahman to toil without pay."

"Come, we had better slip away at once: why should we run anymore risk when there is nothing to be gained by it?"

XXI

MATILALL ON THE GUDDEE

P eople did not think much of Baburam Babu's *shraddha*. The rain, as the proverb has it, was out of all proportion to the thunder. Oil fell on a good many heads that were oiled already, while heads that were dry and destitute of oil only got cracked. Their disputation was all the profit that the pandits got. The uneducated city Brahmans had it all their own way. The harsh discipline of all kinds to which pandits subject themselves, creates in them a stubbornness of nature: they follow their own opinions and do not agree with all and everything they find. The Brahmans of a lower order, *habitués* of the city, suit their conversation to the minds of the Babus: in the words of the proverb, they adapt their strokes to the quality of the wood. If it suits them to be Gosains, Gosains they can be; and the characters they can assume are as varied as the ingredients of a curry mixture; is it surprising then that they generally get the best of everything? The managers of the *shraddha* had taken every precaution to fill their own pockets: they were keen chiefly on their own share of the gifts: what did it matter to them whether the pandits or the poor received anything worth mentioning? There was a great flourish of trumpets over things that would be matter of public observation and could not be avoided, but equal consideration was not shown throughout. Management such as that is a mere playing to the gallery.

The stir which the *shraddha* had caused gradually died away.

Bancharam and Thakchacha took to flattering Matilall to an extraordinary extent, and Matilall, being of a very weak nature, was enthralled by their seductive language, and thought that he had no other friends on earth like them. With a view to increasing his importance they one day said to him:—"Sir, you are now master: it behoves you to take your seat on the *guddee* of the master now in heaven: how otherwise will his dignity be maintained?" Matilall was highly delighted at the idea. As a child he had heard bits of the *Ramayana* and *Mahabharata*, and so it occurred to him that he would be seated on the *guddee* with the same pomp and circumstance with which Yudhishthira and Ram Chandra were anointed to the throne of their ancestors. Bancharam and Thakchacha saw that Matilall's face shone again with delight at the suggestion they had made, so the next day they settled on a date for the ceremony, and calling together all his kinsmen and friends, seated Matilall upon his father's *guddee*. In the village the report got about that Matilall had attained to this honour: The news soon spread: it was told in the market-place, in the bazar, at the *ghât*, and in the fields. A choleric old Brahman, when he heard it remarked, "Oh, he has attained the *guddee*, has he? What a fine expression! And whose *guddee*, pray? That of the great Jagat Sett, or of Devi Dass Balmukunda?"

When a man of sound sense attains to a high position or to great wealth, he is not liable to be lightly swayed hither and thither; whereas a man who lacks solidity of character, should he attain to a higher position than he is accustomed to, is as unstable as the waters of a flood. And so it proved with Matilall. Day and night, unceasing as a torrent, arose the hubbub of boisterous amusement. His companions did not diminish; on the contrary, their number daily increased, rapidly as the fabulous *Raktabij*. Was there anything surprising in this? When rice is scattered there is no lack of crows, and a whole army of ants will come together at the scent of molasses.

Bakreswar Babu visited Matilall one day to try and get something out of him, and used all his arts to fascinate Matilall by his talk. But Matilall had been acquainted from his boyhood with Bakreswar's crafty cajolery, and so he gave him this answer:—"Sir, you have destroyed all my chances in the next world by the partiality and favour you showed me in the past. I never failed to give you enough presents when I was a boy: why do you keep bothering me now?" Bakreswar went away with his head bent low, muttering to himself. Matilall was now as one inebriated with pleasure: though Bancharam and Thakchacha went occasionally to see him, he would have little to do with them in the way of business. Owing to the power-of-attorney he had given them, they had entire command over everything, and now and again they made the Babu a liberal advance, but nothing in the way of detailed accounts of expenditure was forthcoming from them.

As for the rest of his family, he never took the slightest notice of them: he never even troubled himself to enquire where they were or where they went. The ladies endured much hardship on this account, but Matilall by his riotous living had become so lost to all sense of shame that he paid no heed to the reports that reached him on the subject. To have to mourn for a husband is the greatest affliction that a faithful wife is called on to endure. It is some alleviation to her in her trouble, if she have good children; but if on the contrary they disappoint her it adds intensity to the bitterness of her grief, as melted butter thrown upon fire. Matilall's evil behaviour was a terrible grief to his mother, but she never spoke openly of it. one day, however after long deliberation, she approached him and said:—"My child, what was to be my lot, that has been: now, for the few remaining days that I have to live, let me not have to listen to this evil report of you. I cannot lend my ears to people's abuse of you. Have some little regard for your younger brother, your elder sister, and your stepmother: they are not getting half enough to eat. Ah, my child, I ask nothing for myself: I lay no further burden upon you." To these words of his mother, Matilall, his eyes inflamed with passion, replied: "What? will you be always chattering and abusing me? Do you not know that I am now master in my own house? What is this evil report about me?" As he said this, he struck his mother a blow on the face and pushed her down. She got up from the ground after a short interval, and wiping away her tears with the border of her *saree*, said to her son: "Ah, my son! I never heard of children beating their mothers before, but it has been my destiny for this to happen to me. I have nothing further to say: I only pray that all may be well with you." Next day, without saying a word to anyone, his mother left the house with her daughter.

Since the death of his father, Ramlall had made many efforts to be on good terms with his brother, but had had to suffer many indignities. Matilall was in constant anxiety lest he should have to give up the half of the property, and so be unable to continue his *rôle* of the grandee; and as life would be but a sorry farce if he had to give up that *rôle*, he must, he considered, take the necessary steps to mulct his brother of his share. Having settled on this plan, by the advice of course of Bancharam and Thakchacha, he forbade Ramlall the house. Thus shut out from the home of his fathers, Ramlall, after long deliberation, without having had an interview with his mother, sister, or anyone, proceeded to another part of the country.

XXII

Matilall in Business

Matilall saw that his mother, his brother, and his sister, had now all gone from the house. "A good riddance!" thought he: his path was at length cleared of thorns; all bother was at an end. This had come about by a slight display of passion on his part,—'Dhananjoyas got rid of by a blow!' True it was, a single blow had sufficed to get rid of them all, but his resources were now exhausted. What was to be done? How could he go on living in such style? The small retail shopkeepers would not be put off with excuses anymore, and no one would supply him with anything on credit: just too as the great bathing festival of the *Snan Jatra* was coming off. The expenses of engaging a *budgerow* had to be provided: earnest money would have to be advanced to the nautch girls: sweetmeats must be ordered: tobacco, *ganja*, and liquor all had to be procured for the occasion; and for these preliminary arrangements he had no money at his disposal. In such anxious thoughts Matilall was wrapped when Bancharam and Thakchacha arrived. After exchanging a few remarks, they said to Matilall: "Well, sir! why this melancholy? It makes us quite sad to see it. At your age you should be always lively and cheerful. Why this anxiety? Fie! be merry." Affected almost to tears by this sweet language, Matilall told them. all that was in his mind. Bancharam said: "Why be so anxious on that account? Are we mere grass-cutters that we cannot help you out of a difficulty? What brought us to see you today was a splendid idea that has occurred to us. Within a year you will have paid off all your liabilities, and be able to enjoy yourself at your leisure, and your sons and your grandsons in their turn will be able to play the rich man on a grand scale. Is it not written in the *shastras?*—

'Lakshmi, fair godddess,
'Of commerce is queen.'

There is a fortune to be made in trade: by it people spring to sudden affluence. Why, look at the numbers of people I have known,—many of them of very low origin and blessed with no brains to speak of,—who have sprang to sudden importance by trade! It makes me quite envious to see them. What troubles me is that we are wasting all our energies with only one string to our bow. This is not as it should be! 'Chandi Charan gathers cow-dung while Ram is riding on horseback.'"

Matilall.—Ah, a brilliant notion! I am daily in need of money. Does commerce flourish in the bazar, or does it grow in an office? Is it merely the buying and selling that goes on in a sweetmeat-maker's shop? My business will lack all importance unless I am to be the chief agent of some English merchant.

Bancharam.—You need only sit at home on the *guddee*, sir! The burden of business will devolve entirely upon us. A Mr. John, a friend of one Mr. Butler, has but recently arrived from England. You might make some arrangement with him and become his agent: he is a very shrewd business man.

Thakchacha.—I shall be with you to help you, whether it be the courts of law or the Treasury Office, or the police department, or commerce. They none of them have any secrets for me: I know all the ins and outs of them! My Shena also understands all these matters. Ah, sir, it is a grief to me that my great capacity for business has been lying dormant all this time! it has never been roused into action or had full play. I am not the kind of man to sit idle: if I find an enemy in my way, I promptly assault him and put him to the rout. If I once put my hand to business I shall get on like the famous Rustem Jol.

Matilall.—And who is Shena, Thakchacha?

Thakchacha.—Shena is your humble servant's wife. How can I possibly extol her qualities adequately? Her beauty is as the beauty of Zuleeka, and her understanding as that of an angel of light.

Bancharam.—Enough of this talk for the present: let us to business. We shall have to advance Mr. John ten or fifteen thousand rupees, but there need be no risk. I have arranged to find this money by mortgaging the Kotalpore Taluk. I will deposit the necessary deeds in Mr. Butler's office: the expense will not be very great; it will come to between four and five hundred rupees. Besides this, you have to give five hundred rupees to the money-lender's *amlah*. Ah, those *amlahs*! they are our mortal enemies: our enterprise may all come to nought if they put any obstacle in our way. When we have smoothed away all the preliminary difficulties, we shall find the auspices favourable for our success. I am just going off to Calcutta with Thakchacha. I have a variety of commissions to execute, and shall be in a fever till I have finished them. Do you, sir, for your part, ascertain from friend Tarka Siddhanta a propitious day for the commencement of the enterprise, and then come at once under the auspices of Durga, to my house in Sonagaji. You will have to remain a few days in Calcutta; but only a short time will elapse before, like Chand Sadagar, you will return to Vaidyabati Ghât with seven vessels laden with wealth, drums beating, young men and old men, women and children, as they gaze on the splendour of your return, greeting you with blessings. Oh, may the day speedily dawn!"

Bancharam then proceeded on his way, and took Thakchacha with him.

Matilall reported the whole of the conversation to his companions. They danced with delight when they heard it. Want of means had almost entirely put an end to their fun. Now there was every chance of the treasury being replenished. Mangovinda at once hurried off to the *tol* of Tarka Siddhanta; he was puffing and blowing with his exertions when he arrived there. Tarka Siddhanta was a very old man. He was taking snuff, and alternately sneezing and coughing; his pupils were ranged all round him; in front of him lay a Sanscrit work written on a palm leaf. Every now and then he would glance at the manuscript through his spectacles, then give out a passage to his pupils and explain it to them. The cow of the establishment had not had its rack supplied, there being a scarcity of straw, and it lowed continuously. From inside the house the wife of the old pandit was screaming: "The old man is rapidly losing his wits: he does nothing all day and all night but mind his books: he never once turns his attention to household matters." His pupils, hearing all this, nudged each other and winked. Tarka Siddhanta flew into a towering rage, and taking hold of a stick, with which to keep the old women quiet, was just getting up very slowly and deliberately, when suddenly Mangovinda caught hold of him, and said: "Oh, Tarka Siddhanta, respected sir! we are all going into trade. Do ascertain for us an auspicious day." Tarka Siddhanta got up in great wrath, his face distorted with passion. "A curse light upon you and your trade; could you find no other time but when I had just risen from my seat, to call me behind my back? So you will go into trade, eh? May you and your father's house come to ruin, bad luck to you. You want to know what day will be auspicious, eh? When you cease vexing people as you do, they will have their *Ganga Snan* in peace. Off, away with you this minute! The day you clear out of this will be the auspicious day." Somewhat disconcerted by the old man's abuse, Mangovinda went and told his companions that the next day would be auspicious.

Sounds of preparation straightway arose, and there was all the bustle that attends arrangements for a festival: it was the *Udjog Parba* over again. While one of the party fixed the wire for playing the *sitar* on his fore-finger, another tested the *baya*, tapping it to see whether it had any pitch or not: another examined the *tabala:* another tightened the rings round the drums: another put resin on a fiddle and tested the strings: another packed up the clothes: another prepared small parcels of tobacco, *ganja* and other stimulants, along with bundles of firewood: another selected, with great care, balls of opium and sweetmeats: another examined the different purchases to see whether they were of correct weight. All day and all night the bustle and noise of preparation went on without any diminution. It had got about in the village that the young Babus were about to go into trade, and next day, when all the shopkeepers of the place, the poorer sort of people, and the beggars and loafers, were out in the roads looking out for them to pass, they came swaggering down to the *ghât*, like so many wild elephants. There were a number of pandits at the *ghât* engaged in their early morning devotions: hearing the stir and bustle, they looked behind them, and at once shook with fright. Seeing them so terrified, the Babus only jeered at them and laughed. Then they showered upon them Ganges mud and brick-bats, and insulted them generally, and the Brahmans, interrupted in this rude way at their devotions, went their way, calling upon Krishna in their distress. The young men having embarked on board a boat, all caught up a popular love-song, screaming it out at the top of their voices. The boat glided quickly down stream on the ebb. The Babus could not keep still for a moment; one would get on the deck of the cabin; another would work the rudder; one would pull an oar, and another strike a light with a flint. They had not gone very far when they met with Dhanamala. Now Dhanamala never cared what he said to anyone: he called out to them: "Having reduced a whole village to ashes, are you now going to set the Ganges on fire?" To which they angrily replied: "Shut up, you idiot! Do you not know hat we are all going into business?" Dhanamala's only answer to this was:—"If you ever become traders, may your business come to grief! may it perish with a halter on its neck!"

XXIII

MATILALL AT SONAGAJI

At Sonagaji there was a Mahommedan mosque: it had long since become the abode of ghosts, and was everywhere covered with lichen, while jungle crows and mynahs had built their nests in different parts of it. These were now bringing food to their young ones, who were chirping merrily. The mosque had been left unrepaired for many a long day: the only sounds heard there at nightfall were the cries of jackals and the howling of dogs: no one remembered having ever seen a light in any part of it.

Near this ruin a village teacher used to instruct some of the village children, whose necks were generally enveloped in woollen comforters; and whatever the extent of the education they were receiving, they were at least frightened out of their lives by the sound of the cane. It was only necessary for a boy to lift his eyes off his book, or to eat something out of his lap, for the stick to fall at once with a whack on his shoulders. It is a human failing for a man armed with authority in any matter, to think that he must constantly display that authority in various ways lest his dignity should suffer; and so it was that the old village school-master loved to collect a crowd round him, in order to make a display of his sovereignty. When he saw people going by, he would look in their direction and raise his voice to its highest pitch, and then, if a crowd collected, his self-importance increased till there was no limit to it: no wonder therefore that there was a very heavy punishment for any trifling fault on the part of the boys. A village school under such a master pretty nearly resembles the Hall of Yama. Besides the constant sounds of slapping and screaming, and cries of "*Oh Guru Mahashay! Guru Mahashay!* your pupil is present," one boy will get his nose tweaked, another his ear pulled, another will have to carry a brick in one hand, another will be caned, another may be strung up by his thumbs, while a stinging nettle will be applied to another: some form of punishment or other is continually in force. The honour and glory of Sonagaji used to be kept up solely by the village school-master whom I have mentioned. Just on the outskirts of the village, a few beggars, who had been at it all day long, used to congregate in the evening, wearied by their day's labour, and lie down, singing snatches of songs softly to themselves.

Such was Sonagaji. Since Matilall's auspicious arrival, however, the destiny of the place had undergone a revolution: there was all the stir and bustle attending a great man's movements: the air was full of the prancing of: horses, the loud beating of drums: there was an eternal munching of delicate sweetmeats: feasting and revelry went on unceasingly by night and by day, and the people of the place began to prostrate themselves before the great man.

It is very difficult to know Calcutta people well: to the outer world, many of them appear all that is respectable, like mangoes with a fair outside. They can assume a vast variety of characters. Money is at the bottom of all this: where that is in question, countless are the shifts and turns resorted to. Man's nature is so frail that he worships wealth out of all proportion to its worth. People make herculean efforts to become recipients of the favour of any man reputed to be wealthy; and whatever may be necessary for them to say or to do to accomplish their object, there are no shortcomings on their part.

People of all grades took to visiting Matilall. Now there are some men, like the Brahmans of Ula, who at once go to the point with unblushing frankness, so that there is no mistaking their meaning. Others, again, like the good people of Krishnaghar, expend much ingenuity in embroidering their remarks, and only after a good deal of beating about the bush will they introduce the real object of their visit, and then very delicately. Others, like our friends of Eastern Bengal, are very careful and deliberate in their procedure: they at first assume an appearance of indifference and disinterestedness, plunging their real object deep in the Dvaipara Lake, and when after a long interval their special intention is revealed, it turns out that the real object of all their coming and going was after all a pecuniary one,—some present or other that might hereafter be exchanged for cash. Matilall had only to sigh, and the visitor with him at the time would snap his fingers, by way of warding off the evil omen: if he but sneezed, his visitor would say: "May your life be prolonged." If Matilall called for a servant, the sycophant would scream out: "Ho there! Ho there!" and in answer to every remark of Matilall's, no matter what it was, he would say: "Whatever your honour says must be right."

From early dawn till long after midnight people crowded about Matilall: every single moment of the day they were either coming or going: the staircase leading to his reception-room was constantly creaking beneath the heavy tramp of their shoes. Every moment fresh supplies of tobacco were arriving; smoke issued from the room at all times as from the funnel of a steam ship: the servants were so terribly worried, they were at their wits' end. Night and day, in one continuous succession, dancing, music and all sorts of boisterous fun were kept up.

The dignity of the village school-master was quite eclipsed by all this stir: till now he had been the turkey-cock; now he had become but the tiny tailor-bird. There would be a good deal of noise at times when he was teaching his boys, and Matilall, hearing this one day, said to his companions:—"Why is that idiot making so much noise? I escaped in boyhood from the annoyance of a school-master: why must have I another near me now? Away with him quickly." The young Babus taking the hint, very soon brought about the disappearance of the village school-master from the scene by the simple expedient of throwing brickbats at him; and the village school was in consequence broken up. The boys of the school, thinking it a happy release, took up their bundles of palm leaves, and having ridiculed their old school-master to their heart's content, ran breathlessly home.

Just about this time, Mr. John opened his house of business: the firm was known as John and Company. Matilall was the chief agent of the house, Bancharam and Thakchacha managers. The Saheb showed great attention to his chief agent for the sake of his money, and the chief agent for his part would pay occasional visits to the office with his companions. He generally came about three or four in the afternoon, chewing *pán*, his eyes red and inflamed, and after walking about and prying into everything, would go home again. The Saheb had not a pice to his name, and depended entirely upon Mr. Butler for his support: but he rented a house in Chowringhee, and filled it with a great variety of furniture and pictures: he also bought splendid carriages, fine horses and dogs, all on credit, and amused himself by training and running race-horses. Later on he married, and frequented the best society of the place, wearing a gold chain and a diamond ring. Seeing all this display, many people were firmly persuaded that Mr. John was a wealthy man, and had no hesitation in having monetary transactions with him; but a few persons, of higher intelligence, knowing the real state of his affairs, were more cautious, and would have nothing to say to him. Many of the Calcutta merchants get their living by brokerage: they may be either freight brokers, or they may buy and sell Government paper or goods generally, their commission being several rupees in every hundred. Many ethers, acquainting themselves with the market prices current in Calcutta and elsewhere, do affairs on their own account; but to manage this, they must have already learned the details of business, as otherwise their business cannot prosper. Mr. John had no capacity for business at all: he was persuaded that he only had to purchase goods to dispose of them at a profit: as a matter of fact, his only object was to enjoy himself and play the rich man at the expense of others. He thought trade a very simple thing: he only had to fire enough bullets, and game was sure to fall to one or other.

The chief agent was even worse in this respect than the Saheb: he was blankly ignorant, without any education to speak of, and understanding nothing whatever of accounts: consequently, to do business with him was so much lost labour. *Mahajans,* brokers, and shopkeepers were continually going to him with patterns of their goods, informing him of the fluctuations in prices, and giving him the latest market intelligence: all the time they were talking business, he would be gazing vacantly about him, completely at sea. He never answered any of their questions, doubtless for fear that anything he might say would betray his ignorance: he would refer them to Bancharam and Thakchacha.

There were a few clerks in the office, who kept all the accounts in English. Matilall having one day expressed a wish to have a thorough examination of the English cash-book, had it fetched for this purpose by one of the clerks, then having just looked into it casually, shoved it aside. He generally occupied a room below the office: this being rather damp, the cash-book, having been kept there over a month, soon got completely ruined. The young Babus too used to tear leaves out of it and twist them up into spills for daily use; and very soon they were all used up in this way, the cover only remaining. When search was afterwards made for it, it was found to be the mere shadow of its former self: it was reduced to a mere skeleton,—bones and hide, as the saying is, sacrificed in the service of others.

Mr. John bewailed and lamented the loss of his cash-book, but kept his grief locked in his own breast. He exercised no discrimination in the purchases he made, when he began to export largely to England and to other countries, and took no trouble to find out the real cost of the goods, or what would be the margin of profit. Bancharam and Thakchacha saw their opportunity, and made many a successful stroke of business for themselves: they soon waxed fat on their gains. A small draught is never sufficient to relieve great thirst. These two, as they sat together in secret consultation, had only one object in view, and that was to increase their gains by every possible means in their power. They well knew that the opportunity would never recur again. The springtide of their gains would soon pass, and the winter of want might come: no time like the present.

Within a year or two, very bad news arrived of the sale of the goods: instead of a profit there would be a loss, which Mr. John, to his confusion and dismay, estimated at a lakh of rupees. He had himself been spending nearly a thousand rupees a month, and was besides heavily in debt to several banks and money-lenders. For some months past, indeed, the firm had only been kept going by a variety of shifts: now the fair bark of outward respectability was altogether swamped. It was impossible to keep up appearances any longer, and it soon became notorious that John and Company had failed. The Saheb went off with his wife to Chandernagore, a place under French rule, to which, even to this day, debtors and criminals betake themselves to escape imprisonment. The money lenders and other creditors thereupon came down upon Matilall. Look where he would, Matilall could see no way out of his difficulties: he had not a single pice he could call his own: he had been living entirely on credit. He could come to no decision one way or the other at this juncture. He was constantly on the look out for a visit from Bancharam Babu or Thakchacha, but "confidence in a dear friend is as a knife in the left hand" says an old proverb: it was idle to look for any aid from them: they had vanished before the smash.

When the creditors were referred to them they only answered that all the accounts were in Mati Babu's name: they had had no dealings with the others, regarding them as agents only. Owing to all this confusion in his affairs, Matitall fled one night in disguise with his companions to Vaidyabati. The people of that place, when the news reached them of the outcome of Matilall's trade enterprises, all clapped their hands, and cried: "This is grand news: there is still justice on the earth: what meaning would the terms right and wrong have, if such a fate had not befallen so wicked a man,—a man who has cheated mother, brother, and sister,—a man to whom no sinful action has come amiss?"

It so chanced that Premnaryan Mozoomdar was bathing the next day at the Vaidyabati Ghât: seeing Tarka Siddhanta there, he remarked to him: "Those wretched fellows, after having squandered all their substance, have had to take to flight, to escape a warrant for their apprehension, and have returned here: they are not ashamed to appear in public again. A fine instrument for the ruin of his family has Baburam bequeathed to the world." Tarka Siddhanta replied: "The village has been tranquil all the time those boys have been away: alas! that they should have returned at all. Had mother Ganga only shown us a little favour, how happy we might have been!" Several other Brahmans were bathing at the *ghât* at the same time: their teeth began to chatter in terror when they heard the news of the return of the young Babus, and they thought to themselves:—"Henceforth we may expect to have to confide into Sri Krishna's keeping our daily ablutions and devotions." Some small shop-keepers, as they looked towards the *ghât*, said:—"Ah sir! we heard that drums would beat when Mati Babu returned with his seven ships laden with treasure: yet we cannot see so much as a fisherman's dinghy approaching, let alone a cargo-boat." Premnarayan replied:—"Do not be anxious; Mati Babu, like Srimanta Saudagor, has obtained a place of temporary retirement, because of the difficulties caused by Kamala Kamini. Is not the Babu a very estimable person? Is he not the chosen son of the fair Lakshmi! His dinghies, his cargo-boats, and his ships will soon appear, and you will hear the sound of the drums, while preparing your parched rice and pulse."

XXIV

THAKCHACHA APPREHENDED

The morning breeze was blowing softly: the *champac*, the *sephalika,* and the *mallika* were diffusing sweet odours abroad: birds were chirping merrily. Beni Babu had taken Barada Babu home with him to his house in Ghatak, and was engaged in converse with him, when suddenly to the south of where they were, the dogs began to bark violently, and some boys came laughing loudly along the road. During a temporary lull, they heard the charming accents of a nasal voice, expostulating with the boys, and singing a Vaishnava song:—

> *"In Brindabun's woods, and the sweet-scented bowers*
> *"Of Brindabun's maidens, O waste not your hours."*

Rising from their seats, Beni Babu and Barada Babu saw that it was Becharam Babu of Bow Bazar who had just arrived: he was rapt in his song, and was snapping his fingers by way of accompaniment: dogs were barking about him, and boys laughing derisively, and the man of Bow Bazar had been angrily expostulating with them. Beni Babu and Barada Babu greeted him very courteously and invited him to be seated. When they had enquired after each other's welfare, Becharam Babu, putting his hand on Barada Babu's shoulder, said to him:—"My good friend, I have seen a great many people in my day since I was a boy, and many of them possessed of good qualities, but after all I can only regard them as moderately good, their standard little above the average. Be that as it may, I have never seen anyone with modesty, sincerity, moral courage, simplicity and straightforwardness, equal to yours. I am somewhat modest myself; but still there are occasions when my pride manifests itself: the sight of another man's pride is sufficient to evoke it, and with the manifestation of my pride my anger rises, and my pride is increased still more by my anger. I can never abate a jot of my claims on others. I always say what comes uppermost in my mind, but to tell you the truth, I am never sincere enough to be willing to acknowledge openly any mean action I may have been guilty of, for I always fear that I may have to endure mortification, if I acknowledge the truth. I have a very limited amount of moral courage: I may be convinced in my own mind that I ought to take a particular course, but I lack the moral courage to act uniformly up to my convictions. I find it very difficult, too, to maintain a straightforward attitude in dealing with others. True, I am aware that a man should always exert himself for the welfare of mankind, but I find it very hard to carry the conviction into actual practice. It is only necessary for a man to speak harshly to me for me to lose all respect for him, and to regard him as utterly beneath contempt. Now a man may have done you an actual injury, but your feelings towards him are still sincere and kind. I mean to say, that you would never think of doing him an injury, but on the contrary a kindness; and even abuse does not make you angry. Can qualities such as these be considered trifling?"

Barada.—Any man who loves another sees nothing but good in him, whereas a man who cannot know another intimately only misinterprets his conduct. It is pure kindness on your part to speak as you have of me: it cannot be owing to my own qualities. It is well-nigh an impossibility for man to maintain a mind that shall be simple and honest at all times, in all respects, and towards all men. Our minds are full of passion, envy, malice, and pride, and is it an easy task to hold all these in restraint? If one's character is to be simple and unaffected, humility is the one thing necessary. Some persons display a mock modesty: some are made humble by fear, others by trouble and misfortune. Humility of this kind is but transient. If humility is to be an enduring and permanent quality, such sentiments as these should be firmly fixed in our minds. Our Creator, He is all-powerful, omniscient, without spot, or stain: ourselves, we are here today, gone tomorrow. Our strength, what is it? Our learning, what is it? Every moment of our lives we are subject to error, evil thoughts and evil deeds: where then is the ground for pride? Such humility as this being implanted in the mind, passion, envy, malice, and pride, all are dwarfed, and the mind becomes simple and sincere. Where this is the case, we derive no pleasure from a display of our own learning or intelligence, our own pride of wealth or place, which can only anger others; neither is our envy excited by the sight of the prosperity of others. We have no desire, either to abuse others, or to think meanly of them; neither does an injury we may have received from another arouse our anger or hatred against him. Our thoughts are directed solely to the purification of our own minds, or to other's welfare. But much harsh self-discipline is necessary before this result can be attained. It is wonderful, the pride that springs up in the mind of the man possessed of but a modicum of wit: his own words, his own deeds, stand forth, in the estimation of such a man, as superior to those of all others; nothing that others may say or do is worthy of the slightest attention on his part.

Becharam.—Ah, my dear friend, how it refreshes me to hear you talk! I have been all along wishing to have such an opportunity.

Their conversation was suddenly interrupted by the hurried arrival of Premnarayan Mozoomdar, with the news that the Calcutta police had apprehended Thakchacha and taken him off to prison. Becharam Babu was immensely delighted when he heard the news, and exclaimed: "This is indeed good news to me." Barada Babu was astounded, and fell into deep thought. Becharam Babu said to him: "Why are you so deep in thought? Why, there is nobody I know who would not be delighted if so wicked a man were to be transported."

Barada.—What grieves me is the thought that the man from his youth upwards should have done evil and not good. Besides, there is his family to think of: they will die of starvation if he is put in chains.

Becharam.—Ah, my good friend! why do people reverence you but for all your qualities? Thakchacha never lost an opportunity of maligning and injuring you: he never ceased insulting and abusing you. Why, it was he who fabricated that charge of illegal confinement and assault against you, and he made every effort to press the charge home by means of forgery. And yet there is not a trace of anger or enmity in your mind against him on that account. The very meaning of retaliation is unknown to you. Your idea of retaliation was to restore him and his family to health again when they fell sick, by administering medicines, and by unremitting attention on your part; and even now all your anxiety is for his family. Ah, my dear friend, you may be a Kayasth in caste, but I should be willing to take the dust off the feet of such a Kayasth and put it on my head!

Barada.—Do not, sir, I pray you, talk like this to me. I am contemptible, and of no reputation amongst men, and am in no way worthy of your praise. Ah, sir! if you keep on saying this to me, my pride will increase.

Meanwhile, in Vaidyabati, a police sergeant, some constables, and an inspector, were hurrying Thakchacha, his arms tied behind his back, away to prison. A great crowd had collected in the streets. One man said, quoting an old proverb:—"As the deed, so the fruit." Another man exclaimed:—"We shall never have any peace until the wretch is put on boardship and transported." While another remarked:—"My only fear is that he may after all get off, and become as mischievous as ever."

As, with head bent low, beard fluttering in the breeze, and eyes glaring, Thakchacha was going along with the police, he quietly offered the sergeant half a rupee to loose his bonds: the sergeant had a capacious paunch, and at once tossed the half rupee away in contempt. Thakchacha then said to him: "Take me for a short time to Mati Babu: get him to give bail: let me go for a day only, I will put an appearance tomorrow." The sergeant only replied: "You jabbering idiot: you will get a smack on the face, if you speak to me again." Thakchacha then folded his hands in humble supplication before the sergeant, and begged and prayed to be let off. The sergeant refused to listen to him, and put him into a boat; About four o'clock in the afternoon he arrived with him at the police court; but as the police magistrate had left the court by that time, Thakchacha had to spend the night in the lock-up.

Matilall, when he heard of the evil plight of Thakchacha, became very anxious for himself. He dreaded the fall of the thunderbolt in his direction. Thakchacha having been caught, his turn he thought was safe to come next: the whole affair, he imagined, was connected with John Company, but anyhow extreme caution on his part was necessary. Acting upon this determination, he fastened the main door of the house very securely. Ramgovinda said to him: "Thakchacha has been apprehended, sir, on a charge of forgery: if there had been a warrant out against you, your house would have been surrounded long ago: why entertain such causeless alarm?" Matilall replied. "Ah! none of you understand: unluckily for me misfortunes are cropping up all round me: as the old proverb has if, 'The burnt *shal* fish has slipped out of my hands.' If I can only get through today somehow or other, I will go off the first thing tomorrow to my estates in the Jessore district. It is not safe for me to remain at home any longer: I am encompassed with portents, obstacles, fears, and misfortunes of every kind, and besides all this my money is all gone, my hand is mere dust."

Just as he had finished speaking, there was a loud knocking at the door, and somebody shouted out: "Open the door, friend! Ho there! Is there anybody there?" Matilall said very quietly: "Hush! just what I expected has happened." Mangovinda peeped out from above, and saw a messenger pushing away at the door: he went quietly to Matilall and said to him: "It is high time for you to be off, sir! you had better get away at once; I rather fancy that a second warrant has come in connection with Thakchacha's case. Who can foresee the end of a spark of fire? If you can find no other deserted spot, go and get into the dirty tank at the back door, and stand like a pillar in the middle, as did King Durjyodhan." Dolgovinda said: "Why anticipate evil? why swamp the boat at the first sight of waves? Find out the true state of affairs first: if you wait a second I will make enquiries." Saying this, he called out: "Ho there! you messenger! from what court have you come? The messenger replied! "Sir, I have brought a letter from Mr. John," and saying, "Here, take the letter!" he threw it up to them. They all shouted "Aha! we are saved! we breathe again!" Then Haladhar and Gadadhar, who were behind the others, caught up the refrain:—"Protect us, O Lord, in this world." The news to the young Babus was like an autumn cloud: it was rain, it was sun, it was warmth, it was joy. Matilall enjoined them to be quiet a little and asked for the letter, telling them that it was possible that someone opportunity for trade might be presenting itself. When he had opened the letter, the young Babus all stooped over him: there were a good many heads collected together, but not an atom of learning amongst the lot of them: reading the letter was a sore trial to them. At last they had a man called from the house of a neighbour of theirs, a Kayasth, and they ascertained the substance of the letter to be that Mr. John was almost starving, and that he was very badly in want of money. Mangovinda remarked:—"What a shameless wretch! So much money already thrown into the deep on his account, and yet he does not leave us alone; I like his impudence!" Dolgovinda said: "It is a very good thing to have an Englishman in our power, for their luck is sure to turn: there are times when a handful of mud in their hands may become a handful of gold." Matilall said to them: "Why are you chattering like this? You may cut me up and not find any blood in me: you may whittle me away, and get no flesh off me."

One evening, about this time, Becharam Babu, having crossed over from Bally, was proceeding along in a northerly direction in a gharry. He was singing a song, the refrain of which was—

"*Mahadev! thou, by thy great might,*
"*Upholdest all things day and night.*"

Bancharam Babu was driving his buggy from a southerly direction: when the two were alongside each other, they both peeped out to see who was passing. As soon as Bancharam caught the outline of Becharam's figure, he whipped up his horse. Becharam thereupon, holding the door of his gharry tight with his hand, put his head hurriedly out of the window and shouted out: "Ho! Bancharam! Ho Bancharam!" Upon this summons, the buggy was brought to a stop, and the gharry drew up to it with many a creak and a groan. Becharam Babu then said to Bancharam: "Aha, Bancharam! you are indeed a lucky fellow! The vessel of your gains is like Ravan's funeral pile, ever blazing. At one stroke you have successfully carried out your trade ventures. Your friend and ally, Thakchacha, is now ruined; and I fancy that even out of that circumstance some trifling gain will accrue to you, perhaps the price of a goat's head. But you have only worked your own future ruin by all your *vakeel's* practices and stratagems. Has this thought, that you must die sometime or other, never occurred to you?" Bancharam Babu was exceedingly angry at all this: he frowned and bit his moustache in his vexation, and venting his rage on his horse's back, drove away.

XXV

MATILALL IN JESSORE

The *taluk* that belonged to Baburam Babu in Jessore had been more profitable to him than all his other estates. At the time of the Permanent Settlement the land on that portion of the property had been mostly uncultivated, and the rent of it had been fixed at one rate; but once under tillage, it became very productive and was let out in fields: in fact it proved so fertile that hardly any portion of it remained common land or waste.

At one period the ryots, after cultivating it for sometime, used to make large profits by a succession of crops of different sorts, but they were now in a very bad way, owing to oppression on the part of the proprietor of the estate, acting entirely on Thakchacha's advice. Many of the *lakherajdars*, finding that their lands had been included in the estates of the zemindar, and not having any proofs of possession, came now and again to give their customary offerings to the zemindar, and then gradually left the estate altogether. Many of the headmen of the different villages, too, finding themselves disturbed in their possession by forgeries and oppression, abandoned their rights to their own lands, without getting any compensation, and fled to other estates. So it came about that for a space of two or three years the income of the *taluk* had considerably increased, and Thakchacha would remark to Baburam in a swaggering tone: "See how great my power is!" But, says the old Sanscrit proverb;—"The course of virtue is a very delicate thing." Within a very short time, many of the ryots, alarmed at the state of affairs, left the estates, taking with them their draught cattle and their seed-grain, and it became very difficult to let their land: they were all afraid that the proprietor would, either by force or by craft, seize upon the little profits they might make, and that the toil and labour of cultivation would be carried on at the risk of their lives: what was the use then, they argued, of remaining any longer on the estate? The *naib* of the estate, for all his soft language and insinuating address, could not succeed in calming them down. So it was that a good deal of land remained unlet, and nobody could be found willing to take it even at a low rent: much less would anyone take it at a fixed permanent rent.

The proprietor had now some difficulty in raising the revenue from it when he took it into his own hands, and paid labourers to cultivate it. The *naib* kept the proprietor constantly informed of the state of affairs, and he would write back the customary reply;—"If the revenue is not collected, as it always has been hitherto, you will have to starve, and no excuse will be attended to." Now there are times when severity, under special circumstances, may be of avail; but what can it profit when misfortunes have occurred entirely beyond its reach? In this dilemma, the *naib* went about his duties, anxious and perplexed. Meanwhile, as the revenue had fallen into arrears for some two or three years past, an order was issued for a sale of the property; in order to save his property, Baburam Babu had paid the Government revenue, borrowing money by a mortgage upon the land.

Matilall now came and took up his abode on this estate, accompanied by his band of boon companions. His intention had been to get all the money he could out of the *taluk* to pay off his debts with, and so keep up his state and dignity. The Babu had never seen a paper connected with estate management, and was entirely ignorant of the ordinary terms used in keeping estate accounts. When the *naib* said to him one day: "Just look, sir, for a moment at these different heads of the records"; he would not even glance at the papers, but gazed vacantly in the direction of a tree near the office. On another occasion, the *naib* said to him: "Sir, there are so many Khodkast and so many Paikast tenants." "Don't talk to me," said the Babu, "of Khodkast and Paikast, I will make them all Ek-kast." When the tenants heard of the arrival of the proprietor of the estate at his head-quarters, they were delighted, and said to each other: "Ah, now that that old wretch of a Mussulman has gone, our destiny after all these days has changed its course!" And so these poor empty-handed, empty-stomached and poverty-stricken tenants came with joyous and confident faces, to offer him the customary gifts, making profound obeisance the while. Matilall, enraptured by the jingling sound of the silver, smiled softly to himself. Then the ryots, seeing the Babu so happy and cheerful, began to shout out their various grievances. "Somebody has removed my boundary mark, and ploughed up my land," said one. "Somebody has put his own pots on my date palm, and stolen all my toddy," said another. "Somebody has loosed his cattle into my garden," exclaimed another, "and they have done a lot of damage in it." "My grain has all been eaten up by somebody or other's ducks," cried another. Another said, "I have brought back the money I borrowed upon a promissory note; please give me my bond back." "I have cut down and sold some *babul* trees" said another, "and as I wish to repair my house, please pass an order to have the fourth part of the price remitted to me." Another said, "My land has not been properly made over to me yet: the old tenant's name has not been cut out of the deed: I shall be unable to give the customary offering till this is done." And another cried out, "The present measurement of the land in my occupation is short: allow me to pay rent in proportion, or else let another measurement be made." Such were some of the grievances the ryots gave vent to, but Matilall, not understanding in the least their purport, remained sitting like a painted doll. The young Babus, his companions, made fun of the strange sounds, which they had never heard the like of before, and made the office ring with their laughter, striking up a song the refrain of which ran:—

> "A bird is soaring in the air:
> "Oh, let me count its feathers rare!"

The *naib* was like a log, and the ryots sat round in utter dejection, resting their heads on their hands. Where the master is a competent man, there is not much chance of the servant carrying on his tricks. The *naib*, seeing how utterly dense Matilall was, soon began to show himself in his true colours. The proprietor being altogether incompetent to enter into the numerous cases that had come before him, his agent threw dust in his eyes, to effect his own ends; and the ryots soon got to know that to have an interview with the Babu was a mere waste of breath. The *naib* was wholly master.

The high-handedness of the indigo planters of Jessore had greatly increased at this time. The ryots had no mind to sow indigo, as more profit was to be got out of rice and other crops, and besides, any of them who chanced to go to an indigo factory to get an advance, was ruined once for all. True, the ryots cultivating indigo at their own risk might clear off the advances made to them, but their accounts would go hanging on and increase, yearly and the maw of the planter's *gomashtha*, and the other people about the factory, was never satisfied with a little. Any ryot therefore who had once drunk of the sweet waters of an advance from the factory, never, to the end of his life, got out of its power. But it would be a heavy calamity to the planter if his indigo were not ready: the working expenses of the factory were annually advanced by one or other of the merchant firms in Calcutta, and if his wares were not forthcoming, his expenses would be very largely increased: the factory might even have to be closed, and the planter be compelled to retire from the concern. These English managers might be very ordinary sort of people in their own country, but at their factories they lorded it like kings. Their great fear was lest obstacles should be put in the way of the working of their concerns, and they, in consequence, should become as mean as mice again: naturally, therefore, they exerted themselves to the utmost, by all the means in their power and at all seasons, to have their indigo ready in time.

One day, Matilall was amusing himself with his companions. The *naib*, with spectacles on his nose, had just opened his office, and was busily engaged in writing, drying the ink on his papers with lime, when suddenly some ryots came running up, shouting: "Sir! those brutes from the factory have ruined us entirely! the manager has come on our land in person, and is now ploughing over some of our sown lands, and he has taken off our draught cattle. Oh sir! the brute is not content with destroying all our seed, he must needs too have his barrows drawn over our ripe paddy." The *naib* at once assembled about a hundred *paiks,* and, hurrying off to the scene, saw the planter, with his sun-helmet on his head, a cheroot in his mouth, and a gun in his hand, standing there, and urging on his men. Upon the *naib* approaching him, and gently remonstrating, the planter only called out to his men: "Drive them all off, and beat them well." The men on both sides thereupon wielded their clubs, and the planter himself hurried forward, quite prepared to fire. The *naib* slipped off, and concealed himself in a hedge of wild cotton.

After the fight had lasted a considerable time, the zemindars' people fled, some of them badly wounded. The planter, after this exhibition of his might, went off to his factory in great glee, while the ryots returned to their homes, crying out for justice, and exclaiming, amid heir tears: "We are ruined: we are utterly undone." The indigo planter proceeded home to his factory after the row, his dog running before him and playing, poured himself out some brandy and soda, and drank it, whistling the while, and singing—"*Taza ba Taza.*" He knew that it was hard to control him; the magistrate and the judge constantly dined at his house, and the police and the people about the courts held him in great awe because of his associating so much with them! Besides even if there was any investigation made, in a case of homicide, his trial could not take place in the Mofussil courts. Any black people accused of homicide or any other great offence, would always be tried and sentenced in the local courts; whereas any white man accused of such offences would be sent up to the Supreme Court; in which case the witnesses or complainants in the case being quite helpless owing to the expense, trouble, and loss their business that would be entailed, would fail to put to in an appearance; and naturally, when the cases against such persons came on for trial at the High Court, they would be dismissed.

It happened just as the indigo planter had anticipated. Early next morning the police inspector came and surrounded the zemindar's offices. Weakness is a great calamity: in the presence of a man of might, the poor man is powerless. When Matilall saw the state of affairs, he withdrew inside his house, and secured the doors. The *naib* then approached the inspector, and having arranged matters by a heavy bribe, got most of the prisoners set free. The inspector had been blustering loudly, but as soon as he received the money, it was as though water had fallen on fire: having completed his investigation, he made a report to the magistrate, exonerating both parties—actuated on the one hand by avarice, on the other by fear. The planter was at the same time busily engaged in arranging the affair, and the magistrate for his part was firmly convinced that the indigo planter, being an Englishman, and a Christian to boot, would never do what was wrong; it was only the black folk who did all the mischief. This was an opportunity the *sheristadar* and the *peshkar* did not neglect: they took a heavy bribe from the indigo planter, and suppressing the depositions of the opposite party, read only the depositions of the party they favoured themselves: thus by very delicate and skilful manœuvring, they succeeded in their object. The indigo planter seized the opportunity to address the court:—"Ever since I came to this place, I have been conferring endless benefits on the Bengalis: I have spent a great deal upon their education and upon medical treatment for them; how can such an accusation be brought against me? The Bengalis are very ungrateful, and very troublesome." The magistrate, having heard everything, proceeded to tiffin: he drank a good deal of wine after tiffin, and came into court again, smoking a cheroot. When the case came on again, the magistrate looked at the papers before him as if they had been so many tigers, evidently wishing to have nothing more to do with them, and said all at once to the *sheristadar:* "Dismiss this case." The planter's face beamed again with delight, and he glared at the *naib*, who went slowly away, his head bent low, and his whole frame trembling, exclaiming as he went: "Ah, it has become very difficult for Bengalis to retain their zemindaries! the country has been ruined by the violence of the brutal planter: the ryots are all calling out in fear for protection: the magistrates are entirely under the influence of their own countrymen, and the laws are so administered as to provide the indigo planter with many paths of escape. People say that it is the oppression of the zemindars that has ruined the ryot: that is a very great error. The zemindars may oppress the ryot, but they do keep him alive after their fashion: his ryots are to the zemindar his field of *beguns*. Very different is the action of the indigo planter; it does not much matter to him whether the ryots live or die: all he cares about is to extend the cultivation of indigo: to him the ryots are but a common field of roots."

XXVI

Thakchacha in Jail

S leep will never come when fear and anxiety have entered the mind. Thakchacha was exceedingly uncomfortable in the lock-up: he had thrown himself on a blanket, and was tossing restlessly from side to side: now and again he got up to see what hour of the night it was. Whenever he heard the sound of carriage-wheels, or a voice, he imagined it must be daybreak: he kept getting up in a hurry, and saying to the sepoy guard: "Friends, how far advanced is the night?" They were very angry, and said to him: "Ho, you there! the gun will not be fired for two or three hours yet! Keep quiet now; why do you keep on disturbing us like this every hour?" Thakchacha, at these words, began to toss about on his blanket again. Conflicting emotions rose in his mind, and he revolved a variety of plans: his reflections continually taking this turn;— "Why have I been so long conversant with craft and trickery? Where is now the money that I have earned in this way? I have nothing left of all my sinful gains. The only result, so far as I can see, is that I got no sleep at night for fear of being detected in some crime or other. I lived in constant terror: if the leaves of a tree only shook, I imagined someone was coming to apprehend me. How often did my sister-in-law's husband, Khoda Buksh, warn me against all this trickery and craft! His words to me were: 'It would be much better for you if you would get your living by agriculture or trade or service: you can come to no harm so long as you walk in the straight path: by such a course you will keep body and mind alike in sound health.' And Khoda Buksh, because he does himself walk thus, is happy. Alas! why did I not listen to his words? How shall I find a release from this present alamity unless I can secure a pleader or a barrister, I shall never succeed in doing so. But if there is no evidence against me, I cannot possibly be punished. How will they find out where the forgery was committed, or who committed it?" He was still revolving all these thoughts in his mind when the day began to break, and then from sheer weariness he fell asleep. Soon however he began to dream about his many misfortunes, and to talk in his sleep. "Ah Bahulya! take care that no one gets a glimpse of the pencil, the pen and the other instruments: they are all in the tank in the house at

Sialdah: they will be quite safe there: be very careful now not to take them out again, and get off yourself as soon as you can to Faridpore; I will meet you there, when I have been set free."

It was now morning, and the rays of the sun fell through the venetians full on Thakchacha's beard. The *jemadar* of the lock-up had been standing near Thakchacha, and had heard all he said. He now shouted: "Ho, you old rascal! what! have you been asleep all this time? Get up, you have revealed all your secrets yourself." Thakchacha got up in a great flurry, and rubbing his eyes his nose and his beard with his hand, commenced repeating his prayers: and again, he looked at the *jemadar* with eyes half-open, and then closed again. The *jemadar* frowned, and said: "You are a fine hypocrite, you are! sitting there with a whole sack of virtue! Well, well! your virtue will be fully manifest when we have taken the instruments out of the tank at Sialdah." At these words Thakchacha trembled all over like a plantain leaf, and said: "Ah, sir! I have a heavy fever on me; hence the lies I told in my sleep." "Well," replied the *jemadar,* "we shall soon know the meaning of all you have said: get ready at once." With these words, he departed.

As soon as it struck ten, the officers of the court took Thakchacha and the other accused into court. Bancharam had been walking up and down the police court with Mr. Butler, long before nine. He was thinking—"If we can only get Thakchacha off this time, we may still secure a good deal of business through his agency: he is an extremely useful person in many ways, through his power of talking people over, and his special knowledge and experience in every kind of business, legal or otherwise; but I have always for myself acted, on the principle;—'No rupees, no investigation.' I cannot, as the saying is, 'drive away the wild buffalo at my own expense;' and again, as another saying has it, 'I have sat down to dance, why then a veil?' Why conceal my sentiments? Besides, Thakchacha has bled a good many people, what harm then in bleeding him? But a good deal of skill is necessary to get the flesh of a crow to eat, and it will not be easy to make anything out of so wary an individual as Thakchacha. Mr. Butler, seeing Bancharam so absent-minded, asked him what he was anxious about. Bancharam replied: "Ah, dear Saheb, I am thinking how to get money to enter my house!" Mr. Butler, who had moved away a little distance, exclaimed: "A capital idea, capital."

As soon as he saw Thakchacha, Bancharam ran up to him, and catching hold of his hands said to him, with tears in his eyes: "Ah, what a misfortune this is! I sat up the whole of last night in consequence of the bad news; not once did I close my eyes, and after I had in a fashion performed my religious duties, I slipped away before daylight, and brought the Saheb with me. But why be afraid? Am I a mere child that you cannot trust me? A man's life has many vicissitudes: moreover, it is the big tree that the storm strikes! But no investigation can be made, and nothing done, unless money is forthcoming: I have none with me: but if you would have some of your wife's heavy ornaments fetched, business can proceed: only get off scot-free this time, and you will get plenty of jewelry afterwards." It is very hard for a man who has fallen into any misfortune to deliberate calmly. Thakchacha at once wrote off a letter to his wife. Bancharam took the letter and with a wink and a smile at Mr. Butler handed it to a messenger, saying: "Run with all speed to Vadyabati, get some heavy ornaments from Thakchacha's wife, and return here or to the office in the twinkling of an eye; and look you, be very careful how you bring the ornaments! Look sharp, be off like a shot." The messenger testily replied: "It is easier said than done, sir! I have to get out of Calcutta first, then I have to get to Vaidyabati and then find Thakchacha's wife. I shall have to wander and stumble about in the dark, and besides, I have not yet had my bath, let alone a morsel of food: how can I possibly get back today?" Bancharam lost his temper and abused the man, saying: "The lower orders are all alike: each acts as he thinks proper: courtesy is wasted upon them: there is no hurrying them up without kicks and blows! People can go as far as Delhi when they have an object in view: cannot you then go as far as Vaidyabati, do your business, and come back again? You know the proverb: 'A hint is sufficient for a wise man:' now I have actually had to poke my finger into your eye, and yet you have not had wit enough to see." The messenger hung his head down, and without saying a word in reply, went slowly off like a jaded horse, muttering as he went: "What have poor persons to do with respect or disrespect? I must put up with it in order to live, but when will the day arrive when the Babu will fall into the same snare as Thakchacha? I know that he has ruined hundreds of people and hundreds of homes, and hundreds he has rendered houseless and destitute. Ah indeed, I have seen a good many attorneys' agents, but never a match for this man! See the sort he is! a man who can swear black is white, a man who can compass anything he likes by his trickery and craft, and yet all the time keeps up his daily religious duties, his Dol Jatra and his Durga Pujah, his alms to the Brahmans and his devotions to his guardian deity! Bad luck to such Hinduism as his, the unmitigated scoundrel!"

Meanwhile Thakchacha, Bancharam and Mr. Butler had all taken their seats: the case had not yet been called on, and their impatience only increased with the delay. Just as it struck five o'clock, Thakchacha was placed before the magistrate, and soon saw that the instruments wherewith he had committed the forgery had been brought into court from the tank at Sialdah, and that some villagers from that quarter were also present in court. After examination into the case, the magistrate passed these orders:—"The case must be sent up to the High Court: the prisoner cannot be admitted to bail: he must be imprisoned in the Presidency Jail." As soon as these orders had been passed, Bancharam ran up quickly, and shaking the prisoner by the hand, said: "What cause for alarm is there? You don't take me for a child that you cannot trust me? I knew all along that the case would go up to the High Court: that is just what we want."

Thakchacha's face looked all at once pinched and withered from anxiety. The constable seized him by the arms, dragged him roughly down, and sent him off to the jail. Thakchacha proceeded along, his fetters clanging as he went, and his throat parched, without so much as lifting up his eyes, for fear of seeing somebody who might recognise and jeer at him.

It was evening when Thakchacha first put his foot into that 'House of Beauty,'—the Presidency Jail. All those who are in for debt or civil cases are imprisoned on one side, those who are in on criminal charges on the other; and after trial they may have either to work out a fixed sentence there, or grind *soorkey* in the mill-house, or else chains and fetters may be their lot. Thakchacha had to remain on the criminal side of the jail. As soon as he entered, the prisoners all surrounded him. Thakchacha looked closely at them, but could not recognise a single acquaintance amongst them. The prisoners exclaimed: "Ah, Munshi Ji! what are you staring at? You are in the same plight as we are: come then, let us associate together." Thakchacha replied: "Ah, gentlemen I have fallen into unmerited trouble! I have taken nothing from any man: I have touched nothing belonging to any man: it is but a turn of the wheel of fortune." One or two of the old offenders said: "Ha! And is that really so? A good many people get overwhelmed by false charges." One rough fellow said harshly: "Are we to suppose then that the charge against you is false, while those against ourselves are true?

Ha! what a virtuous and eloquent man has come amongst us! Be careful, my brothers: this bearded fellow is a very cunning sort of individual." Thakchacha at once became more modest, and began to depreciate himself, but they were long engaged in a wrangle on the subject: any trifling matter will serve when people have nothing else to do, as a peg whereon to hang an argument.

The jail had been shut for the night: the prisoners had had their food and were preparing to lie down to sleep. Thakchacha was just on the point of seizing this opportunity to throw into his mouth some sweetmeats he had brought with him tied up in his waistcloth, when suddenly two of the prisoners, low fellows, with whiskers, hair and eyebrows all white, came up behind him and snatched away the vessel containing the sweetmeats, laughing loudly and harshly the while. They just showed them to the others, then tossed them into their mouths, and demolished them, coming close up to Thakchacha as they ate, and jeering at him. Thakchacha remained perfectly dumb, and keeping the insult to himself, got quietly on to his sleeping mat, and lay down.

XXVII

THE TRIAL AT THE HIGH COURT

The cutting of the rice-crops had already begun in the Soonderbunds: boats were constantly coming and going with their loads. There was water everywhere: here and there were raised bamboo platforms to serve as refuges whence the ryots could watch their crops; but, for all their produce the people were no better off. On the one hand there was the *mahajan*, who made them advances, to be satisfied, on the other, the zemindar's *paik* with his extortion: if they succeeded in selling their crops well, they might perhaps have two full meals a day, otherwise all they had to depend upon was fish or vegetables, or what they could earn as day labourers. On the higher lands only the autumn rice-crops are grown, the spring crops being generally raised on the lower lands. Rice is very easily grown in Bengal, but the crops have many obstacles to contend with: they are liable to destruction from excess of rain and from want of it; then there are the locusts and all kinds of destructive insects, and the late autumn storms: the rice-crop, moreover, requires continual attention for without very great care being exercised, blight attack the plants.

Bahulya, after looking after his little property all the morning, was sitting in his verandah smoking, a bundle of papers before him. Near him were seated certain scoundrels of the deepest dye, and some persons connected with the courts: the subject of their conversation was the law as administered by the magistrate, and certain suits-at-law then pending. One of the men was hinting at the necessity of getting some fresh documents prepared and some additional witnesses suborned: another was loudly applauding his successful devices, as he unfastened rupees from his waistcloth. Bahulya himself seemed somewhat absent-minded and kept looking about him in all directions: now and again, he gave some trivial orders to his cultivators. "Ho there! lift that pumpkin on to the *machan*." "Spread those bundles of straw in the sun." Then again he would gaze all about him, evidently restless and agitated. One of the company remarked: "Moulvi Saheb! I have just heard some bad news about Thakchacha. Is there not likely to be some trouble?" Bahulya had no wish to tell any of his secrets, so shaking his head from side to side he

PEARY CHAND MITRA

replied in a light sententious manner: "Man is encompassed about with every danger; why should you be in any fear?" Another man remarked: "That is all very true, but Thakchacha is a very clever man: he will escape from the danger by the mere force of his intelligence. But be that as it may, we shall be very glad if no calamity befalls you: we have no allies, no resources save you, in this Bhowanipore. Talk of our strength, of our wisdom; why, you are all in your own person: if you were not here we should have to remove our abode hence. It was most fortunate for me that you fabricated those papers for me, for I managed to give that idiot of a zemindar a good lesson by their means: he has done me no injury since: he knows very well that all the weight of your influence has been thrown into the scales on my behalf against him." Bahulya, contentedly puffing away at his *hooka*, with its pedestal of *Bidri* ware, and letting the smoke out of his eyes and mouth, laughed gently to himself. Another man remarked: "When a man has to take land into his own hands in the Mofussil there are two ways of keeping the zemindar and the indigo planter quiet; the first is to get the protection of a man like the Moulvi Saheb here: the second to become a Christian. I have seen a good many ryots, under the protection of the *padri*, lording it over their fellows, like so many Brahmin bulls among a herd of cows: there is power in the *padri's* money, in his signature, and in his recommendation. 'People always look after their own,' says a proverb. I do not say that the ryots are all really Christian at heart, but those that go to the *padri's* church get a good may advantages, and in police cases a letter from the *padri* is of great service to them." Bahulya replied: "That may be all very true, but it is a very bad thing for a man to renounce his faith." They all at once said: "Very true, very true, and on this account we never go near the *padri*."

They were all gossiping away merrily like this, when suddenly a police inspector, some *jemadars*, and sergeants of police, rushed forward and caught hold of Bahulya by the arms, saying: "You have committed forgery along with Thakchacha: there is a warrant for your apprehension." The men who had been with Bahulya were seized with terror when they heard these words, and ran off as fast as they could. Bahulya appealed to the avarice of the inspector and the sergeant of police, but they would not listen to the offer of a bribe for fear of losing their appointment; they seized him and took him off with them. As the news spread in Upper Bhowanipore, a great crowd collected, and some of the more respectable people in the crowd exclaimed;—"The punishment of crime must come sooner or later: if people who have been perpetrating crimes pass their lives in happiness, then must the creation be all a delusion and a lie; but such can never be." As Bahulya proceeded on his way, with his head bent low, he met a good many people, but he affected to see no one. Some there were who had at sometime or other been victimised by him: seeing that their opportunity had now come, they ventured to approach him, and said: "Ah, Moulvi Saheb! how deep in thought you are—Krishna pining for Brindabun! you must have some very important business on hand." Bahulya answered not a word. After having crossed over from Bansberia Ghât he arrived at Shahganj. Some of the leading Mahomedans of that place remarked when they saw him, "Ah! the rogue has been caught: that is a very good thing, and it will be still better thing if he is punished." All these remarks directed against him seemed so much added to his disgrace: they were as the strokes of a sword upon a dead body. Exceedingly mortified by all the insults he had been exposed to, he at length reached Bhowanipore.

From a short distance off it appeared as if there was a crowd of people standing on the left side of the road. When they came nearer, the police sergeant stopped with Bahulya, and asked why there was such a crowd there: then, pushing his way into the circle, he saw a gentleman seated on the ground with an injured man in his lap: blood poured in a continuous stream from his head, and the clothing of the gentleman was all saturated with it. Upon the sergeant asking the gentleman who he was and how the man got injured, he replied:—"My name is Barada Prasad Biswas: I was coming here on business, and, as it happened, this man was accidentally run over by a carriage, and I have been looking after him. I am trying to find some means of taking him to the hospital at once: I sent for a *palki*, but the *palki*-bearers refuse on any consideration to take the man, as he is of the sweeper caste. I have a carriage with me, but the man cannot get into a carriage: if I can only get a *palki*, or a *dooly* I am fully prepared to pay the hire, whatever it may amount to." The heart even of the most worthless may be melted by the sight of such goodness. Bahulya marvelled to see this behaviour of Barada Babu's, and a feeling of remorse rose in his mind. The sergeant of police said to Barada Babu: "Sir, the people of Bengal never touch a man of the sweeper caste: it must be no easy matter for you, being a Bengali, to do as you are doing: you must be no ordinary person." As he said this, he put the prisoner in the charge of a constable and went off himself to a *palki* stand, where by a liberal expenditure of threats and promises, he managed to get a *palki*, and sent the injured man off to the hospital in charge of Barada Babu.

At one time, criminal cases were tried at the High Court at intervals of three months in the year; now, they are held much more frequently. Two kinds of juries are empanelled for the purpose of deciding upon criminal cases. First, there is the grand jury, who, after due deliberation as to whether an indictment framed by the police or others is a true bill or not, inform the court; secondly, there is a petty jury, who help the judge to come to a decision in cases that have been found to be true bills, in accordance with the deliberate opinion of the grand jury, and find the accused guilty or not guilty. At every sessions of the Criminal Court, twenty-four persons are called on the grand jury: any person with property of the value of two lakhs, or any merchant, may be on it. During the sessions, the petty jury may be empanelled everyday, and when their names are called on, the defendants or the plaintiffs may raise objections to them if they please: that is to say, they may have someone appointed on the jury in place of anyone about whom they have any doubts; but when the twelve persons have once been sworn in as the petty jury, no change can be made. On the first day of the sessions, three judges preside, and as soon as the grand jury have been empanelled, the judge, whose turn of duty it may be, charges them, that is to say, explains to them all the cases on for trial at the sessions. After the charge has been delivered, the two other judges, who are not on duty, depart; and the grand jury will then withdraw to record their deliberate opinion on the cases before them, and when they have sent it in to the judge, the trial will commence.

The night had nearly come to an end: a gentle breeze was blowing. At this beautifully cool morning hour Thakchacha was fast asleep and snoring loud, with his mouth wide open: the other prisoners were up and smoking, and some of them hearing the sound of snoring kept whispering into Thakchacha's ears: "Eat a burnt buffalo!" but Thakchacha went on sleeping as soundly as the famous Kumbha Karna;—

> "Oh! the thunder of a snore;
> "How it terrifies me sore!"

Not long afterwards the English jailor came and told the prisoners that they must get ready at once, as they were all wanted at the High Court immediately.

Upon the opening of the sessions, the verandah of the High Court was crowded with people, even before the clock struck ten. Attorneys, barristers, plaintiffs defendants, witnesses, attorneys' touts, jurymen, sergeants of police, *jemadars*, constables, and others were all collected there. Bancharam was pacing up and down with Mr. Butler, and any rich man he saw, no matter whether he knew him or not, he would greet with hands uplifted, in order to parade his Brahmanical degree; but he deceived no one who knew him well by this assumption of courtesy. They would perhaps speak with him for a moment or two, and then on some imaginary plea or other slip away from him. Soon the jail van arrived, with sepoys on it before and behind: everybody looked down on it from the verandah above. The police removed the prisoners from the van and placed them in an enclosure in a room below the court-room.

Bancharam hurried below to have an interview with Thakchacha and Bahulya. "You two are Bhima and Arjuna," said he to them; "have no fear; you may put full confidence in me, I am not a child you know."

Aboute twelve o'clock, a space was cleared down the middle of the verandah, and the people all stood on either side of it: the *chuprassis* of the court commanded silence: all were eagerly expecting the arrival of the judges; then the sergeant of police, the *chuprassis* and the mace-bearers, bearing in their hands staves, maces, swords, and the royal silver-crowned insignia, went outside the court: the sheriff and deputy sheriff appeared with rods, and then the three judges, clothed in scarlet, ascended the bench with dignified gait and grave faces, and, after saluting the counsel, took their seats on the bench, the counsel making profound obeisance as they stood up in their places. The moving of chairs, the whispering and chattering of people, made a great noise in the court, and the *chuprassis* of the court had repeatedly to call out: "Silence in the court!" The sergeants of police also tried to keep the people quiet, and then, as the town crier called out: "Oh yes! oh yes!" the sessions opened. The names of the grand jury were then called over, and they were duly empanelled. They then appointed their foreman, that is, their president. It happened to be Mr. Russell's turn to sit as judge: turning to the grand jury he thus addressed them:—"Gentlemen of the jury, an inspection of the cases for trial shows me that forgery is on the increase in Calcutta: I see that there are five or six cases of that kind, and amongst them a case against the two men Thakchacha and Bahulya. It appears from the depositions in their case that they have for some years past been forging Company's paper at Sialdah, and selling it in this city. Take this case first, please, and be good enough to inform me whether it is a true bill or not: it is superfluous for me to bid you do your duty in examining into the other cases for trial."

The grand jury, having received this charge, withdrew. Bancharam looked very despondently at Mr. Butler. After about a quarter of an hour had elapsed, the indictment against Thakchacha and Bahulya was returned to the court as a true bill. Thereupon the jail sentry produced Thakchacha and Bahulya and made them stand within the railed enclosure before the judge. As the petty jury were being empanelled, the court interpreter called out loudly: "Prisoners at the bar! you have been charged with forging Company's paper: have you committed this crime or not?" The accused replied: "We do not even know what is meant by forgery, or by Company's paper: we are only simple cultivators: we do not concern ourselves with things of this kind: that is the concern of our English rulers." The interpreter then said rather angrily to them: "Your language is all very fine: have you done this thing or have you not?" The only reply of the accused was: "Our fathers and our grandfathers never did such things." The interpreter then, in a great rage struck the table with his fist and said: "Give an answer to my question: have you done this thing or not?" "No, we never did such a thing," the accused at last replied. The reason for putting these questions was that, if the accused acknowledged his crime, his trial proceeded no further: he was at once sentenced. The interpreter then said: "Attention! These twelve men, all good and true, who are seated here, will try you: if you have any objection to raise against any of them, then speak at once: he will be removed, and another man substituted." The accused, not understanding anything that was being said, remained silent, and the trial then commenced: by means of the depositions of the complainants, and the witnesses, the Crown prosecutor established a clear case of forgery. The counsel for the accused did not produce any witnesses, but did his best, by the ingenious twistings and turnings of cross-examination and by the chicanery of the law, to mislead the jury. When the speech for the defence was finished, Mr. Russell gave the jury a summary of the proofs of the case and explained the evidence of the forgery.

Having received their charge, the petty jury withdrew to consult. Unless the jury are unanimous, they are unable to record a verdict. Bancharam seized this opportunity to draw near the prisoners to encourage them. A few words had passed between them, when there was a sudden stir in the court, caused by the re-entry of the jury. When they had all entered and taken their seats, the foreman stood up: there was at once silence in the court: all craned their necks and strained their ears to catch what was said. The clerk of the Crown, the chief conductor of all criminal cases in the court, put the question:—"Gentlemen of the jury! Are Thakchacha and Bahulya guilty or not guilty?" "Guilty" was the reply of the foreman of the jury. As soon as the accused heard this, their hearts died within them. Bancharam then hurried up to them, and said: "Ha, ha! what, guilty? Put your trust in me, I am no child as you know: I will petition for a new trial, that is, for another verdict." Thakchacha only shook his head, and said: "Ah, sir! what must be, must: we cannot afford anymore expense." Bancharam then explained, with some irritation, "How much do you suppose I shall make by binding leaves in an empty vessel? In business like this, is clay to be moistened by tears only?" Mr. Russell then, examining his records very carefully, looked fixedly at the prisoners, as he passed this sentence upon them:— "Thakchacha and Bahulya, your guilt has been well established, and all who commit such crimes as yours should be heavily punished: I sentence you therefore to transportation for life." No sooner was the sentence delivered then the guards seized the prisoners by their hands and took them below. Bancharam had slipped back and was standing to one side; some people remarked to him, "Is this your case that has been lost?" "You might have known that," he replied; "let me never again have anything to do with so bad a one: I have never cared for cases like this."

XXVIII

A Philanthropist

The Vaidyabati house was enveloped in gloom: there was no one to superintend affairs or look after the maintenance of the household; the family was in a very bad way, and had great difficulty even in procuring food. The villagers began to say amongst themselves: "How long can an embankment of sand last? A virtuous house hold is as a building of stone." Matilall was all this time an exile from home, and his companions had also vanished; nothing more was heard of all their display. Great was the delight of Premnarayan Mozoomdar. He was sitting one day in the verandah of Beni Babu's house, snapping his fingers and singing a popular song:—

> "The babul's sweet flower doth its petals unfold,
> "While it swings in your ear with its colour of gold.
> "Your talk is of silver rupees and of rice,
> "Of sweetmeats delicious, and all that is nice."

Inside the house, Beni Babu was playing on the *sitar* and devising a special song for it, in accompaniment to the tune of "*The Champac Flower.*" Suddenly, Becharam Babu was seen approaching; causing great excitement among the children in the street, as he caught up the popular measure of Nara Chandri:—

> "With dice in my hand, all prepared for the game,
> "Born into the world as a gambler I came."

The boys were all laughing and clapping their hands, and Becharam was angrily expostulating with them. When Nadir Shah attacked Delhi, Mahomed Shah was absorbed in listening to music and singing; and even when Nadir Shah appeared suddenly before him in the full panoply of war, Mahomed Shah said not a word, and for a time ceased not drinking in with his ears the sweet nectar of song; at last, and still not speaking a word, he left his throne. Not thus did Beni Babu behave upon the arrival of Becharam Babu; he at once put down his *sitar*, and rising quickly from his seat, courteously invited him to be seated. After a somewhat lengthy exchange of courtesies, Becharam Babu observed: "Ah, my dear friend Beni, we have at last reached the end of the chapter! Thakchacha has come to utter grief by his wicked conduct: your Matilall too, by his lack of intelligence has gone to the bad. Ah, my friend! you have always told me some terrible misfortune is sure to happen to a boy when he has not been so educated from his early childhood as to have a cultivated intellect and a knowledge of rectitude: Matilall is an instance of this. It is a sorrowful subject: what more can I say? The whole fault was Baburam's; he had only the wit of a Muktar: he was sharp enough where trifles were in question, but blind in the really important concerns of life.

Beni.—What is the good of casting reproach upon him by saying this all over again: it was demonstrated a long time ago. When there was such an utter want of attention in the matter of Mati's education, and no means adopted for keeping evil companions from him, it was a foregone conclusion. "It is the Ramayana without Ram." Be that as it may, it is Becharam who has been the chief gainer. Bakreswar has got nothing by all his importunities. No school-master has ever been seen with an equal capacity for flattering the children of the rich: the education he was supposed to give was all a sham: his thoughts day and night were directed solely to getting gain, while appearing still to the outside world to be doing a great work. Anyhow the Vaishnava's hopes of making a good thing out of Matilall were never extinguished; like the little *chatak* bird, he rent the heavens with his cry: "Give me water! give me water!" but not even a cloudlet could he ever see, much less a shower.

Premnarayan Mozoomdar.—Have you, gentlemen, nothing else to talk about? Have you nothing to say on the subject of Kavi Kankan, or of Valmiki, or of Vyasa? Have you nothing to say on business? I am tired to death of discussing the troubles connected with the name of Baburam. Mati has only met with the fate which so wicked a boy deserved: let him go to perdition: need we feel any anxiety on his account?

Meanwhile Hari, the servant, who had been busy preparing tobacco, brought a *hooka*, and putting it into Beni Babu's hands, said:—"That Babu from Eastern Bengal is just approaching." Beni Babu at once rose from his seat and saw Barada Babu approaching rather hurriedly with a stick in his hand. Both Beni Babu and Becharam Babu greeted him courteously and invited him to be seated. When they had enquired after each other's welfare, Barada Babu said:—"Now at length what has been long expected has come to pass. I have a request to make of you just now; I have been living for a long time past at Vaidyabati, and for this reason it became my duty to help the people of the place to the best of my ability. I have no great wealth, it is true, but when I consider what I am, the Lord has given me plenty: if I were to hope for greater abundance, I should be finding fault with His good judgment, and that is not a proper course for me to take: it was my duty to help my neighbours, but whether from laziness, or ill fortune, I have not discharged my duty thoroughly of late.

Becharam.—What language is this? Why, you have assisted all the poor and afflicted people of Vaidyabati in a hundred different ways, with supplies of food, with clothing, with money, with medicines, with books, with advice, and by your own personal exertions on their behalf. In no single detail have there been any shortcomings on your part. Why, my dear friend, they shed tears when they proclaim your virtues. I know all this well: why do you try to impose on me like this?

Barada.—My dear sir, it is no imposition; I am telling you the plain truth: if any have derived any help from me, I am humiliated when I think how trifling that help has been. However, the request I have now to make is this; the families of Matilall and Thakchacha are starving; it has come to my knowledge that they often have to fast for days. It has been a great grief to me to hear this; I have therefore brought two hundred rupees that I had by me, and I shall be exceedingly gratified if you will somehow contrive to have this money sent to them without revealing my name.

Beni Babu was astounded on hearing these words, and Becharam Babu, after a short interval, looking towards Barada Babu, his eyes filling with tears of emotion, said to him, as he put his hand on his shoulder: "Ah, my dear friend! you know what rectitude really is: as for us, we have spent our lives in vain: it is written in the *Vedas* and in the *Puranas:* 'The man whose mind is pure and upright, he shall see God.' What shall I say about your mind? I have never hitherto seen even the slightest taint of impurity in it. God keep you in happiness acceptable to yourself. But tell me, have you had any news of Ramlall lately?

Barada.—Some months back I received a letter from Hurdwar: he was well: he did not say anything about returning.

Becharam. Ramlall is a very good boy: the mere sight of him would refresh my eyes: he is bound to be good, and it has all come about by reason of his association with you.

Meanwhile, Thakchacha and Bahulya had passed Saugor on a vessel. The pair were for all the world like two cranes: they sat together, ate together, slept together, and were perfectly inseparable: their mutual woes formed the continual theme of their conversation. One day Thakchacha, with a deep sigh, said to his companion:—"Our destiny is a very hard one: we have become mere lumps of earth: our trickery is of no further avail, and as for my stratagems, they have all escaped from my head. My house is ruined: I did not even have an interview with my wife before leaving: I am very much afraid that she will marry again." Bahulya replied: "Friend, pluck all these matters out of your heart: life in the world is after all but a pilgrimage: we are here today, gone tomorrow: no one has anything he can call his own. You have one wife, I have four. Throw everything else to the winds, consider only carefully the means whereby it may go well with self." The wind soon began to blow hard, and the ship went on her way with a strong list to one side. A terrible storm then got up. Thakchacha, trembling all over with fright, said to Bahulya: "Oh, my friend, I am in a terrible fright! I think my death must be very near." Bahulya replied: "Are we not already within an ace of death? We are but ghosts of our former selves. Come, and let us go below, and say our prayers to Allah and his prophet: I have them all by heart: if we are swamped, we shall at any rate have the name of our patron saint to accompany us on our journey."

XXIX

Bancharam in Possession

Bancharam Babu's hunger had not yet been appeased: he was always looking out for the chance of a successful stroke, or else revolving in his mind the kind of stratagem it would be best for him to adopt in order to accomplish his wished-for object. His cunning intellect became keener than ever by this practice. He was one day overhauling all Baburam Babu's affairs which had passed through his hands, when a fine plan suddenly presented itself to him: in the midst of his calculations, as he sat there propped up by a cushion, he suddenly slapped his thigh, and exclaimed. "Ah! at last I see before me a toad to a fine fortune. There is an estate in the China Bazar belonging to Baburam, and there is the family house too: they have both been mortgaged, and the limit of time has expired. I will speak to Herambar Babu, and have a complaint lodged in court, and then for a few days at any rate my hunger may be appeased." With these words, he threw his shawl over his shoulders, and making a visit to the Ganges the nominal excuse for his departure, he tramped off with a firm determination to succeed in his plan, or perish in the attempt.

He soon reached Herambar Babu's house. Entering at the door, he enquired of a servant where the master of the house was. Hearing Bancharam Babu's voice Herambar Babu at once descended the stairs. He was a very open-hearted and generous man, and he always acceded to every suggestion made to him. Bancharam took him by the hand and said to him very affectionately:—"Ha, Choudhury Mahashay! you once lent some money to Baburam upon my recommendation. The family and their affairs are now in a very bad way: the honour and reputation of his house have departed with Baburam: the elder boy is a perfect ape, and the younger a fool: they have both gone abroad. The family is deeply involved in debt: there are other creditors all prepared to bring suits against the family, and they may put many difficulties in the way of a settlement: I can therefore no longer advise you to keep quiet. Give me the mortgage papers. You will have to record a complaint in our office tomorrow: kindly give us a full power-of-attorney." In similar circumstances, all men alike would be afraid of losing their money. Herambar Babu was neither deceitful nor artful himself, and so the words which Bancharam had just spoken at once caught his attention: he agreed straightway, and entrusted the mortgage papers into Bancharam Babu's hands. As Hanuman, having obtained the fatal arrow of Ravan, all gleefully hurried away from Lanka, so Bancharam, putting the papers under his arm as if they had been a cherished charm, hurried off smilingly home.

Nearly a year had elapsed since Matilall's departure. The main door of the Vaidyabati house was still close shut: lichen covered the roof and the walls and all about the place there was a dense jungle of thorns and prickly shrubs. Inside the house, were two helpless young women, Matilall's stepmother, and his wife, who when it was necessary for them to go out at anytime, used the back door only. They found the greatest difficulty in getting food, and had only old clothes to wear. For fifteen days in the month they went without food altogether. The money they had received at Beni Babu's hands had all been expended in the payment of debts, and in defraying the cost of their living for some months. They were now experiencing unparalleled hardships, and being utterly without resources, were in great anxiety. One day, Matilall's wife said to his stepmother:—"Ah, lady! we cannot reckon the number of sins we must have committed in our other births: I am married, it is true, but I have never seen my husband's face: my lord has never once turned to look at me: he has never once asked whether I am alive or dead. However bad a husband may be, it is not for a woman to reproach him: I have never reproached my husband. It is my wretched destiny: where is his fault? I have only this much to say, that the hardships which I am now suffering would not appear hardships, if only my husband were with me." Matilall's step-mother replied: "Surely there are none so miserable as we are: my heart breaks at the thought of our misery: the only resource of the helpless and poor is the Lord of the poor." Men-servants and maid-servants will only remain in service with people as long as they are well off. Now that these two girls had been reduced to their present state, their servants had all left them. One old woman alone remained with them out of pure kindness of heart: she herself managed to pick up a living by begging.

The mother-in-law and daughter-in-law were engaged in the conversation we have recorded, when suddenly this old servant came to them, trembling all over, and said, "Oh, my mistresses, look out of the window! Bancharam Babu, accompanied by a sergeant of police and some constables, has just surrounded the house. On seeing me, he said, "Go and tell the ladies to leave the house." I said to him, "Sir! And where will they go?" Then he got angry, and threatened me, adding, "Do they not know that the house is mortgaged? Do they suppose that the creditor will throw his money into the Ganges? Well, I am only acting upon his wish; let them go away at once, or shall I have to put them out by the scuff of the neck?" The two women trembled all over with fright when they heard this. The house was soon full of the noise made by the men who were breaking in the front door: a crowd of people too had collected in the street. Bancharam was ostentatiously ordering the men to hammer at the door, and was gesticulating and saying: "No one can possibly prevent me from taking possession: I am not a child that I can be easily trifled with: it is the order of the Court: I will force an entry into the house: is a gentleman who has advanced money on the house to be called a thief? What wrong is being done? Let the members of the family depart at once." A great crowd had now collected, and some of the people were very angry, and exclaimed: "Ho, Bancharam! No baser wretch exists on earth than you: by your counsel you have ruined this house altogether. You have had heaps of money out of this family by your long-continued malpractices, and now you are turning the household adrift: why the very sight of your face would render it necessary to perform the *Chandrayan* penance: no place will be found for you even in hell." Bancharam paid no heed to their remarks; and when he had at last burst in the door, he rushed into the house, with the sergeant of police, and went into the zenana.

Just at that moment, Matilall's wife and his stepmother, taking hold of the hands of the old woman, and wiping the tears from their eyes, as they exclaimed, "Oh, Lord God, protect these poor helpless women!" went out of the house by the back door. Matilall's wife then said, "Friends, we are women of good family: we are utterly ignorant: where shall we go? Our father and all his race are gone: we have no brothers: we have no sisters: we have no relatives at all: who will protect us? Oh, Lord God, our honour and our lives are now in Thy hands. Welcome death by starvation before dishonour." When they had gone a few paces, they stopped beneath a banyan tree, and began to consider what was to be done. Just then Barada Babu approached them with a *dooly*: with bowed head and sorrowful face he said to them: "Ladies, do not be anxious: regard me as you would a son: I beg that you will get into this *dooly* at once, and go to my house: I have separate quarters ready for you:

stay there for a while, until your plans are arranged." When Matilall's wife and stepmother heard these words of Barada Babu, they were like people just rescued from a watery grave. Overwhelmed with gratitude, they said: "Sir, how we should like to be prostrate at your feet: we have no words to express our gratitude to you: you must surely have been our father in a previous birth." Barada Babu hurriedly placed them in the *dooly*, and sent them to his house; while he himself, fearing he night meet someone on the road who would question him, hurried home by back streets.

XXX

Matilall at Benares: Home Again

A good disposition is created by good advice and good associations: to some it comes early in life, to others later; and from lack of it in early youth great harm happens. As a fire, when it has once caught hold of a jungle, blazes furiously, destroying everything in its path, or as a wind, when it has once got up with any force, on a sudden increases in violence, and hurls down in its course large trees and buildings, so an evil disposition, when it has once been formed in childhood, gradually assumes fearful proportions, if roused into activity by the natural passions of the blood. Bad examples of this are constantly seen; but examples may also be seen of persons long given over to evil thoughts and evil ways becoming virtuous all of a sudden, quite late in life. A conversion like this may have its origin either in good advice or in good companionship. However, it occasionally happens that people come suddenly to their right mind; it may be by chance, it may be by an accident, it may be by a mere word. Such conversions, however, are very rare.

When Matilall returned home from Jessore in despair, he said to his companion: "It is evidently not my destiny to be rich: it is idle therefore for me to seek further for wealth. I am now going to travel for a time in the North-West: will any of you accompany me? The darling of Fortune may call all men his friends: when a man has wealth he has no need to summon anyone to his presence: numbers will crowd to him uninvited, but a poor man finds it very hard to get companions. All those who had been in attendance upon Matilall had made a show of friendship for him because of the amusement and profit they had derived; but, as a matter of fact, they had not a particle of real affection for him. As soon as they saw that his means were exhausted, and that he was hampered on all sides by debt, and that, far from being any longer able to maintain his old style of living, he could hardly keep himself, they began to ask themselves what possible benefit they could derive from keeping on friendly terms with him,—far better drop his acquaintance altogether! When Matilall put that question to them then, he saw at once that none of them would give him any answer. They all hummed and hawed, and pleaded all sorts of excuses. Matilall was very angry at their behaviour, and said: "Adversity is the real test of friendship: at last, after all this time, I have got to know your real character: however, go to your respective homes,—I am about to proceed on my journey." His companions replied: "Oh, sir! do not be angry with us: nay, go on in advance, we will follow you as soon as we have settled all our affairs."

Matilall, paying no heed to what they said, proceeded on his way on foot, and being hospitably entertained at some of the places on the road, and begging his way at others, he reached Benares in three months. Having fallen into this pitiable condition, the course of his mind began to be changed, from his long solitary meditations. Temples, once built at great expense, *ghâts*, and buildings of all kinds, all sooner or later begin to crumble away: sooner or later some vigorous old tree, whose great branches spread far and wide, is seen to decay: rivers, mountains, valleys, none continue long the same. Indeed, time brings change and decay to all alike. Everything is transient; all is vanity. Man, too, is subject to disease, old age, separation from friends, sorrow and troubles of every kind; and in this world, passion, pride, and pleasure are all but as drops of water. Such were Matilall's meditations, as day after day he made the circuit of Benares, sitting, when evening came, in some quiet spot on the banks of the Ganges, and meditating again and again on the unreality of the body, and the reality of the soul, and on his own character and conduct. By such a course of reflection, the evil passions within him became dwarfed, and he was roused in consequence to a sense of his former conduct and his present evil condition. As his mind took this direction, there sprang up within him a feeling of self-contempt, and, accompanying that self-contempt, deep remorse. He was always asking himself this question, "How can I attain salvation? When I remember all the evil I have committed, my heart burns within me like a forest on fire." Absorbed in such thoughts, paying no attention to food or clothing, he went wandering about like one demented.

Sometime had been spent by him thus, when one day he chanced to see an old man sitting deep in meditation, under a tree, glancing at one moment at a book, and at the next shutting his eyes, and meditating. To look at the man one would at once imagine him to be a very learned person, and one, too, who had attained to perfect knowledge and complete subjection of mind. The mere sight of his face would arouse a feeling of reverence in the mind. Matilall at once approached him, and, after making a most profound salutation, remained standing before him.

After a while, the old man looked intently at Matilall, and said, "Ah, my child, from your appearance I should imagine that you belong to a good family; but why are you so sorrowful?" This gentle address gave Matilall confidence, and he acquainted the old man with the whole story of his life, concealing nothing. "Sir," he said, "I perceive you to be a very learned man: now, and from henceforth, I am your humble servant: pray give me some good advice." The old man replied, "I see that you are hungry: we will postpone our conversation till you have had some food and rest." That day was spent in hospitality. The old man was pleased at the sight of Matilall's simplicity and straightforwardness. It is a characteristic of human nature that there cannot be any frank interchange of thought amongst men where they receive no mutual gratification from each other's society; but where there is this mutual gratification, then the thoughts of each man's heart are revealed in quick succession. Moreover, when one man displays frankness, the other, unless he is exceedingly insincere, can never manifest insincerity. The old man was a very worthy person; pleased at Matilall's fankness and sincerity, he began to love him as a son, and, at a later period, he expounded to him his own notions about the Supreme Being. He often used to say him:—"My son, to worship the Almighty with all our powers, with faith, affection, and love, is the main object of all virtue: meditate always on this, and practise it in thought, and word, and deed: when this advice has taken firm root the course of your mind will be changed, and the practice of other virtues will naturally follow; but to have a constant and uniform love of the Almighty, in thought, word, and deed, is no easy thing; for, in this world, such enemies as passion, envy, avarice, and lust, put extraordinary obstacles in the way, and therefore there is every need for concentration of thought and steadfastness." Matilall, after receiving this advice, engaged everyday in meditation on the Almighty, and in prayer, and endeavoured to examine into all his faults, and to correct them. As a consequence of a long-continued course of action like this, faith and devotion towards the Lord of the Universe sprang up in his mind. The honour due to good companions is beyond the power of words to express: pre-eminent amongst the virtuous stood Matilall's instructor; was it then in anyway astonishing that Matilall's mind should have so changed from association with such a man? A feeling of brotherly kindness towards all men developed itself in the mind of Matilall as one consequence of his very great faith in God, and then, in quick succession, a feeling of affection for his parents, and for his wife, and a desire to alleviate the sorrows of others, and to confer benefits upon others, grew in intensity. To see or hear anything opposed to truth and sincerity made him intensely unhappy. He would often tell the old man the thoughts that were passing in his mind, and his former history; and he would sometimes say in a mournful tone, "Oh, my teacher! I am very wicked: when I think of what my behaviour has been towards my father, my mother, my brother, my sister, and others, I sometimes think that no place can be found for me even in hell." The old man would console him by saying, "My child, devote yourself to the practise of virtue at any cost: men are constantly sinning in thought, in word, and in deed: our only hope of salvation is the mercy of Him who is all mercy: the man who displays heartfelt grief for his sins, and who is sincerely zealous for the purification of his soul, can never be destroyed." Matilall would listen attentively, and meditate with bowed head upon all he heard. Sometimes he would exclaim, "My mother, my stepmother, or my sister, my brother, my wife, where are they all? My mind is exceedingly anxious on their account."

It was a day at the commencement of the autumn season; the time was the early dawn. Who can give expression to the amazing beauty of Brindabun? Palms and trees of every kind flourished everywhere in abundance; thousands of birds were singing in every variety of note, perched on their branches. The waves of the Jumna, as if in merry play, embraced its banks. The boys and girls of Brindabun, in arbours and in the roads, were playing their *sitars*, and singing as they played. The night had come to an end, and all the temples, now that the hour for waving the lamps before the shrines had come, resounded with the hoarse murmur of tens of thousands of *conch* shells, and with the clanging of innumerable bells, shoals of tortoises played around the Kashi. Ghât: hundreds of thousands of monkeys were leaping and jumping about on the trees, now curling their tails, now stretching them out, and now and again plunging headlong down with hideous grimaces, and carrying off some poor people's stores of food. Hundreds of pilgrims were wandering about the different groves, and as they gazed on the different objects of interest, were talking about the sports of Sri Krishna. As the sun grew hot, the earth got baked with the heat; it became irksome to walk about any longer on foot, and the majority of the pilgrims sat about under the shade of the trees, and rested.

Matilall's mother had been wandering about holding her daughter by the hand; soon overcome with fatigue, she lay down in a quiet spot with her head in her daughter's lap. The girl fanned and cooled her wearied mother with the border of her *sari*. The mother, feeling at length somewhat refreshed, said to her, "Pramada, my child, take a little rest yourself. Now I will sit up awhile." "Now that your fatigue is removed, mother," said the girl, "mine also has gone: continue lying down, and I will shampoo your feet." Tears rose in the mother's eyes as she heard her daughter's affectionate address, and she said, "My child, the mere sight of your face has revived me. How many must be the sins that I committed in my other births, or why should I be experiencing this grief? It is no pain to me that I should myself be dying of starvation: my great sorrow is that I have not the wherewithal to give you even a morsel of food: the world is too small to contain such sorrow as mine. My two sons, where are they? I know not what has become of them. My daughter-in-law, how is she? Why did I display such anger? Matilall struck me, he actually struck me, his mother! My soul, too, is in constant anxiety on Ramlall's account, as well as on Matilall's." The girl, wiping away her mother's tears, tried to console her; after a while, her mother went to sleep, and the girl, seeing her asleep, sat perfectly motionless, gently fanning her: though mosquitoes and gadflies settled on her person, and annoyed her with their bites, she moved not for fear of interrupting her mother's sleep. A marvellous thing is the love and endurance of women? Herein are they far superior to men. The girl's mother dreamt in her sleep that a youth clothed in yellow came near her, and said, "Lady, weep no more! You are virtuous: you have warded off sorrow from many of the afflicted poor: you have never done anything but good to any: all will soon be well with you: you will find your two sons and be happy again." The sorrowful woman started out of her sleep, and, on opening her eyes, saw only her daughter near her: without speaking a word to her she took her by the hand, and they returned in great trouble to their hut of leaves. The mother and daughter were constantly conversing together: one day the mother said to her daughter, "My child, my mind is very restless: I cannot help thinking that I ought to return home." Not seeing her way to that, the girl replied, "But mother, we have amongst our stock of supplies but one or two cloths, and a brass drinking vessel: what can we get by the sale of these? Remain here quietly for a few days, while I earn something as a cook, or as a maid-servant somewhere, and then we shall have got something together to defray the expenses of our journey." The girl's mother at these words sighed heavily, and remained motionless: she could restrain her tears no longer: seeing her distressed, the girl was distressed also.

As luck would have it, a resident of Mathura, who lived near them, and who was constantly doing them small kindnesses, came up at that moment: seeing them in such sorrow, she first consoled them, and then listened to their story: the woman of Mathura, sorrowing in their sorrow, said to them, "Ladies, what shall I say? I have no money myself I should like to alleviate your distress by giving you all I possess: let me now tell you of a plan you had better adopt: I have heard that a Bengali Babu has come to live at Mathura, who has amassed a fortune in service, and by making advances to agriculturists: I have heard, too, that he is very kind and liberal: if you go to him, and ask for your travelling expenses, you will certainly get them." As the two distressed women could see no other resource open to them, they agreed to adopt the plan proposed; so they took their leave of the woman of Mathura, and reached Mathura in about two days.

On arrival there, they went to the vicinity of a tank, where they found collected together the afflicted, the blind, the lame, the sorrowful and the poor, all in tears. The girl's mother said to an old woman amongst them: "My friend, why are you all in tears?" "Ah, mother!" replied the woman, "there is a certain Babu here: words fail me to tell of his virtues: he goes about among the homes of the poor and afflicted, and is continually attending to their wants, supplying them with food and clothing, and, moreover, he watches by the bedside of the sick at night, administering medicines and proper diet. He sympathises with us in all our joys and all our sorrows. Tears come into my eyes at the mere thought of the Babu's virtues. Blessed is the woman who has borne such a child in her womb: she is certainly destined for the joys of heaven. The place where such a one lives is holy ground. It is our miserable destiny that this Babu is just leaving the country: our tears are flowing at the thought of what our condition will be when he has gone." The two women, hearing this, said to each other: "All our hopes appear to be fruitless: sorrow is our destined lot. Who can rub the writing off our foreheads?" Seeing their despondency, the old woman already mentioned said to them, "I fancy you are ladies of good family who have fallen into misfortune: if you are in want of money, then come with me at once to the Babu, for he assists many persons of good family as well as the poor." The two women at once agreed to this, and following the old woman they remained outside, while she entered the house.

The day was drawing to a close: the rays of the setting sun gave a golden tinge to the trees and to the tanks. Near where the two women were standing was a small walled garden, in which every variety of creeper was growing, carefully trained on trellis work: the turf in it was nicely kept, and at intervals raised platforms had been erected to serve as seats. Two gentlemen were walking about in this garden, hand in hand, like Krishna and Arjuna; as their gaze chanced to fall upon the two women outside, they hurried out of the garden to meet them. The two women, out of confusion, veiled their faces and drew a little to one side. Then the younger of the two men said to them in a gentle tone: "Regard us as your sons: do not be ashamed: tell us fully the reason of your coming here: and if any assistance can be rendered by us, we will not fail to render it." Hearing these words, the mother, taking her daughter by the hand, moved forward a little, and briefly informed them of the plight they were in. Even before she had finished telling her story, the two men looked at each other, and the younger of them, in the enthusiasm of his joy, fell to the ground, exclaiming, "My mother! my mother!" The other, and the elder of the two, made a profound obeisance to the sorrowful mother, and, with his hands humbly folded, said, "Dear lady, look, look! He who has fallen to the ground is your precious one, your treasure: he is your Ram! and my name is Barada Prasad Biswas." When she heard this, the mother unveiled her face, and said: "Oh, dear sir, what is this that you are saying? Shall such a destiny as this befall so miserable a wretch as I am?" On coming to himself, Ramlall bowed down to the earth before his mother, and remained motionless. Taking her son's head into her bosom and weeping the while, his mother poured the cool waters of consolation over his heated mind; and his sister, with the edge of her *sari*, wiped away his tears and the dust that had collected on him, and remained still and silent.

By-and-by the old woman, not finding the Babu in the house, came running into the garden, and when she saw him lying on the ground with his head in the lap of the elder of the two women, she screamed out: "Dear me, what is the matter? Oh dear! Oh dear! Is the Babu ill? Shall I go and fetch a Kabiraj?" Barada Prasad Babu said to her, "Be quiet, the Babu has not been taken ill: these two women that you see are the Babu's mother and his sister." "Oh Babu!" exclaimed the old woman, "Must you make fun of me because I am a poor old woman? Why, the Babu is a very rich man: is he not the chosen lord of Lakshmi? and these two women are but poor tramps: they came with me. How can one be his mother, and the other his sister? I rather fancy they are witches from Kamikhya who have deceived you by their magical arts. Oh, dear! I have never seen such women. I humbly salute their magic." And the old woman went away in high dudgeon, muttering to herself.

Having recovered their composure, they all went into the house, and great was the satisfaction of the mother when she found Mati's wife and her own co-wife there. Having received full particulars of all the other members of her family she said: "Ah, my son, Ram! come, let us now return home: as for my Mati, I do not know what has become of him, and I am very anxious on his account." Ramlall had been already prepared to return home: he had a boat, and everything ready at the *ghât*. Having, in accordance with his mother's instructions, ascertained an auspicious day for the journey, he took them all with him, and prepared to depart. The people of Mathura all thronged round him at the time of his departure: thousands of eyes filled with tears: from thousands of mouths issued songs in celebration of Ramlall's virtues: and thousands of hands were uplifted in blessing. As for the old woman, who had gone away in such dudgeon, she drew near Ramlull's mother, with her hands humbly folded, and wept. All remained standing on the banks of the river Jumna, like so many lifeless and inanimate beings, until the boat had passed away out of their sight. As the current was running down, and the wind was not blowing strong from the south, the boat glided quickly down, and they all reached Benares in a few days.

Early morning in Benares! Oh the beauty of the scene! There in their thousands were Brahmans of two Vedas, and Brahmans of four Vedas, worshippers of Ram, worshippers of Vishnu, worshippers of Shiva, followers of Shakti, worshippers of Ganesh, religious devotees and Brahman students, all devoutly engaged in reciting their hymns and prayers. There too in their thousands were men reciting portions of the Samvedas, and hymns to Agni and Vaya: crowds of women, hailing from Surat, from the Mahratta country, from Bengal, and from Behar, all clothed in silk garments of various hues, were engaged in perambulating the temples after due performance of their ablutions: beyond calculation in number were the temples sweetly perfumed with the odours of aromatic tapers, of incense, of flowers, and of sandal. Devotees in countless numbers crowded the streets puffing their cheeks, and shaking their sides, as they shouted aloud in enthusiasm: "Oh, Mahadeva! Lord of the Universe!" Women, devotees of Shiva, carrying tridents in their hands, and wearing scarlet raiment, were perambulating in their hundreds, about the temple of Shiva, engaged in their devotions to Shiva and Durga, and laughing madly the while. Ascetics there were in great numbers, who striving hard to subdue their bodies, and their passions, sat solitary with their hands uplifted, hair all matted, and bodies covered with ashes. There, too, in countless numbers, were religious devotees, each sitting apart by himself in some secluded corner, engaged in various mystic ceremonies, now emitting their breath, now holding it in: musicians and singers with their lutes and their tabors, their violins and their guitars, were there in great numbers, all completely absorbed in every variety of tone and tune.

Ramlall and his companions remained four days in Benares, bathing and performing other ceremonies at the Mani Karnika Ghât. He was always with his mother and sister, and in the evening he used to roam about with Barada Babu. One day, in the course of their walks, they saw a beautiful pavilion before them. An old man was sitting inside gazing at the beauty of the Bhagirathi: the river was flowing swiftly by, its waters rippling and murmuring in their course; and so transparently clear was it that it seemed to bear on its bosom the many-hued evening sky On the approach of Ramlall, the old man addressing him as an old acquaintance said: "What was your opinion of the Upanishad of Shuka when you read it?" Ramlall looked intently at the old man, and saluted him respectfully. The old man a little disconcerted said to him: "Sir, I perceive I have made a mistake: I have a pupil whose face is exactly like yours. I mistook you for him when I addressed you." Ramlall and Barada Babu then sat down beside the old man and began to converse on a variety of topics connected with the Shastras. Meanwhile a person with a somewhat anxious expression of countenance came and sat beside them, keeping his head down. Barada Babu, gazing intently at him, exclaimed: "Ram! Ram! do you not see? It is your elder brother sitting by you." On hearing these words, Ramlall's hair stood on end with astonishment, and he looked at Matilall, Matilall, looking at Ramlall, suddenly started up, and embraced him: and remaining for sometime motionless, he said: "Oh, my brother! will you forgive me?" and then winding his arms round his younger brother's neck, he bathed his shoulders in his tears. For sometime both remained silent: no words issued from their mouths, and they began to realise the real meaning of the word 'brother.' Then Matilall, prostrating himself at the feet of Barada Babu and aking the dust off his feet, said, as he humbly folded his hands: "Honoured sir, now at length I have come to know your real worth: forgive me, worthless wretch that I am." Barada Babu, taking the two brothers by the hand, then took leave of the old man, and they all proceeded on their way, each in turn telling his story as they went. When Barada Babu, after a long converse, perceived the change that had taken place in Matilall's mind, his delight knew no bounds. On coming to where the other members of his family were, Matilall, while still some distance off, exclaimed with a loud voice: "Oh, mother, mother, where are you? Your wicked son has returned to you: he is now alive and well, he is not dead: ah, mother! considering what my behaviour towards you has been, I do not wish to show you my face; it is my wish to see your feet only just once before I die." On hearing these words, his mother approached with cheerful mind, and tearful eyes, and found priceless wealth in gazing on her eldest son's face. Matilall at once fell prostrate at her feet: his mother then raised him up, and as she wiped away his tears with the border of her *sari* said: "Oh, Mati, your stepmother, your sister, and your wife are all here: come and see them at once." After greeting his stepmother and sister, Matilall, seeing his wife, wept at the remembrance of his previous history, and exclaimed: "Oh my mother, I have been as bad a husband as I have been a son and a brother. I am in no way worthy of so estimable a wife: a man and woman, at the time of marriage, take a form of oath before the Almighty that they will love each other as long as life lasts, and that they will never forsake each other, even though they may fall into great trouble; the wife, too, that she will never turn her thoughts to another man, and the husband that he will never think of another woman, as in such thoughts there is grievous sin. I have acted in numberless ways contrary to this oath: how is it then that I have not been deserted by my wife? Such a brother and a sister as I have too! I have done them an irreparable injury. And such a mother! than whom a man can have no more priceless possession on earth. Ah, mother, I have given you endless trouble. I, your son, actually struck you! What atonement can there be for all these sins? If I were only to die at this moment I might find deliverance from the fire that is burning within me, but I almost think that death has been the cause of its own death; for I see no sign of disease even, the messenger of death. However, do you now all of you return home. I will remain with my teacher in this city, and depart this life in the practice of stern austerities." After this Barada Babu, Ramlall, and his mother, summoned to them Matilall's spiritual teacher, and explained matters to him at length, and then took Matilall away with them.

While their boat was tied up to the shore at nightfall, off Monghyr, someone, resembling a boy in form, came close up to the boat, and raising himself up called out: "There is a light, there is a light." Seeing this peculiar behaviour, Barada Babu, bidding them all to be very careful, got on to the deck of the cabin, and saw about twenty or thirty armed men in ambush in the jungle, all ready to attack as soon as they should get the signal. Ramlall and Barada Babu got their guns out at once, and began firing: at the sound of the firing, the dacoits withdrew into the jungle. Barada Babu and Ramlall were eager to follow them up with swords and apprehend them, and give them in charge to the neighbouring inspector of police, but their families forbade it. When Matilall saw what had happened he said: "My training has been bad in every way: I have been utterly ruined by my life of luxury. I used to laugh at Ramlall when he was practising gymnastics, but now I recognise that without manly exercise from one's boyhood courage cannot exist. I was in a terrible fright just now, and if it had not been for Ramlall and Barada Babu we should all have been killed."

In a few days they all arrived at Vaidyabati, and proceeded to Barada Babu's house. Hearing of the return of Barada Babu and Ramlall, the villagers came from all parts to see them: joy uprose in the minds of all, and their faces beamed with delight: and all, eager for their welfare, showered down upon them prayers and flowers of blessing. On the following day, Herambar Chandra Chaudhuri Babu came, and said to Ramlall: "Ram Babu! without understanding the full circumstances of the case, and acting on Bancharam Babu's advice, I have obtained possession of your family house: I am really sorry that I should have entered into possession, and so driven away the members of your family: take up your abode there, whenever it suits your good pleasure." To this Ramlall replied: "I am exceedingly obliged to you: and if it is really your wish to give me the house back, we shall be under an obligation to you if you will accept your legitimate claims." Upon Herambar Babu agreeing to this proposal, Ramlall at once paid the money out of his own pocket, and drew up a deed in the name of the two brothers, and then, accompanied by the other members of the family, returned to the family house; raising his eye to heaven, and with heartfelt gratitude, he exclaimed: "O Lord of the world, nothing is impossible with Thee."

Soon after this Ramlall married, and the two brothers passed their lives very happily, striving, with exceeding affection, to promote the happiness of their mother and the other members of their family. Under the favour of Durga, the granter of boons, Barada Babu went on special employment to Badaraganj. Becharam Babu, becoming by the sale of his property the true Becharam, went to live at Benares. Beni Babu, who had been for sometime the independent gentleman without much training, turned his attention to the practice of law. Bancharam Babu, after a long course of trickery and chicanery, was at length killed by lightning. Bakreswar went roaming about, making nothing for all his obsequious flattery. Thakchacha and Bahulya, transported for life to the Andamans for forgery, were set to hard labour, chained hand and foot, and at length died after enduring unparalleled sufferings. The wife of Thakchacha, being left without resources, roamed about the lanes singing the song of her craft as a seller of glass bracelets:—

"Bracelets, fine bracelets have I.
Come and buy, come and buy!"

Haladhar, Gadadhar, and the rest of Matilall's old boon companions, seeing Matilall's altered character, looked out for another leader. Mr. John, after his bankruptcy, commenced business again as a broker. Premnarayan Mozoomdar assumed the distinctive dress of a religious mendicant, and roamed about Nuddea, shouting out:—

"To faith alone 'tis given below
Mahádev's secret mind to know."

The husband of Pramada having accepted many hands in marriage in different places, becoming at length himself empty-handed, came to Vaidyabati, and lived at the expense of his brothers-in-law, indulging, to his utmost bent, in every variety of sweetmeat pleasant to the taste. All that happened afterwards must be left to be related hereafter.

"Thus my story ends:
The Natiya thorn withereth"

FINIS

Page

16. *Kulins.*—Mr. Phillips, in a note to his excellent translation of "Kopal Kundala," says:—

> "Large sums are paid by fathers of girls for Kulin bridegrooms. A Kulin Brahmin girl, to preserve her caste and social position intact, must be married to a Kulin bridegroom. So it happens that Kulin youths are sometimes married to ten or twenty different wives. They can visit the houses of their numerous fathers-in-law, and are not only well entertained when there, but expect a present on coming away. There have been cases in which poor fathers of Kulin girls have taken them and had them wedded to old men on the point of death. They cannot afford to pay for a young and suitable bridegroom, and it is an indelible disgrace for their daughters to remain unmarried. On the other hand, Brahmins of lower family have to pay for a bride. The state of things is not so bad as it used to be. The feeling of the upper classes of Hindoos is strongly in favour of monogamy, and a Kulin who marries many wives is regarded with some contempt and aversion."

16. *Literally*—"He has drank down Mother Saraswati at one gulp."

17. "When a Hindu boy is first initiated into school life, he is presented with a piece of chalk, a tal leaf and a plantain leaf"—Bose—"The Hindoos as they Are."

18. The bracelet on the right hand is one of the signs that a woman is married, and that her husband is still living; another sign is a mark on the forehead called the 'sindhu.'

21. *Sakhishamvad*—"Songs expressive of news conveyed to Krishna by Brinda, one of the Gopis, of the pangs of separation felt by the milkmaids of Brindabun"—Bose's—"The Hindoos as they Are."

25. *The Shalgram.*—A flinty stone with the impressions of an ammonite, which Hindoos think represents Vishnu: it is worshipped as Vishnu. Some Hindoos make large collections: one man was reputed to possess a collection of nearly eighty thousand.

26. *Literally*—"Has cut a fine canal, and brought all the waters upon us."

29. The cat watching for a mouse, the heron and paddy birds for fish, are all alike regarded as types of hypocritical saintliness, and as such are largely used as figures in Sanscrit and Bengali literature.

32. "A field of *beguns*" is a popular expression for a source of continual profit, as 'a field of roots' is used for a temporary source of profit.

36. *Literally*—"He had a big heavy hand": the opposite phrase used of a generous man is—"His hand is always turned palm upward."

37. The veneration with which Hindoos regard Benares is expressed in the Sanscrit *sloka*:—"The heaps of your sins will all be burnt to ashes if you only name the name of Kashi."

All orthodox Hindus in their inmost hearts, look forward to spending the evening of their days, if possible, in "the Holy City," where, after having passed the two periods of their lives in the world as students and householders, they may pass the last as ascetics, in reading and meditation.

39. Gambling has always been popular in the East, and was evidently so amongst the ancient Aryans. In a translation of Kaegi's Rigveda, by Arrowsmith, there is a song called "The Song of the Gambler."

40. The favourite expression of Bancharam, which occurs often in this book, means literally: "Is this a cake in the hands of a small child?" The idea being that a cake is easily snatched out of the hand of a child.

49. *Literally*—"Many undertakings getting as far as the 'h' turn back when just short of the 'Ksha'." In some old grammars Ksha, instead of being the first of the compound consonants, as now, was put as the last of the simple consonants.

52. An old Aryan proverb corresponding to this is: "Even an ugly man may be found beautiful, when he is rich."

54. The following vivid description of a nor'wester, as the storms so common in Bengal in the hot season are called, occurs in Mr. Vaughan's "The Trident. The Crescent, and The Cross." "For days, it may be for weeks, the sky has been burdened with clouds charged with the needful watery stores. Millions of longing eyes have watched their shifting course and changing forms. Ever and anon it has seemed as if their refreshing streams were about to descend, but, as if pent up, and

restrained by an invisible hand, the clouds have refused to pour down the desired blessing: at length one point of the sky gathers darkness: a deep inky hue spreads over one-half the heavens: the wild birds begin to shriek and betake themselves to shelter: for a few moments an ominous death-like calm seems to reign: Nature appears to be listening in awful expectancy of the coming outburst: in another instant a dazzling flash of lightning is seen, followed by terrific rolls of thunder: a hurricane sweeps across the plains: sometimes uprooting massive trees in its course, and darkening the air with clouds of sand and dust: a deadly conflict seems to rage amongst the elements: the lightning is more brilliant: the crashes of the thunder more awful: yet the rain does not come. But the strife does not last long. Now isolated big drops begin to fall: then torrents of water pour down from the bursting clouds: driven along the wings of the storm, the rain sometimes appears like drifting cataracts, or oblique sheets of water. Speedily parched fields are inundated, and empty rivers swollen. All this takes place in less than an hour: then the storm abates, the darkness passes away, the sun once more shines forth: the atmosphere is cooled and purified, thirsty Nature is satisfied, and all creation seems to rejoice."

56. Before court-fee stamps came into use, attorneys were personally liable for fees payable to the court, and in default of payment they were punished with suspension.

57. The name given to a continuous supply of *Ghi* dropping through seven courses at certain of the Hindoo ceremonies, such as a child's first eating rice, at investiture with the sacred thread, and at marriage.

63. On one night in the month of Phalgun a lamp is kept burning in all Hindoo households, and if it is extinguished misfortunes are expected to happen.

63. The fear that a Hindoo feels lest he shall have no one to offer the customary libations to his manes and those of his ancestors is expressed in "Sakuntala." King Dushyanta says:—

> *"No son remains in King Dushyanta's place*
> *To offer sacred homage to the dead*
> *Of Purus' noble line: my ancestors*
> *Must drink these glistening tears the last libation*
> *A childless man can ever hope to make them."*

—Sir M. Monier-William's Translation

66. A local name for Durga: most towns in Bengal have some local deity representing Durga: at Krishnaghur the local deity is Ananda Maye.

66. *Literally*—"Were performing the *shraddha* of Vedavyasa," the reputed author of the *Mahabharata*.

70. It was no uncommon thing formerly at great men's houses for uninvited guests to attend in some numbers, solely for the purpose of creating a disturbance.

70. One of the preliminary ceremonies of a Hindoo marriage, is for the bridegroom elect to put a thread on his right hand, on the day preceding the night of the marriage (a Hindoo marriage cannot take place before the evening twilight).

71. Kankan was the name of a Bengali poet: this name is assumed for the nonce by the poetaster.

80. Prahlad is ever a favourite with Hindoos: his story is told in the Vishnu Purana: there is a capital ballad on him in Miss Toru Dutt's "Ballads of Hindustan." The story of Prahlad has been supposed to point to the gradual absorption into the Hindu system of the aboriginal tribes. The resistance long offered to that absorption, is supposed to be hinted at in the treatment of Prahlad by his Daitya parents.

81. Repetitions of the name of Hari, or Vishnu, made with the beads of the Tulsi plant: the rosaries are of different lengths: the common one consists of 108 beads: a pandit once told me he had seen one of 100,000 beads.

85. *Literally*—"They see all round them only the yellow flower of the mustard plant"—a man at the point of death being supposed to see everything with a yellow tinge upon it.

86. *Literally*—"To lose his drinking pot, and all for a cowrie"—the pot being either of block-tin, or of silver for holding drinking water, and carried by every Mussulman, and largely by Hindoos when moving about.

86. The *Kabiraj* means that the sick man should be taken to the banks of the Ganges, that he might die happily with his feet in the water. People are often taken to the river bank when very ill, and left in as ual hut, which will be erected for them there, where, if they are rich enough to afford it, a Pandit is engaged to watch the pulse; and when the pulse becomes so feeble as to show death to be at hand, the

Brahmin in atten lance takes the sick person to the river and places the feet in the water: the sick person will then die happy in the full assurance of salvation. Death is often actually hastened by the zeal with which the relatives of sick persons hurry them to the river-side, or, if they are too far from a river, outside the house, for it is regarded as an happy augury if the sick man dies being able to think of the sacred waters or even speak of them with his latest breath. Indeed the phrase: 'He died conscious' is practically equivalent to, 'He died happy, in the full assurance of salvation.'

Benares is regarded as so holy a place to die in that consciousness at death is not regarded as a *sine qua non* of a happy death: the mere fact of dying in Benares is of itself sufficient to ensure the feeling of happiness and assurance.

92. An evil spirit is supposed to depart in a *sirish* seed thrown over the shoulder.

95. "He is utterly unscrupulous": literally—"His orthodoxy is killing cows and making presents of shoes."

104. The wooden frame is here referred to in which the heads of goats are put to be cut off with one stroke of the broad sacrificial knife, with the eye of Kali on it, used for the purpose; the literal word is "The Bone Cutter."

104. *Stri-Achar.*—The name given to certain ceremonies which are gone through amongst the women of a household where a marriage is being celebrated, the object being to promote conjugal felicity: one of the ceremonies consists in the ladies of the family taking pan and betel in their hands and offering up prayers for the welfare of the bridegroom.

105. Ram Prasad was a popular poet who flourished at the same time as Bharat Chandra Raya, who was one of Maharajah Kishen Chandra's "Five Jewels." Maharajah Kishen Chandra was Maharajah of Nuddea at the time of Lord Clive: he was a Sanscrit scholar, and a great patron of learning.

106. *Literally*—"Before he had got as far as the initial mystic salutation to Ganesh, the sacred Om." All business is commenced with this mystic invocation: it is written at the top of letters in the form of a crescent with a dot in the centre.

107–108. For an explanation of this, see note 30.

108. These questions were simply put to see if the patient was still conscious—see note 30.

108. To die conscious in the full possession of all his faculties is regarded as of supreme importance with a Hindoo, and as ensuring a happy hereafter; even though a Hindoo may not be dying in the waters of the sacred Ganges, if he is able to ask the question as he dies—"Is this the Ganges that I am dying in?"'tis enough: the priest in attendance will reply: "It is the Ganges."

110. A place supposed to be famous for witchcraft. Some say it is an old name for Assam.

114. One of the features of a *shraddha* ceremony is the assembly of Pandits, who engage in a dispute more or less factitious, in the course of which a point arises when they all get so excited that they almost come to actual fisticuffs; an arbitrator then steps forward, and the excitement subsides as suddenly as it had arisen.

114–115. The point in the supposed argument is to create amusement amongst the by-standers by the difference in pronunciation of certain words by Pandits from different districts. The whole sentence is a jumble of more or less nonsense, designed to give the speakers credit with the audience for great learning. The ordinary arguments for discussion amongst Pandits who are adepts in the Nyaya Philosophy as taught in the Nuddea schools are on the difference between objects perceived by the Senses and those perceived by the Intellect: it is Gnan *versas* Vidya. The discussion here is a humorous travesty.

116. Tales from the *Mahabharat* and the *Ramayan* form almost the entire mental food of Bengal children.

117. Jagat Sett was the famous banker of the Nawab Nazims of Bengal.

117. The reference is to a story how each drop of blood as it fell from the Demon Raktabij produced a new demon, and how Debi and her companions put their tongues out and licked up the blood.

119. The reference is to an old story about a joint-family: there were four sons-in-law in the family of whom Dhananjayas was one. Efforts were constantly made to annoy them to get them to leave, and three went because their feelings were offended. Dhananjayas would not go until he was actually beaten.

119. It is a very common practice in India to give earnest-money in advance, when making any arrangement with a small tradesman; it is

commonly asked for with the excuse of buying materials, but the idea really is that of binding or closing a bargain.

120. This proverb practically means that gentlemen are doing menial acts, while beggars are riding on horseback.

121. "Seven" seems a favourite number when reference is made to wealth. "The Wealth of Seven Kings" is a favourite expression in Bengali Fairy Tales.

"Ten" in Bengali seems to be used for the whole world, as "Five" in Sanskrit.

Dash Jan—"Ten people" in Bengali means everybody.

121. It is regarded as of evil omen to call a man back when he has just started anywhere.

123. The indigenous village schools used to be noted for the severity of discipline in vogue there: various stories are told of the ingenuity of the village school-masters in devising ever-fresh punishment. One punishment was adopted from the illustrations of Bala Krishna, who is generally represented as kneeling on one knee, holding something in his right hand, and something on his head; the poor boy who was to be punished was made to kneel on one knee, and hold a brick in his upturned hand.

126–127. Literally—"Day and night there were cries of 'Let us eat,' 'Let us eat.'—Today we will eat the elephants out of the elephant stables, and tomorrow the horses out of their stalls."

The reference is to the popular stories current in Bengal about the *Rakshashas* and *Rakshashis,* the ogres and ogresses of our English childhood.

127. Literally—"Day and night are still with us."—The idea seems to be that the Universe is still in its place, and that there is still justice in the earth; the popular tradition apparently being that justice is gradually disappearing from the earth.

128. The reference is to a rich merchant, who, having on one of his journeys seen Durga sitting in the form of a woman on a lotus, in the sea off Ceylon, was punished with solitary confinement for sometime; he was at length released through his son's efforts and returned home with all his wealth.

133. Literally—"Their luck is a covering of leaves,"—the idea being that as leaves are easily blown about, so any slight circumstances may cause

an Englishman's luck to turn: he may be in bad luck at one moment, but he will be in good luck the next moment.

134. There is a reference here to a popular belief that Ravan's funeral pile is ever blazing, and in Bengal people closing their ears can imagine that they hear the sound of the blazing and crackling, just as children in England imagine they can hear the sound of the ocean waves that encircle the island, when they apply a shell to the ear.

136. "Don't talk to me of Khod-kast and Pai-kast: I will make them all Ek-kast."

The remark shows utter ignorance on the part of Matilall of terms used in connection with landed property in Bengal. Khod-kast is a cultivator who cultivates his own land: "Paikast is one who cultivates land for another: Ek-kast is simply a term invented by Matilall, and would mean one who cultivates for one."

136. These are all signs of poverty in the East: oil has always been regarded in the East as a sign of prosperity, and we find it constantly referred to in the Hebrew Bible—"It is like the precious ointment upon the head."

The absence of oil on the head is a distinct mark of poverty in the East. A thin stomach would also be regarded as a sign of poverty in a country like Bengal, especially where "The fair round belly" of Shakespeare, and "The front like the front of Ganesh" of the Bengali, is regarded as a mark of prosperity. A good story is told of an Indian client who had full confidence in the English barrister to whom he had entrusted his case because he was a very fat individual.

138. There is a reference here to a story, found in the Puranas, a familiar child's tale in Bengal, of a sage who was disturbed in his quiet meditation by seeing a cat pursuing a mouse: he turned the mouse into a tiger that it might escape from the cat, but he very speedily had to turn the tiger back into a mouse again, as the beast was about to attack and kill him.

142. Many are the stories told of the wariness of the Indian crow.

143. There is a beautiful figure taken from a large tree in Sakuntala; in reference to a king's responsibilities, it is said:—

> "Honour to him who labours day by day
> "For the world's weal, forgetful of his own,
> "Like some tall tree that with its stately head

"Endures the solar beam, while underneath
"It yields refreshing shelter to the weary."

—*Sir M. Monier-Williams' Translation*

144. The Harinbati was at one time the place where prisoners used to pound soorkey, and the phrase "Go to the Harin bati" is still used in Bengal as equivalent to "Go to jail."

149. It is a common tradition that if this expression is whispered in the ear of anyone snoring three times, the snoring will cease.

149. The reference is to the stories told of a brother of Ravan who was famous as a great sleeper: he is said to have slept the whole year, except on one day, when he would wake, and eat a hearty meal of some thousand animals: his name is taken from the tradition that his ears were as large as water jars.

150. The first salutation of a Brahman is in the form of a blessing: his hands are held out before him, palms upward: his second salutation is the ordinary one with hands folded together against his forehead, the fingers upwards: this is after his first salutation has been acknowledged.

150. The story of these two is found in the Bhagavadgita, which, with the Chandi or Hymn to Durga, forms the favourite reading of the class of Pundits. Many Brahmins make a living as itinerary readers of the Bhagavadgita, or Ramayana: they halt for weeks at a time at various places, and erect a temporary booth, where they read and explain to all who may come to hear them: at the end of a course of reading they are presented with presents: one man in Patna is reputed to make as much as five hundred rupees for one course of reading the Ramayana which may take him about six weeks.

153. One of the verses I have referred to in note 12. "The Song of the Gambler," runs:—

> *"The gambler hurries to the gaming table,*
> *"Today I'll win, he thinks in his excitement,*
> *"The dice inflame his greed, his hopes mount higher,*
> *"He leaves his winnings all with his opponent."*

153–154. The reference seems to be to the last of the divisions of the Mahabharat: the divisions are called Parbba.

154. Literally—"He is sharp enough in the *buri,* but blind in the *kahan,*" — a *buri* is equal to 20 cowries: a *kahan* to 1,600 cowries.

154. It is a popular tradition that Valmiki, the author of the Ramayana, wrote his famous epic before Ram was born: thus the expression practically means: "It was a foregone conclusion."

154. There is a popular tradition about a small bird, called in Bengal the Chátak, which sings in the hot weather months: the tradition is that it drinks only rain-water, and that its song is a cry to Heaven for rain: this is only one of the many traditions pointing to the eagerness with which in India the annual rains are expected. The bird is a small black-plumaged bird, and its cry exactly resembles "Phatik Jal," which the people interpret as "Sphatik Jal," "Water clear as crystal." It is supposed to drink with its beak raised in the air; a synonym for an anxious man is—"He is like a Chátak."

154. Kankan, the name of the poet, the author of the Bengali Version of the Chandi, or Hymn to Durga: in the poetical effusion in the Tale the poetaster assumes the name of Kankan. Valmiki, the reputed author of the Ramayana. Vyasa, the reputed author of the Mahabharat.

158. A reference to the popular tradition how Hanuman won from Ravan's wife the arrow presented by Brahma to Ravan, and how Hanuman presented it to Ram for Ravan's destruction.

158. The wearing of charms is very common amongst all classes in Bengal: it is still a matter of popular belief that sickness may be cured, and harm averted, by their use. The actual charm is often a piece of bark on which a sacred text is written: this is folded in paper into a very small compass, and is worn on a delicate silk string round the neck, or round the arm.

161. The author had doubtless read the lines in "Hamlet":—

> "Let the candied tongue lick absurd pomp,
> "And crook the pregnant hinges of the knee,
> "Where thrift may follow fawning."

162. In Hindu Philosophy, the name given to the third and lowest of the inherent natural qualities of man,—is Tamas—Gloom or Darkness.

162. The most profound salutation that a Hindu can make, and one that denotes absolute devotion of a man's whole body to the service of another, is one "with the eight members": the members on which Hindus make religious marks,—the two hands, the chest, the forehead, the two eyes, the throat, and the middle of the back.

167. Women keep their money tied up in a corner of their *saris*: the expression here means literally "the riches of your skirt"; men keep their money in a small bag stitched into their waist cloths.

168. No orthodox Hindu will commence any undertaking of importance, and some will not undertake even a short journey, without having first ascertained whether the day will be an auspicious one or not. The family Guru will be consulted; and even when an auspicious day has been fixed, the ladies of the zenana will always insist upon the observance of certain ceremonies. A gentleman of position, when inviting a guest to visit him, will often send him by special messenger a slip of paper with the auspicious days for his journey written down by his Guru either in Sanskrit, or in the current language of the district.

169. Shuka was the author of the Commentary on the Vedas, and has sometimes been identified as Vishnu himself: he is said to have been the only one amongst many hundred millions of Hindoos who ever obtained perfect Nirvana: that is complete absorption into the Deity: the full expression is "Nirvana Mukti," that is, Redemption, a salvation which consists in perfect absorption into the Deity.

172. There are several plays upon words in this concluding passage of the book: in this particular passage the word 'Pani' is used both for "Hand" and for "Wife": it came to be used in the latter secondary sense because one of the ceremonies, rendering a Hindu marriage legitimate, is the ceremony in which the bridegroom takes the bride by the hand. The use of words and phrases capable of a double meaning, is very common in Sanskrit writings.

172. According to a not uncommon custom of ending stories in Bengal, the author ends his story with the first lines of a song, which in full is:—

"Thus my story endeth,
The Natiya thorn withereth:
Why, oh Natiya thorn, dost wither?
Why does thy cow on me browse?
Why, O cow, dost thou browse?
Why does thy neat herd not tend me?
Why, O neat herd does not tend the cow?
Why does thy daughter-in-law not give me rice?
Why, O daughter-in-law, dost not give rice?

Why does my child cry?
Why, O child, dost thou cry?
Why does the ant bite me?
Why, O ant, dost thou bite?
Koot, koot, koot."

Glossary

Amlah.—A name for the whole establishment of an office; sometimes simply for a clerk.

Arjuna.—His story is told in the Bhagavad Gita.

Ashwar.—The month corresponding to the English June-July:—The first month of the rainy season.

Astrologer.—An important person in Hindu households, where his chief duty is to cast horoscopes on the birth of children.

Bidri.—The name given to finely-chased metal ware, which was originally made at Bidri in the Deccan.

Bhagirathi.—A name given to that branch of the Ganges which lower down becomes the Hooghly. Sometimes used for the Ganges proper.

Baya.—A drum played with the left hand only.

Bhisma.—A great warrior of the Lunar Race, whose story is told in the Sanscrit Epic—Mahábhárata.

Bael.—A Egle Marmelos. The fruit of this tree has a very hard rind, almost as hard as the cocoanut.

Budgerow.—The name given to a large house-boat used on the rivers of Bengal.

Champac.—Michelia Champaka. A flowering tree that flowers in the rains: it bears large and yellow fragrant flowers, and is a very popular tree.

Chowkidar.—A kind of rural policeman.

Durga Poojah.—The great Autumn festival in honour of the goddess Durga, wife of Siva, during which all business is suspended in Bengal for ten days: it affords an opportunity for a re-union of families.

Dampati Baran—A form of Shraddh.

Dan Sagar.—Literally "Ocean of Gifts." A form of funeral ceremony where every guest receives some present.

Daroga.—An Inspector of Police.

Druva.—A boy of four years old, who went in search of Vishnu and received a sacred mantra of twelve letters from Narad. Upon the repetition of this mystic mantra Vishnu appeared to the boy.

Durryodhan.—One of the heroes of the Mahábhárat who was obliged to hide in a Lake called the Dvaipana Lake, to avoid capture; he was the eldest of the hundred sons of Dhritarastra.

Eed.—A Mahomedan Festival.

Ghat.—The name given to a landing or bathing-place on the bank of a river, also to a place for burning the dead.

Gosain.—A class of Hindu religious mendicants.

Gāriwan.—Hackney coachman.

Guddee or Couch.—The principal seat at an assembly of notables. "To attain the guddee" is a synonym for succeeding to a title or to estates.

Golden Age.—The first of the four Hindu Ages. Literally—The Age of Truth.

Ghi.—Melted butter specially prepared for household cooking purposes.

Gomashtha.—A land agent, or steward, the headman of the employés on an estate, or in a factory.

Hunuman.—The monkey-god, a great favourite with Hindus. His story is told in the great epic—the Rámáyana, which, in its Hindi version by Tulsi Dass, is annually acted in Northern India.

Hom.—An offering of ghi, barley-meal, sandal and rice, fried over a fire.

Hori Bol.—A cry to Vishnu, as "The Saviour."

Jelabhi.—A sweetmeat made in twists.

Krishna.—The favourite Incarnation of Vishnu.

Kalidas.—The Author of the popular Sansrkit Drama, "Sakuntala."

Kodali.—A kind of broad hoe, used for breaking up the ground.

Kabiraj.—A Hindu physician.

Kayasth.—A man of the writer caste.

Lanka.—A name for Ceylon in the Ramayana.

Lakshmi.—Goddess of fortune and good luck.

Lathial.—One armed with a heavy stick, often employed by landlords in disputes with neighbours.

Mohurrir.—A clerk.

Mantra.—A verse from the sacred hymns of the Vedas.

Mahadeva.—A name of Siva.

Mahajun—A money-lender.

Machan.—A platform of bamboo, raised on piles above the ground.

Mallika.—A species of Jessamine.

Muktar.—An agent, or broker.

Moulvi.—A Mahomedan title of respect meaning 'Learned.'

Nala Raja.—The hero of the Sanskrit Drama, "Nala and Damayanti."

Naib.—An agent, or deputy of the landlord of an estate.

Pandit.—A learned Brahman, learned in Sanskrit literature. Regular titles are conferred on Pandits according to the extent of their knowledge, as tested from time to time by an assembly of Pandits; one of these meets at the old Sanskrit University of Nuddea, or Navadwip.

Phalgun.—The month corresponding from February to March.

Paik.—Originally "a runner":—Men employed by landlords as messengers.

Ryot.—A cultivator.

Radha.—The wife of Krishna.

Ramzan.—The name given to the Mahomedan Lenten Fast.

Shravan.—The month corresponding to July-August, the second month of the rainy season, when the rainfall is heaviest.

Shástras.—The name given to some of the Hindu Sacred Books especially to the Philosophical works.

Sari.—The usual dress of women, made of cotton, or silk, or muslin.

Sati.—A woman who threw herself on her husband's funeral pile was known as Sati, "The Chaste One." Sati was abolished under Lord Bentinck.

Satya Pir.—A Hindu deity regarded by Mahomedans as one of their saints.

Saraswati.—The Hindu goddess of learning.

Shorash.—A kind of funeral ceremony where sixteen different kinds of presents are distributed, six kinds being of silver.

Sephalika.—Nyctantes Arbor Tristis, flowering only at night.

Shraddha.—The Hindu funeral ceremony; see Wilkins' "Modern Hinduism."

Shal Fish.—A fish used in religious ceremonies; it is first roasted.

Sheristadar.—The Head Clerk in charge of the records of an office.

Tol.—The name of the indigenous Sanskrit schools.

Tulsi.—Ocymum Sanctum. The basil honoured by all Hindus.

Tauba.—The Mahomedan cry of grief meaning, "I repent me of my sins."

Tabala.—The name for the drum that is played with the right hand only.

Taluk.—A portion of an estate, consisting of several villages.

Udjog Parvva.—One of the cantos of the Mahábhárat, giving the preliminary incidents of the Kurukshetra Battle.

Veda.—The name given to the oldest sacred books of the Hindus meaning "Revelation."

Vaishnava.—A follower of Vishnu; see Wilkins' "Modern Hinduism."

Yudishthira.—Surnamed "The Incarnation of Virtue." One of the heroes of the Mahábhárat.

Yama.—The Hindu god of Death.

A Note About the Author

Peary Chand Mitra (1814–1883) was an Indian writer. Born in Calcutta to a wealthy Bengali family, Mitra studied Persian as a boy and began learning English at the Hindu College, where he enrolled in 1827. In 1836, he found employment with the Calcutta Public Library as a deputy librarian, eventually reaching the position of curator. A frequent contributor to the *Englishman, Indian Field, Calcutta Review,* and *Bengal Spectator*, Mitra was a major force in the development of Bengali literature and journalism. Although several of his novels and essays were written in English, Mitra was known for his use of accessible Bengali prose in order to expand readership beyond the fortunate few who had received an education in Sanskrit. His novel *Alaler Gharer Dulal* (1857), or *The Spoilt Child: A Tale of Domestic Life*, is considered a classic of Bengali literature that set the standard for writing in the language that would be adapted and virtually finalized in Bankim Chandra Chatterjee's monumental first novel, published in 1864. Towards the end of his life, Mitra became a successful businessman as director of several hospitality, investment, and import-export ventures.

A Note from the Publisher

Spanning many genres, from non-fiction essays to literature classics to children's books and lyric poetry, Mint Edition books showcase the master works of our time in a modern new package. The text is freshly typeset, is clean and easy to read, and features a new note about the author in each volume. Many books also include exclusive new introductory material. Every book boasts a striking new cover, which makes it as appropriate for collecting as it is for gift giving. Mint Edition books are only printed when a reader orders them, so natural resources are not wasted. We're proud that our books are never manufactured in excess and exist only in the exact quantity they need to be read and enjoyed.

bookfinity™

Discover more of your favorite classics with Bookfinity™.

- Track your reading with custom book lists.
- Get great book recommendations for your personalized Reader Type.
- Add reviews for your favorite books.
- AND MUCH MORE!

Visit **bookfinity.com** and take the fun Reader Type quiz to get started.

Enjoy our classic and modern companion pairings!

Classic & Modern